Praise for
Phantom's Touch

"When Hollywood magic meets real magic, the collision leads to a sexy and thrilling tale. Leto's got the touch."
—*Romantic Times*

"Leto has penned one hot paranormal! 4 stars!"
—Romance Novel TV

"Readers will relish Julie Leto's outstanding touch!"
—Genre Go Round Reviews

**Praise for the Other Novels
of Julie Leto**

"A sexy page-turner you won't want to miss!"
—Gena Showalter, *New York Times* bestselling author

"Nobody writes a bad girl like Julie Leto!"
—Carly Philips, *New York Times* bestselling author

"She loves pushing the envelope, and dances on the edge with the sizzle and crackle of lightning."
—The Best Reviews

continued . . .

KISS OF THE PHANTOM

JULIE LETO

A SIGNET ECLIPSE BOOK

SIGNET ECLIPSE
Published by New American Library, a division of
Penguin Group (USA) Inc., 375 Hudson Street,
New York, New York 10014, USA
Penguin Group (Canada), 90 Eglinton Avenue East, Suite 700, Toronto,
Ontario M4P 2Y3, Canada (a division of Pearson Penguin Canada Inc.)
Penguin Books Ltd., 80 Strand, London WC2R 0RL, England
Penguin Ireland, 25 St. Stephen's Green, Dublin 2,
Ireland (a division of Penguin Books Ltd.)
Penguin Group (Australia), 250 Camberwell Road, Camberwell, Victoria 3124,
Australia (a division of Pearson Australia Group Pty. Ltd.)
Penguin Books India Pvt. Ltd., 11 Community Centre, Panchsheel Park,
New Delhi - 110 017, India
Penguin Group (NZ), 67 Apollo Drive, Rosedale, North Shore 0632,
New Zealand (a division of Pearson New Zealand Ltd.)
Penguin Books (South Africa) (Pty.) Ltd., 24 Sturdee Avenue,
Rosebank, Johannesburg 2196, South Africa

Penguin Books Ltd., Registered Offices:
80 Strand, London WC2R 0RL, England

First published by Signet Eclipse, an imprint of New American Library,
a division of Penguin Group (USA) Inc.

First Printing, June 2009
10 9 8 7 6 5 4 3 2 1

PUBLISHER'S NOTE
This is a work of fiction. Names, characters, places, and incidents either are the
product of the author's imagination or are used fictitiously, and any resemblance
to actual persons, living or dead, business establishments, events, or locales is
entirely coincidental.
    The publisher does not have any control over and does not assume any re-
sponsibility for author or third-party Web sites or their content.

If you purchased this book without a cover you should be aware that this book is
stolen property. It was reported as "unsold and destroyed" to the publisher and
neither the author nor the publisher has received any payment for this "stripped
book."

The scanning, uploading, and distribution of this book via the Internet or via any
other means without the permission of the publisher is illegal and punishable by
law. Please purchase only authorized electronic editions, and do not participate
in or encourage electronic piracy of copyrighted materials. Your support of the
author's rights is appreciated.

Here's hoping that what they say is true:
Third time's the charm!

And to Tim and Terri,
I hope your lives together are as exciting and
romantic as the ones in my books.

ACKNOWLEDGMENTS

First and foremost, this book is dedicated to Dr. Richard Dillon and the nurses and staff of both Tampa Bay Women's Care and the Women's Center at University Community Hospital. Your excellent care led to the rapid writing of this book, because apparently, healing the body also frees the creativity of the mind. Thank you and bless you all!

As always, I owe so much to the Plotmonkeys: Janelle Denison, Leslie Kelly and Carly Phillips, for loving this series and helping me so much with every aspect from the plotting (obviously!) to the characterization and the actual business of putting words on paper. Also, to Susan Kearney, Diana Peterfreund, Anne-Marie Carroll and Kathy Carmichael, and my family in TARA, who are always instrumental in ensuring that I have a writer's support group that is second to none.

I also have to give a special shout-out to my family, who support me in so many ways and make it entirely possible for me to follow my dreams. And I couldn't have written this story without my agent, Helen Breitwieser, whose unwavering enthusiasm for my work gets me through the roughest times. And last, I want to thank and acknowledge the wonderful team at NAL, especially my editor, Laura Cifelli, for her incredible insight into story and character. Also Lindsay Nouis, her ever-efficient assistant, and the absolutely, positively amazing team in the art department, who have graced my books with some of the most gorgeous covers I've ever seen.

PROLOGUE

Gemma Von Roan dangled the antique keys in front of Paschal Rousseau's face, shaking them enticingly, her back to the door he'd anticipated entering for more than six months. Inside a room hidden beneath this centuries-old manse in upstate New York was the secret horde of the K'vr, a cult founded to plunder the bounty of the eighteenth-century sorcerer Lord Rogan. Even through the thick oak door, Paschal sensed the blackguard's bloody fingerprints on the cache within.

Gemma, young and stylish and cunning beyond measure thanks to a bloodline that she could trace back to the wizard himself, knew how badly Paschal yearned to explore the collection. Undeterred by his advanced age, she'd pulled out all the stops to entice him away from his family, promising him unlimited access to the vast assemblage of Gypsy-wrought artifacts.

All she wanted in return was the very thing Paschal had sworn he'd never give away.

"So we have a deal, yes?" Gemma asked. "I let you in and give you open access to my family's store and you'll show me how to do what you do."

He frowned, his expression lost in the dim light. "It won't be that easy."

Gemma fussed with the keys, inserting one in the rusted lock as she spoke. "If my life were ever easy, we'd have had access to this place six months ago."

"The radon and asbestos report really was genius," Paschal complimented.

But Gemma only snorted in disgust. Having to resort to chicanery in order to gain entrance to a building owned by her family since the Civil War had chafed her pride raw.

Discounting her brother, currently awaiting trial for murder in Florida, Gemma was the last living descendant of Lord Rogan. And yet, because she was a woman, she'd been denied the leadership of the K'vr. For the past year and a half, the top spot of grand apprentice remained unclaimed while the council of elders determined if Keith Von Roan, the incarcerated brother, or Farrow Pryce, a wealthy businessman whose father had long served the Von Roan family, was better suited to serve.

But with Keith Von Roan looking at a long jail term and Farrow Pryce missing and presumed dead, the K'vr was in disarray. Never had there been a better time for Gemma to step in and fight the patriarchal attitudes of the elders. But instead she was helping Paschal, someone she'd once had a hand in kidnapping, in order to break into her family's most secret and treasured storehouse. Paschal wasn't sure why she'd chosen this course of action, but he had no doubt she'd betray him at the first opportunity.

Trouble was, he did not care. He just wanted her to find the right key.

"Need help?" he asked.

She flipped through the key ring again. "You'd think we already had the Source, with all these damned locks."

Paschal cleared his throat unnecessarily. They'd carefully avoided this topic over the last six months. Both of them recognized that any conversation regarding the mysterious fire opal would go nowhere. She wanted it, but could not find it. Paschal knew precisely where it was—certainly not in this secret storeroom—but he would die before he gave away the location. The stone possessed a frightening amount of dark magic. In the wrong hands, the potential for devastation was too terrifying for Paschal to contemplate. ·

The Source had been the Holy Grail to the K'vr since Rogan's disappearance in 1747. Gemma had probably been told bedtime stories about its limitless power. Yet, oddly enough, she did not seem to be after it at the moment. But even the powerful stone could not help Paschal in his quest. He needed whatever was inside the locked room, calling to him. Beckoning to him. Luring him to a fate that might just equal crashing on sharp and pitiless rocks.

"Let me try," he offered.

Ignoring him, Gemma continued to try key after key. Paschal couldn't help admiring how stubborn she was—or how lovely, no matter that she styled her hair like a porcupine. Her attempt to camouflage what amounted to a dollish, pretty face with spiked black and blond hair, dark eyeliner and darker lips revealed more about her true personality than she would ever admit. While on the arm of Farrow Pryce, she'd become a sleek, sophisticated seductress. Since his death, she'd taken on a tougher persona, from the shade of her lipstick to her Morticia Addams wardrobe. Paschal couldn't help but wonder who was truly at the core of this ambitious young woman—or if he'd live long enough to find out.

To her knowledge, Paschal was over ninety years old . . . though he was still as virile as a man half his "age." She no longer tried to use sex as a weapon against him, and for this he was grateful. He might be ancient, but he wasn't dead. Besides, he was on her side now. She'd begun, a little at a time, to treat him more like a mentor than a conquest.

There was a responsibility in that role that Paschal had not experienced in years. While he'd enjoyed being a father to Ben, he'd spent too many years keeping secrets from his son to actually teach him anything of value. Now Paschal had a chance to influence a young woman who unknowingly possessed a unique power—one she could use for either good or evil. Perhaps her choice would depend on how he played this next challenge.

Gemma finally cursed and threw the ring of keys onto the ground, then kicked them until they ricocheted against the scuffed and rat-gnawed baseboard—a rare show of genuine, raw emotion. "What does any of this fucking matter if we can't get inside?"

Paschal *tsk*ed at her colorful language, retrieved the keys and ran them through his fingers, trying to get a reading off the energy embedded in the metal. His talent with psychometry was trained and specific. Accepting energy from every single item he ever touched would be like boarding a bullet train straight to an insane asylum. Instead, he'd taught himself to focus on only the energy signature of members of his own family or on Rogan's dark magic—which over time had become inextricably intertwined.

He found the key on the second pass and inserted it into the lock. He attempted a twist, but while the lock mechanism gave way, the door did not budge.

"Hot damn," she said, nudging him out of the way so she could grab the doorknob. "The lock is sticking. Means no one's been inside for a long time."

"Or someone hasn't used the WD-40 in a while," he offered. "When's the last time you were inside?"

"Years ago. My father used to find me down here and totally lose his mind. If he ever found out I'd taken pictures of some of the items and kept them hidden, he would have died from an aneurysm rather than cancer."

She grunted when the door finally yielded to the pressure of her shoulder. Stale air pressed into the dank tunnel. Almost instantly, Paschal felt the presence of Rogan's magic. He'd had more than fifty years to hone his ability to sense the dark power, even from a distance. The trick would be to focus. According to Gemma, her ancestors had been notorious pack rats. If he did not call upon his psychometric tricks, it could take them weeks to explore every item warehoused in this underground cavern. And they didn't have weeks. According to Gemma, they'd be lucky if they had days.

She flicked on the flashlight she'd brought along, found an ancient light switch and, with effort, flipped it on. After a few protesting flickers and the pop of a bulb somewhere in the distance, feeble amber light glowed above them. Paschal poked his head in and saw what appeared to be rows and rows of shelving. Layers of dust and cobwebs made everything gray and unappealing—to someone who had to rely on his eyes to find what he was looking for. Luckily, Paschal had other skills at his disposal.

Gemma groaned. "How lovely. You'd think the bozos

running this outfit now would assign someone to dust down here every once in a while. My family's legacy looks like piles of old junk."

"You know what they say about one man's trash," he replied.

She snickered doubtfully. "If you can find a treasure in this abandoned trove, you'll be worth the price I paid to get you here."

Flashlight in front of him, Paschal moved through the rows. The shelves, stacked all the way up to the cramped six-foot ceiling, created a maze that snaked deep beneath the house. He found a wild array of vases and urns and boxes crafted in carved wood, fine pewter and even blown glass. Goblets and wineglasses collected inches' worth of dirt and dust inside their sometimes uneven bowls.

Finally, he found the cup he sought—a pewter chalice marked with Rogan's seal. Carved into the side of the dark metal, a hawk soared. A red stone glittered from within its talons. Gemma's photograph of this exact item had lured him here. Could this cup possess the spirit of one of his missing brothers?

He hesitated before lifting it into his hands. He'd anticipated this moment for months. No, years. And yet, when he finally touched the cup, nothing happened; the metal was cold and dead in his hands.

He cursed, then noticed a second, identical chalice on the shelf. In fact, there was an entire collection of seven. Not a single one gave off the vibration he'd awaited for so long.

Yet he'd sensed Rogan's magic even before he'd entered. Something of value had to be here. He simply had to find it.

The K'vr might be in disarray, but the storehouse

of their legacy was divided down distinct boundaries. Household items. Jewelry. Crude mechanical devices and tools. Weapons. Paschal smirked as he looked over the swords, which were not quite as dusty as the rest.

"See anything interesting?" Gemma called, still in the entryway, from the sound of her voice.

"Not yet," he murmured. But then, it wasn't his eyes that were going to assist in finding what he sought.

When he approached a row of musical instruments, a shiver up his spine stopped him cold.

"Paschal?"

A golden circle of light rounded the corner. After a moment, Gemma joined him, holding a lantern as he pawed through a box of flutes.

He didn't need two tries this time around. Not only did he recognize the instrument carved from ebony as belonging to his brother Rafe, but the echo of the half-Romani's psychic signature, a mournful tune, nearly blasted in his ears. Gemma yelped and jumped back.

"Did you hear that?" she asked.

So, the time had come.

"Yes, my dear, I most certainly did."

"Someone else must be down here." She stepped back toward the aisle that would lead outside. He grabbed her arm.

"No," he assured her. "We are quite alone."

Paschal rolled the flute across his palm, blocking the images from overwhelming him, acclimating himself to what must happen next. He was torn between rejoicing in the fact that he'd finally found an item to connect to the past, and lamenting that under the circumstances, he had to show Gemma the secret that might just undo them both.

"But I heard music," she insisted.

"From this flute," he explained. "This once belonged to a man named Rafe Forsyth. He lived more than two hundred and fifty years ago in Valoren."

Her eyes widened so that the whites nearly outshone the shocked blue of her irises. "How do you know?"

"By touch."

"That's impossible," she muttered.

He smiled. "You don't really believe that or you would not have brought me here or struck our bargain. You've lived up to your end. Now take my hand and let me show you what you need to know."

Surprisingly, she hesitated. "I never imagined that you were—"

"There's no time. I need to know what happened to Rafe."

"How?"

"Shh," Paschal said, then grabbed Gemma's quivering hand. "Enough talk. Just hang on for the ride."

1747
The Romani colony at Valoren

Rafe's heart froze, then dropped into the bile-rich depths of his stomach. From atop the *Chovihano*'s *vardo,* where he'd climbed to get an all-encompassing view of the village of Umgeben, he saw a girl running into the forest, pursued by a man in a flapping cloak, shouting her name. For an instant, the flash of dark hair evoked his beloved, Irika. But she was gone, safely hidden by her father along with Rafe's infant son. The village was deserted, but oddly peaceful. Nothing looked out of place.

He had no reason to suspect any danger had touched his family—yet. They were likely in the mountain caves, waiting for the mercenary army sent by King George II of England to find the Gypsy colony abandoned.

But Rafe's sister was another matter. Her name, shouted again by her pursuer, rent the air. Sarina! Only hours ago, he and his brothers had read her hastily scribbled note, announcing her elopement with the Gypsy's patron, Lord Rogan. Coupled with the threat of annihilation by a paid and ruthless army that had already crossed the Hanoverian borders into Valoren and would reach Umgeben by daybreak, Rafe and his father's British-born sons had ridden to the village to find their sister and evacuate the Romani.

But upon arriving in the village, they'd found no one—until now. Sarina was running away from the man she'd so childishly professed to love. Running for her life.

Rafe opened his mouth to call to his sister, but she had disappeared into the trees only seconds before Rogan. The sound of their retreat was instantly swallowed. Even in skirts, Sarina was incredibly fast. Unfortunately, with cursed magic at his greedy disposal, Rogan moved with swiftness not unlike the wind.

Rafe leaped to the ground and shouted for his brothers, who, like him, were searching the village. While the lightning and thunder of the storm they'd ridden through had retreated, time was still their enemy. Why was Sarina running from the man she claimed she loved? No matter how Rafe and Irika had railed against her affection for the stranger, Sarina had defended him. Loved him. She'd abandoned her family to be with him. And now she ran from him as if her life depended on it?

At least Rafe had found her. No matter how many

chase games he'd lost to her as a child, this time he would catch up. This time, he would snatch her away from the man who had spawned this invasion by defying the British king.

Rafe sprinted toward the forest. Over his shoulder he announced his position to the emptiness, hoping Aiden, Damon or another of his other brothers would hear him and pursue. Rafe suspected he could rip the blackguard Rogan apart with his own hands, but if the sorcerer sensed his approach, Rafe would be at a disadvantage. Rafe's magic flowed from a source of tranquillity and stillness. Rogan's power flew forth from hate and rage.

Still, Rafe knew these woods as well as any Gypsy in the colony, even if he had been sired in the *gadje* manor on the other side of the ridge. Rogan rarely ventured farther than the gilded steps of his grand castle.

Once within the copse of trees, Rafe stopped, closed his eyes and concentrated on sound. Even before his ears registered the whispers of the spirits that roamed these woods—spirits he'd communed with since childhood— he heard not only the stomp and crunch of rapid footfalls, but Rogan's cries for Sarina to stop. His anguish was overwhelming, knocking Rafe in the gut like a punch. Why did the *kalo* rat want her so badly? Wisely, his sister did not reply, though he could practically hear her panting as she ran farther, faster, and with desperation to reach some safe haven.

Rafe forced himself to move with deliberation and stealth. The element of surprise might be the difference between Sarina's life and Rogan's death. After sliding around a massive oak, Rafe leaped across the twist of roots knotting the ground beneath a blanket of decaying leaves, then ducked through a snarl of prickly bushes.

He knew Sarina had gone this way—he could smell her perfume, feel her fear in the wind. They were not twins, but, born of the same mother and sharing the same Gypsy blood, Rafe and Sarina knew each other's spirits. They were both wild and unpredictable. Passionate and stubborn. Growing up in a British household, they'd been allowed only a limited number of hours per day in the village. They both hungered for the traditions and the magic of their mother's people. But Rafe had married the *Chovihano*'s daughter and become part of the tribe, while Sarina remained an outsider—which had sent Sarina into the arms of the *o Beng* himself.

"Sarina!"

He could not keep silent any longer. He shouted her name over and over, suddenly aware that the echoes of footfalls no longer crackled through the forest. He considered turning back, finding his brothers now that they finally knew the direction she'd gone, but there was no time. Rogan was on her heels. He'd catch her. Rafe had no idea what the wizard would do once he had her in his grasp.

But after a half hour of searching without hearing another human sound in the dense wood, he was forced to turn back. He circled around to the entrance to the village, his lungs burning from running and climbing, then staggered to the large gates Rogan had been building, but had not yet completed, to protect the colony.

While he pulled in gulps of air, Rafe glanced beyond the tall fence posts to the castle at the other end of the village. Rogan had finished the ostentatious structure, and yet the Romani remained without gates, unprotected and vulnerable. Rafe looked up at the sky. From the position of the moon and stars, finally visible through the swiftly moving clouds, he estimated the dawn would come in less than four hours.

If the army discovered the caves, the Romani would die trapped inside walls, torture for a people who traveled the earth. Confining them to a colony in a deserted corner of Germany had been cruel enough, but at least the first King George had allowed the Gypsies to live. His greedy son, however, had not appreciated Lord Rogan's arrogance. The fool had taken control of the village and declared Valoren free from British rule—which explained the march of the mercenary army toward Rafe's home.

Rafe had started through the gates when a flash of red caught his eye. Carved into a stone marker embedded in the fence posts was Rogan's insignia—a hawk with a fire opal for an eye. With facets more brilliant than a ruby, and decidedly more uncommon, the gem was the sorcerer's favorite amulet. He had them crafted into his most prized possessions, from the brooch he wore boldly on his cloak to the hilt of his favorite sword. It signified the wealth he'd used to achieve his reign over Rafe's people.

Unable to stand the insult of the usurper's signature, Rafe drew his knife, intent on gouging the cursed gem out of the gatepost. With a battle cry from deep in his soul, he stabbed into the marker, connecting with the opal.

Pain shot through Rafe's arms, then centered on his heart. A blast of heat fired his insides, and before he could scream in shock or agony, the world went black. His legs buckled. He collapsed, but the ground never came.

Only nothingness . . .

1

"Don't touch it, Mariah."

With dexterous skill bred from close shaves all over the globe, Mariah Hunter pocketed the stone she'd spent the last half hour digging out of the craggy earth and traded it for the Walther P38 pistol she'd bought in a Berlin pawnshop. The warning had come from the last person she'd wanted to catch up to her. And considering the dangerous and desperate people who were currently on her trail even in the middle of this godforsaken wasteland, that was saying a lot.

Bending her knee to cover the gaping hole in the ground, Mariah stood, then slid her boot directly over the spot where she'd found the stone. Ben Rousseau couldn't see that his warning had come too late. She hadn't had a chance to notice anything about the rock other than a glossy red shine in one corner and the odd markings carved along the edges, but the find must be valuable or Ben wouldn't have taken a chance with a confrontation.

He held his open palms at shoulder height. "I'm not armed."

"Then you're an idiot," Mariah replied, flipping off the Walther's safety. She spared a split-second glance at the thick trees directly behind him. The massive pines curved around the tight, oblong clearing. She saw no sign that Ben had brought anyone with him, but she couldn't imagine that her former lover had come after her without backup. At the very least, she expected that Catalina Reyes, the paranormal researcher who'd been sharing Ben's bed for the last year, was out there somewhere, probably training a rifle sight on her while Ben attempted to sweet-talk Mariah out of her hard-earned treasure.

Mariah hoped Cat remembered that she owed Mariah a favor. Mariah had used her aviation contacts to track down some dodgy collector threatening to swipe some Gypsy artifact out from under Ben and Cat.

Ben took a step forward, but Mariah stopped him with a shot that missed his big toe by a quarter inch. He jumped back and cursed, just as Mariah dropped and rolled, bouncing back to her feet with her gun steady.

Maybe Cat isn't here.

"Hey! I said I was unarmed," Ben shouted, sidestepping to the left, arms out, instinctively protective of someone hidden behind him.

Or maybe she is.

"I beat you to this dig, Rousseau. Finders keepers. Back off now, while you still have all your body parts."

Ben's gaze dropped slyly to his crotch. Maybe he wasn't as clueless as she remembered. He'd zeroed in on precisely where she might have shot him ten years ago, after their disastrous relationship and fiery breakup. Now she had no desire to hurt him. She simply wanted to keep what was hers.

Though he didn't lower his hands, Ben's posture relaxed and his mouth curved into an infuriatingly lazy grin. "Threats, Mariah? I'm just trying to keep you from falling into a quagmire of trouble you really don't want right now. From what I'm hearing, you have enough on your plate."

He wasn't talking out of his arse on that, was he? If not for the aforementioned *quagmire* of trouble, she wouldn't be in this godforsaken wasteland digging up rocks and threatening an ex-boyfriend with a gun.

"Listen to the bloody professor," she said haughtily, stepping back and to the right, lining up her body to make the quickest escape. "And whatever trouble I'm in, I'll get out without any help from you. I always have. You may have lost your nerve for the antiquities game, but I haven't."

"Some artifacts are worth coming out of retirement for," he replied, with an annoying hint of cockiness that contradicted his current situation. The man never did know when an ounce of humility would do him good.

"But this place," he explained, "it's cursed, Mariah."

"So was that cave near the Oasis at Dakhla. That didn't stop either one of us from scooping up the statue of Sekhmet and selling it to the collector in Yemen."

"This is different. Trust me—"

She snorted. "Trust *you*?"

"Anything taken from this area," he continued, ignoring her justified doubts, "could contain very powerful black magic. There are some really dangerous—"

Mariah laughed. She couldn't imagine for one minute that Ben thought his warning would scare her off. Not after all they'd seen together. Not after all they'd survived.

"This isn't funny," he insisted.

She raised the gun to his chest. "Look, after what I've been through, I take my laughs where I can get them. Now pipe down. I thought I heard something."

The wind, sharp with an icy nip, whistled through the pines. Tucked in a corner of Germany still relatively undeveloped and surprisingly wild, the area had been dubbed Valoren, which the locals told her translated loosely into "land of the lost." Made perfect sense. From the sharp, jutting ridges of the mountains that surrounded them to the mossy soil beneath their feet, the area was a perfect place to hide treasures like the cricket ball–size stone she now had in her pocket.

Under the circumstances, she didn't imagine that Ben would tell her why this stone—or whatever else she might have found here—was so sought-after. Even the people she'd met in the nearby village had been perplexed by the recent interest in their undeveloped corner of the world. As a result, the locals had become exceedingly suspicious. She'd considered it a major coup that she'd found a local artisan with Gypsy roots who'd provided a hand-drawn map.

"Look," Mariah said reasonably, "like you've said, I've got troubles that have nothing to do with you. Once I pack up, I suggest you don't follow me."

"What makes you think you're leaving?"

"Who's going to stop me, you?"

Mariah fired the weapon again, missing Ben purposely and splintering the trunk of a nearby tree to his right.

Ben spun and started toward the trees on the left, giving Mariah the chance she needed.

She sprinted into the tangled forest. Behind her, Ben

shouted for her to stop. She didn't look back, but focused on leaping over rocks, ducking behind boulders and sliding over fallen tree trunks. Finally she spilled out onto the path where she'd stored her transportation—a dirt bike she'd bartered for in the village. It wasn't pretty and it was as loud as a cyclone, but it would get her out of there in a hurry.

She rode for nearly a quarter of a mile before her pursuers caught up, roaring behind her in an open-topped Jeep. With a curse, Mariah leaned forward, downshifted and swerved off the road, sending dirt and gravel flying. She preferred air travel to ground, but she'd scoped out the area well enough to map a few escape routes. Behind her, the Jeep's horn honked. Did they really expect her to stop?

She careened around an outcropping of boulders and under a canopy of trees that would lead to a river if she could avoid dropping over any of the cliffs that dotted this region. The overhang threw her into shadows. She could hear nothing but the roar of the bike's engine, the kick of the rocks beneath her wheels and the thumping of her heartbeat in her ears.

The path narrowed, forcing her to either slow down or crash. She cursed, wondering yet again why she'd come here. The whole operation had been a lark—a spontaneous grab at an opportunity that might have gotten her arse out of the proverbial sling. She'd jumped at the chance to beat her former lover to a valuable piece of history, which she planned to sell to pay off her debt to a certain collector who wasn't above having her legs broken if she disappointed him a second time. Last month's failed Mayan operation would have been her largest score in years, but she'd had to dump the coins in the

Chiapas jungle rather than risk arrest by the Mexican police. Trouble was, the tracking device she'd attached to the treasure before she tossed it wasn't working. Now, the collector wanted either the coins or the cash he'd paid her up front to facilitate her operation.

She had neither.

But she had the bloody stone. She could only hope that Ben's persistence meant the thing was valuable enough to buy her out of this mess.

Distracted by her worries, she hit a root at top speed and nearly flew over the handlebars. She corrected, scattering twigs, leaves and dirt behind her, but avoided running into a tree and kept the bike upright. The forest undergrowth was too thick for her to continue. She should have chosen another route. *Damn.* She stopped, fighting to catch her breath as she powered down the engine and listened for her pursuers.

She didn't have to listen long. They were getting closer.

She might have offered to sell the stone to Ben right there, but she had no way of knowing a fair price until she'd examined the find more closely. She patted her jacket, surprised that the spot where she'd stashed the rock was warm. Without time to wonder about the phenomenon, she hid the bike behind a thick oak, grabbed her dilly bag and crashed deeper into the brush on foot. She'd find a hidey-hole until they gave up, then make her way back to the bike and hightail it to the next village before trading up to a car that would carry her to the nearest airstrip.

She tried to find a balance between speed and stealth. Spying a narrow ledge she guessed might lead her to a lookout, Mariah moved carefully along the edge, digging her fingers into the mossy rocks for handholds.

When the flat rock beneath her feet curved around an outcropping above a deep ravine, she stopped. Being a pilot, she wasn't afraid of heights, but her many talents did not extend to mountaineering.

She cursed. She'd have to go back down and find another route. But in her hurry to change directions, her ankle twisted and she lost her footing. When she tried to recover, she found nothing beneath her. Nothing but air.

The *gadje* woman was going to get herself killed.

Infuriated, Rafe Forsyth tried to tune out the woman's emotions. For years he'd existed in peace. Centuries. His entrapment within the stone had not, until now, included experiencing the feelings of others as he had so naturally in life. Unpracticed at bearing the onslaught of emotions after all this time, he could not tune her out. Despite his efforts to remain alone, he could not ignore the warmth of her flesh so near his, could not resist reacting when a jolt of fear shot into his soul like a scalding blade.

Suddenly the ground beneath them disappeared. Her terror spiked, and the image of an impending plummet caused him to yell out the Romani word for "fly." A sensation of weightlessness suddenly surrounded him, surrounded her. Movement, sleek and swift, like a bird, propelled them forward. Then her fear gave way to surprise and, a second after her feet gently touched the ground, relief.

He saw none of this, but he sensed it. Sensed it all.

"What the bloody hell?" she said, her voice muffled even as she dug into her pocket. He heard the rustle of fabric, and then a yank of limitless force grabbed at his middle and pulled. She'd wrapped her hand completely around the stone that contained him, and instantly he was injected with an essence of woman that stirred his blood. Spiked his awareness. Tempted him to sin.

Concentrating, he fought the wrench of the magic, the all-encompassing drag of the sorcery that had bound his soul to the stone for what he guessed had been hundreds of years. Rogan had not controlled him in life; nor would he now, despite Rafe's entrapment by the curse.

How had this woman found him?

And why?

From the moment she'd brushed her fingers across the stone that had become his prison, the same dark magic that had entrapped him centuries ago awakened with full force. The urge to expand from the containment of the stone pounded at him, but he refused to succumb.

And yet now, in the open, with sunlight dappling across hair the color of rich mahogany, he couldn't help breathing in the essence of this woman named Mariah. He sensed no fragrances except her own natural musk mixed with the fertile scent of the earth and the sweet smell of torn leaves. For an instant, before he saw her startled amber eyes and the pale arch of her cheek, he wondered if she might be Romani, like himself.

She turned the stone that contained him over in her palms, fascinated by what he imagined was the same fiery glow that had drawn him to the marker so long ago. He pushed the memory aside and concentrated on the woman holding him, examining him, her entire being seized by a boundless curiosity unlike any he'd ever experienced.

What was this stone? Had it given her the ability to

fly and saved her from certain death? Was it magic? Or was it truly cursed?

He had no answers. Only regrets.

At the sound of distant voices, she released him. Sudden darkness engulfed him once more. An intense burst of energy told him she was again on the run.

This time she suppressed her fear with a thrill of adventure and a burst of confidence. The lure of her tugged at his core, but he fought. He had no desire to leave his prison.

No desire for anything but quiet. Peace. Solitude.

Forgetfulness.

Gifts he suspected he'd never experience as long as this woman possessed him.

2

"What the hell just happened?"

Gemma crashed backward, colliding with a collection of dusty knickknacks that rained to the floor and shattered on impact. The sound magnified. She grabbed her temples and pressed hard, crouching into a ball as pain radiated throughout her body. She forced her eyes to squint open. She was still in the repository. She hadn't left? Hadn't actually traveled back to the past?

It had seemed so real.

She caught sight of Paschal splayed on the ground. She crawled across the floor and turned him over. In the uncertain light from the lantern, his skin resembled fine vellum—thick, but translucent. The dark rings beneath his eyes looked nearly black against his ashen complexion. His mouth, parted slightly, was ringed in blue. Was he dying or already dead?

She pressed her cheek to his chest and tried to distinguish the throbbing in her brain from the beating of his heart. He was still alive. Which was good, because when he came to, she was going to kill him.

"Paschal! Wake up. What just happened?"

His eyes fluttered but didn't open. His groan sounded dry and weak.

Visions of her father crushed her with an emotional weight she had worked hard never to bear again. A lifetime clinging to dreams of limitless magic could not save him from mortality. Instead, he died, his beloved organization in disarray, his children pitted against each other in a battle for supremacy, and now, his daughter making pacts with the enemy to regain her family's once-precious status.

But that enemy was going to die, too, if she didn't get her head on straight. With a push of determination, she staggered to her feet and grabbed the lantern, but then decided to leave the light and brave the darkness in case Paschal woke up. She tripped only once, upending a shelf and bringing down an avalanche of dusty books.

At the top of the stairs, she caught her breath. The house was still empty, she was sure. But as she opened the hidden door that led from the underground storage area into the old manse, the atmosphere seemed to shift, as if she'd walked into a dream.

It had been daylight when she and Paschal had gone down into the bowels beneath the house. Now an inky blackness doused the innards of the creepy old house. Though she'd spent much of her childhood in these rooms, she hadn't lived here for more than ten years—hadn't visited for more than three. She couldn't remember where the light switches were, so she concentrated on finding the kitchen from memory. The kitchen had windows. The kitchen was where she'd find something to bring Paschal out of his fugue.

She reached back into her childhood, breaking into the memories she'd so carefully locked away. Her flitting

around the house in the frilly, old-fashioned dresses her
father so adored, trying to stay clean, trying to stay out
of the way while the men talked of things she shouldn't
understand. Magic. Power. Domination.

And perhaps she hadn't understood what those words
in combination truly meant, though she'd operated for
the past three years thinking that she did. What Paschal
had just done—what he'd just shown her, had nothing to
do with magic born of nostalgia or tradition or wishful
thinking. The K'vr viewed magical power as something
their leader had possessed in the past and that they intended to regain. But the magic Paschal wielded was
very real. Very now.

Doubling back after a wrong turn, she finally found
the kitchen. Shiny silver moonlight illuminated the window above the sink, so she pushed back the curtains.
Except for a breeze flitting through the collection of
willows that dominated the front of the property, she
saw no movement. Even if someone from the K'vr had
returned, she'd have no energy to fight him. She had to
focus hard just to fill a large tumbler with ice water from
the refrigerator and then retrace her steps back to the
repository.

Paschal had managed to pull himself up against the
shelf, but his eyes were closed and his face looked as
pale and semitransparent as before.

"Here," she ordered, holding the tumbler to his lips.
"Drink this."

He obeyed, then coughed and sputtered, showering
her with water.

"Damn, woman," he choked out. "Water? Need
brandy."

She shoved the cup to his lips again. "You'll drink this

water and savor every drop, old man. Once your whistle is wet enough, I want a full explanation of what the hell just happened. Then, maybe after that, you'll get your booze."

He didn't argue, but drank as she instructed, resting between sips. She took some of the cold water herself, suddenly feeling the full effects of her exhaustion now that adrenaline had subsided.

She'd never experienced anything so draining and disturbing, and yet so fascinating. Somehow, they'd traveled into the distant past. She'd felt the body of the man named Rafe wrapped around hers, as if he were a thick wool blanket in an icy storm. His emotions flowed through her. His anger. His fear. His rage. He'd lost his sister to her ancestor, Lord Rogan, for whom the K'vr had been founded. And in the end, he'd become trapped within some sort of magical lockbox. Why?

And how on earth had she piggybacked onto Paschal's psychic journey? She'd studied the phenomenon of psychometry since the first time she'd heard rumors of what he could do. But until she'd experienced the sensations for herself, she'd truly had no idea what magic felt like.

"Ready to talk yet?" she asked.

"Didn't you see everything for yourself?"

"Who is Rafe?" she asked, annoyed. She had no time for his coyness now. Not when there was so much she needed to know. "Did he own the flute?"

"Owned it or carved it," Paschal replied. "His connection to the instrument was strong. I felt him the minute I turned into this aisle. We channeled into his last memory."

"How?"

He shrugged, though the motion was barely noticeable. "If I have contact with an item associated with ... certain people ... I can view their final or, at the very least, most powerful experience."

"But he didn't die," she insisted. She wasn't entirely sure how she knew this, except that what happened, though painful, had not felt like death. There was something constraining about the experience. Something tight and dark. But the rage and anger and fear never dissipated. She continued to feel them now, though they were a fading echo, giving way to her own confusion and, truth be told, excitement.

"No," Paschal replied. "No, I don't believe he died."

Crouched beside Paschal until her legs ached, Gemma let him drink the last of the water, then eased onto the stone floor and stretched her limbs until the kinks loosened. A year ago, even six months ago, she would not have anticipated this series of events, all culminating with her sitting on a dirty floor beside a man she'd once considered only a means to an end—a source of information that would lead her closer to authority over the K'vr. But in the time she'd spent with Paschal, he'd become her mentor and teacher—in ways her father never had.

"When did you realize you had this ability?" she asked.

"Since childhood, though I kept it hidden from my family. My stepmother guessed, though, and helped me hone it in secret."

"It's remarkable. And I was able to come with you. Was it because you were holding my hand? Can we do it again?"

Paschal pressed his lips more tightly together, enhancing the blue line circling his lips. Okay, so he wasn't up to another go so soon. Neither was she, truthfully. But she would revisit the idea once they had their energy back. Wasn't like he was going anywhere. Not without her, at any rate.

"Tell me about Rafe," she asked, changing tack. "How did he know Rogan?"

"You heard his thoughts," he replied, the relaxation of his jaw indicating that she'd hit a topic he was willing to discuss. "Rafe's father was the governor of Valoren, the land your ancestor usurped."

"So this Rafe was somehow important to Rogan? An enemy?"

"Important? Hardly. But an enemy to the last. Sarina was Rafe's only full-blooded sibling. They were very close. Until Rogan seduced her away from her family." Paschal's volume dipped to barely a whisper. Even clearing his throat did nothing to strengthen the sound of his voice. "She was young and beautiful and wild as the wind."

For a split second, Gemma thought she heard more in Paschal's voice than the mere repetition of Rafe's emotions. It was almost as if he'd known her himself. But that was impossible. Rogan had disappeared over two hundred and sixty years ago. The Gypsies of Valoren and the family of the governor were all as dead as her forebear.

But Rafe had not died. At least, not in that moment.

"Rogan must have loved Sarina," Gemma insisted. "She must have been the woman to whom he gave the Queen's Charm."

The truth about her ancestor's life was, for the most part, a great unknown, but the stories were endless. Rogan's brother, Lukyan of Hungary, had started the K'vr, and wrote extensively about how his sibling had used his magic to collect great wealth and control the locals.

Then Rogan had left his homeland and migrated first to England, and then to a Gypsy colony named Valoren by King George, its founder, who'd wanted to cleanse the Romani from London. He'd set aside barren Hanoverian lands for the task, lands that, unbeknownst to the monarch, possessed a powerful magic all their own.

According to K'vr archives, Lukyan never saw his brother again. But Lukyan used the villagers' fear of Rogan's power to maintain a position of might over them. And his strength did not die with him. His son kept the K'vr going, as did his son afterward. War and political change forced the K'vr underground, where they remained to this day, amassing wealth in anticipation of the day their legacy of magic would take them out of the shadows and into a position of unyielding strength that armies of the greatest nations would not be able to thwart.

And though Gemma knew that various grand apprentices, as their leaders were called, often wielded psychic abilities that helped them make money and influence others, she'd never seen anything like what Paschal could do—not even in her own father.

"Rogan wanted Sarina, yes," Paschal offered, "but Sarina received the Queen's Charm from her father."

"That's not the story I heard," she contradicted.

Paschal did not argue. He said nothing at all. Then she realized his eyes had closed and he was, undoubtedly, asleep.

She cursed. She shook him once, but when he simply snored more loudly, she gave up. He was in no shape to tell her more right now, but he would. Eventually.

Though Paschal looked uncomfortable sitting on the floor with his head lolling sideways against a dusty shelf, she didn't imagine she could move him without doing more damage. She pulled off her jacket and shoved it under his head. With sleep, he'd recover.

Hopefully, the same would go for her. Exhaustion unlike any she'd experienced was seeping into her bones, clutching at the insides of her eyelids from the base of her skull and yanking them tight like window shades. Still, she resisted. She had so much to think about—so many questions to find answers to.

First, how had Paschal gained this power to peek into the past? He was not, to the best of her knowledge, descended from Rogan. She'd long suspected that Paschal had access to Rogan's magical source, which her brother had tried unsuccessfully to recover, resulting in his conviction for murder, among other charges. But Paschal certainly didn't carry it with him. She'd searched his things on multiple occasions, and since they'd come to New York, they'd traveled light.

Though psychometric talent was rare, it was not unheard-of in her circles. One of the grand apprentices in their long line—a great-great-grandfather, if she remembered correctly—reportedly possessed the ability. Perhaps that was why she was able to see what Paschal saw?

She snuggled beside him and surrendered to sleep with images of Rafe thrashing about in the forest, searching for his sister, replaying in her mind. He'd wanted to find her with a desperation Gemma couldn't quite comprehend. He'd left his wife and son behind to search for an errant sister. He and his brothers had risked life and limb on behalf of a headstrong girl in love with an older, more powerful man. Why?

So many questions . . . and no answers. Until, at least, Paschal awoke and told her the rest of what he knew.

3

Mariah settled into her spacious first-class seat and pulled her fedora down over her eyes. The smell of leather and sweat on the inside band assailed her nostrils, and she couldn't suppress a chuckle. How ironic that Ben Rousseau had given her this very hat. He'd meant the gift as a joke. Called her a female Indiana Jones after she'd flown them to safety following a narrow escape from a Bedouin sheikh who didn't appreciate their liberating a valuable scimitar that had been in his family for twelve generations.

Tonight, she'd proved yet again that she could get out of a tight spot without so much as a whip. She'd upgraded to the best seat on the plane without turning out as much as a quarter. A great trick, since that was about as much cash as she had left. She'd need to restock her wallet as soon as she got home.

Not that she had all that much cash left in Texas, but she always kept a few stashes in various locations around Austin in case she had to make a quick getaway. Escaping Europe hadn't been easy, but she'd managed. Now she had fifteen hours to relax.

Maybe fifteen hours to wonder how the hell she'd managed to get this far.

The incident on the cliff haunted her, but she'd pushed the event out of her mind. She supposed there might be a logical explanation, but Ben's words in the clearing rang loudly in her mind.

Magic.

Black magic.

Black magic that had saved her life.

Black magic that just might get her out of trouble, once she figured out how to harness it.

She cursed, shifted in her seat, double-checked her seat belt and waited for the Boeing 777-200LR to power up. For years, her competitors had called her insane for the risks she took. Now, finally catching her breath after the narrow escape from Valoren, she wondered if they might have been right. Not only had this been a particularly dangerous dig, but since she'd picked up that ruddy stone, something had changed inside her. Or around her. Had she really flown off the face of a mountain and lived to tell the tale? The whole incident was whacked.

And yet, she'd barely looked at the rock since her escape from the woods. She didn't want to take any chances. When she was safe at her place in Texas, she'd examine it closely and find a way to determine what price it might fetch. If she got home. There was a very good chance that either Hector Velez, the Mayan collector, or Ben Rousseau would be waiting for her at the airport. If they hadn't already found her here.

She lifted her hat and took a look around the cabin. No one in first class looked the least bit interested in her. The man in the aisle next to her window seat had a *U*-shaped pillow tucked around his bulky neck, noise-blocking headphones strapped around his ears and a black satin eye mask blocking out any light. His breathing indicated he was already fast asleep, and they hadn't even pulled away from the gate.

Still, Mariah couldn't help but shift closer to the window. With Velez after her for his lost coins and Ben Rousseau likely in pursuit to recover the stone, she couldn't afford to trust any situation. But her best bet for now was to get some rest. Rejuvenate her body and her brain.

After about twenty minutes and two gratis single-malt scotches, however, she realized that relaxation simply wasn't possible. A heat centered in the pit of her stomach kept her awake. Antsy. She shifted, displacing the bag she'd kept clutched in her lap since she'd boarded. After nearly killing herself to retrieve the stone, there was no way in hell she was going to chuck it into the overhead compartment.

"Ma'am, may I take your bag?"

Mariah lifted the brim of her hat. This was a different flight attendant. Not the one who'd asked her the same question first upon boarding and the second time about ten minutes ago, when she'd delivered her second drink.

"No," she replied. "Where's Lisa?"

The flight attendant's seemingly permanent smile did not falter. "You have to store it at your feet, then, until after takeoff. If there's anything I can get you, please don't hesitate to—"

Mariah cut off the rest of the practiced platitude by complying and then lowering her hat. She was rarely rude by accident, having been raised by a woman who considered bad manners to be an abomination only slightly above a lack of education or a misguided fashion sense. On the other hand, her father would have agreed that simply covering her eyes with her hat was a perfectly acceptable way to tell someone that you had no interest in what they had to say. Lord knew the man had done the same thing to her more times than she could count.

With an audible sniff, the flight attendant moved away. Mariah figured she wouldn't be getting another scotch anytime soon, but that was probably for the best. She wasn't much of a drinker anymore. First, her tastes traveled to the expensive, and second, she'd come to value a clear head. Maybe if she'd laid off the hooch in her misspent youth, she might never have fallen for Ben Rousseau's cool gray eyes and silver tongue in the first place.

Just after takeoff, Mariah reclaimed her bag from beneath the seat, surprised by the flare of heat against her lap. She tore off her hat, then dug into the bag to see if the stone was really increasing in temperature. This was the second time the stone had grown hotter—the first time was immediately before she'd nearly fallen to her death. As a pilot herself, she realized that any incendiary device on a plane wasn't a good thing, though the rock had passed through security at the airport without garnering so much as a sideways glance from the screeners. It was, after all, just a rock.

Once her hand closed around a cool stone, she blew out a relieved breath. Flying commercial, even in first class, wasn't her preferred mode of travel. She'd practically been born in the pilot's chair, and she didn't like handing over the yoke of her avionic destiny to some unknown flyer who might or might not have gotten a decent night's sleep before embarking on a transatlantic flight. Still, she supposed she should at least find a way to rest while she could.

The scotch finally reached her bloodstream and, after a yawn, she retrieved her hat, settled it over her eyes and pushed back her seat. With her hand still clutched around the stone inside the bag, she fell asleep.

And then, just as quickly, awoke.

The sound of the plane engine had stopped.

She threw off her hat and slid up the window shade. They were still flying. Soft, cottony clouds, shining silver under the rays of a full moon, streamed beneath them. Mariah yawned, determined to alleviate the pressure in her ears that was blocking out all noise, but it did not work.

Silence pressed in on her, and when she turned to look at her seatmate, she jumped back, slamming against the window beside her.

The man beside her was no longer hefty and co-cooned. Instead, it was Ben.

"You can't have it," she argued. "I found it first."

Ben smirked, but did not answer. He reached out to touch her face, but she slapped his hand away. He'd lost the privilege of touching her a long time ago.

The moment her palm made contact with his skin, he changed. Morphed. His complexion darkened. His hair deepened to the same blue-black as polished ebony and then lengthened until it covered his shoulders. Only his eyes remained similar—but where they were once light gray, they were now the color of a silvery, moonlit sky.

"Who are you?" she asked, though her voice bounced around in her head as if there were nothing to absorb the sound except her skull.

He did not answer. He simply stared at her with an

intensity that made her want to cover herself. She still had clothes on, but felt entirely naked to his gaze. And her arms wouldn't move. Or her legs. She could not turn her head. The seat belt suddenly tugged tight against her midsection, and her blouse pulled across her chest.

"If you work for Velez, I don't have the money. But I'll get it. Soon. I have this—"

His quizzical expression cut off her explanation. He had no idea what she was talking about, and yet he stared at her with a curiosity that, though not threatening, chilled her to the bone. Again, the sensation of being completely exposed washed over her. It was as if he were looking inside her—as if his stare could penetrate not only her clothes, but her very skin.

"Tell me who you are," she demanded.

He shifted nearer, and the unmistakable scent of the forest assailed her. Not just any forest, but the one she'd escaped at Valoren. The sweet aroma of pine, the deep, loamy fragrance of soil, and the musky essence of man struck her hard. He said nothing, but stared at her intently, starting at the top of her head and then sweeping downward. Each trailing of his gaze over her body ignited a sexual awareness she did not want to feel. She'd never seen this man before. He had no right to examine her so . . . intimately.

But she could do nothing to fight him off.

"Please," she begged, thrown into unknown territory by her utter helplessness. He rewarded her weakness with a smile and then lowered his mouth over hers in a kiss that defied everything she'd ever known about kisses.

He was gentle, but not shy. Exploratory, but not inexperienced. His mouth tasted of dry red wine and some exotic fruit—like plum or currant. His lips were warm and his breath intoxicating. She couldn't fight the instinctual pull to wrap her arms around his shoulders and feel the sinews of his muscles through his shirt, but the moment she could move again, she woke with a start.

"What the fuck?"

This time when Mariah ripped off her hat, it sailed all the way to the galley. The flight attendant coming around the corner with a tray full of mimosas screamed, then doused herself and the passengers in the front rows with orange juice and champagne. The man beside Mariah, no longer the dark stranger or Ben but again the hefty, world-weary traveler, stared at her as if she'd sprouted a second head.

"Such language," he muttered, and then returned to buttering his bagel.

Mariah muttered an apology, then sank back into her seat. She'd been dreaming. Only dreaming. But it had felt so real. If she didn't know she was persona non grata with the airplane crew at this moment, she would have ordered enough scotch to keep her occupied until landing. Instead, she gripped the bag tighter, squelching a yelp at the heat of the stone within.

She didn't know what the hell she'd found in Germany, but she now knew one thing beyond a shadow of a doubt—at the first opportunity, she was getting rid of it. And the sooner the better.

Had he possessed corporeal form, Rafe would have grabbed onto something solid to hold himself steady. The pull, particularly when he had wondered what it might feel like to kiss Mariah, had increased to nearly inescapable levels. He'd dreamed of tasting her, imagined the yielding of her lips against his. But as quickly as he'd felt freedom, the stone encasing his soul constricted. Fortunately. While he remained safe within the stone, he defied Rogan's magic and stood firm against the elemental call that could come to nothing good. Rafe had had his chance at love and desire—and thanks to Rogan, it was gone.

Once the sensation of floating on the air ended with a jolt and jostle, Rafe understood that Mariah had returned to the ground. He did not understand, of course, how she could fly without his magical assistance, but he knew that she had. Her emotions, so guarded and controlled with everyone she spoke with, flooded from her heart every time she touched the stone. He knew things about her he did not want to know. How much her resentment toward her former lover had faded. How her disappointment in her failure for a man named Velez gnawed at her. How her heart ached for someone she could share her fears with—someone who would not turn her weakness into a weapon to wield at will.

She was strong, this woman. Strong, but damaged. And with Rafe's own personal history, he was the last man who could offer her solace.

If he was still a man.

At this moment, he knew not what he was. Trapped within the stone, he could think and suffer as a man, but he could not feel the mist of the night on his skin or the ground beneath his feet. Or a woman's mouth pressed intimately to his. And until Mariah, he had not craved the sensations. Not once.

But now it was all he could think about. The kiss had not been real, but the dream had made his blood rush in his ears. As if he had tasted her, the flavors of her lips lingered on his tongue. Strong, smooth whiskey and sweet feminine warmth had intoxicated him for hours.

He could see nothing from inside the bag where she'd stored the stone, but he experienced a change in atmosphere. The stone suddenly grew moist and hot, and he guessed the temperature had changed to match the air outside. He'd never visited a climate such as this, but he did not have to be free of the curse to know that he'd somehow been transported to a foreign land.

Hours had gone by. Only a few days ago, the passage of time would have been inconsequential, but ever since Mariah dug his prison out of the Valoren dirt, he'd suffered every excruciating minute with an awareness he did not want.

He attempted to block out the murmurs and mumblings of conversation outside the bag, but without trying, he understood that she was attempting to find lodging under a name that was not her own. Once the bartering was complete and a swooping upward ride ended, he heard a door open, then close. Locks snapped into place, and the soft bounce of a cushion jolted him. Had she tossed the bag onto a bed?

Again, he heard a succession of opening and closing doors. The slide of curtains. Clicking noises he could not identify. Suddenly he heard a loud, trilling sound, this time from within the bag. Her hand brushed against the stone as she dug inside, and again, he was overwhelmed with emotions he did not wish to feel. Desire. Longing. Lust.

She cursed, then pulled him out. The need to touch her, taste her, possess her, increased to dizzying proportions.

The room was dark. She'd pulled down the shades, and only the golden glow from strangely steady lanterns illuminated the room. Her brown hair caught the light, reflecting a fiery red he longed to slide his hands through. Her eyes, warm as topaz, widened at the sight of him.

The chirping noise stopped. For the first time, she inspected the stone that contained him. Every stop on the route to this place had been quick, and her mistrust had been overwhelming. But here she felt safe.

With the precision of a craftsman perusing the workmanship of a rival, she thrust the stone beneath the light and examined every crevice and curve. When she nicked the center of the stone with her thumbnail, a dizzying shiver ran the length of his spine. She raised the stone to her lips, expelled a mint-infused breath over him, then rubbed the stone vigorously against her breasts, throwing him into a conflagration of need versus resistance. He had to use the entire force of his will to remain inside the stone.

"Just what are you?" she asked.

Your darkest nightmare, he thought.

With a gasp, she dropped the stone and screamed.

4

Had she heard him?

Rafe watched her intently as the trilling noise again broke through the shocked silence. Mariah had already backed away from where he'd landed on a cushioned floor. She tripped near the bed, fumbling as she scooped a slim metal case from her sack on the bed. Her gaze darted nervously between the stone on the ground and the odd case in her hand, which continued to emit noises not unlike the skylarks that had once perched in the willow outside his window.

She flipped open the metal case and then stomped about as if the innards had revealed distressing news. After a long glance in his direction, she pressed the device with her thumb, then held it to her ear. Her eyes, however, darted back to him, entrapped in the stone, every few seconds.

"Hunter here," she said to the device. Her voice held none of the anxiety Rafe felt washing off her body in waves. She was putting on a show, but for whom? There was no one in the room other than him . . . of this he was certain.

After observing her for a full minute, he guessed that the device she spoke into allowed her to communicate with someone who was not there. Someone she knew. Rafe's mind whirled. Did Mariah have magic of her own? How else could she perform such a marvel? And yet, if she possessed powers, why could she not save herself at the cliff in Valoren?

Though Rafe had not ventured from the stone, he understood that she'd traveled a great distance in a short amount of time. Snippets of conversation led him to believe they were in a different country, one far removed from his homeland. To his left, a black box blinked green numbers. Did they represent the time? And though the windows were closed, a cool breeze riffled through the room.

Apparently, the device she spoke into was part of her everyday world, a world that contained many mysteries Rafe had no desire to solve. And yet, he could not help but watch her as she paced about, exchanging conversation as if she communicated with distant compatriots regularly, and without concentration or incantation.

Rafe's learned eldest brother, Damon, had often spoken of many conceived inventions that would have allowed for magic in the everyday world. What would Rafe's ancestors have thought about such marvels as pistols and telescopes? They'd likely be as confused as he was, but at least he knew that he'd been thrust forward in time, into a world wholly unlike his own. Logically, that world must have changed. And with it, so had methods of communication.

He would simply have to listen and learn and observe.

"No, Señor Velez, I haven't found the coins yet," Mariah explained. "I was just in Chiapas last week and I—"

She stopped speaking, and her gaze shifted back to the stone. Rafe could tell from her expression that she was only half listening to the voice speaking directly into her ear through the strange metal box. She approached Rafe's prison with caution, kicking the edge with the toe of her boot, then hopping away as if she expected someone to jump out at her. Well, it would not be him. No matter how the temptation to emerge pulled at him, he resisted. If his speaking had terrified her, he could only imagine the crazed consequences of his appearing from nowhere.

Though she did not seem the fearful type, Mariah Hunter did appear to be a sensible woman who harnessed her fear and turned it to her advantage, but whoever she spoke with now frightened her. And she'd been startled to hear Rafe's voice. Yet despite her apprehension, she approached the stone again and knelt, her elbow on her knee and her chin resting on her fist. Her eyes narrowed with curiosity.

He could hear the tinny sound of a voice emerging from out of the slim silver device, which, now that he could see it more closely, resembled a decorative case often used for snuff. The idea that people could converse over any distance with no more than a piece of metal as their conduit fascinated him.

"Yes, I understand that you invested a lot of money," she said, her tone distracted. "But these things happen. You knew the risks."

With a jolt, she moved the box abruptly away from her ear. The harsh voice inside the box increased in both volume and anger.

"I need more time," she said finally.

Rafe sensed her annoyance increase as she pushed any fear completely aside.

"A week?"

She paced around the room now, stopping once to glance out of the window. When she moved the shade, no light came into the room. Rafe assumed this meant the hour was late. For a split second, he allowed himself to wonder what view existed outside the window, and the thought increased the drag he'd been fighting since she first touched the stone.

He resisted again, something that became easier after she walked away.

"What if I find you something even more valuable than the Mayan coins?" she asked.

Her smile was enhanced by a cunning light in her eyes, a gleam suddenly in balance with the rest of her face. Rafe watched in wonder. Her anxiety dissipated as her sense of control increased. Her excitement and anticipation seeped into the stone, even from a distance, building his curiosity to unbearable levels.

She was no ordinary woman. He sensed that she fed on risk and danger. He couldn't remember experiencing such an intimate connection to someone he'd never yet touched. Never *would* touch.

His resistance to the pull faltered, but did not break.

"Well," she said, "I may have something interesting for you. I'm doing research. I'll be back in touch when I know more. You could end up recouping your investment and making a tidy profit. That's win-win, yes?"

Her smile broadened. She said good-bye, tossed the silver case onto the bed and threw her hands up with an excited whoop. With her exhilaration canceling out her wariness, she scooped the stone into her palm and talked to it directly.

"I don't know what you are, but if you get me out of

this fix, you'll be worth all the added craziness you've brought into my life."

Rafe concentrated on remaining silent. He washed his thoughts of any possible response, focusing instead on the nothingness that had been his only company for centuries. Mariah continued to eye the stone quizzically, then finally tossed it onto the bed, double-checked the lock on the door and then proceeded to remove her clothes.

Rafe knew he should look away. But as she peeled her snug shirt from her skin, revealing a lacy contraption that buoyed her breasts, the distinction between right and wrong disappeared. Like a man, she wore breeches that reached her ankles, but the fabric hugged her hips and buttocks, with shocking emphasis on the parts of her that were, undeniably, female.

She flicked a button at her waist and, seconds later, shimmied and undulated provocatively until only the lace on her breasts and a sheer scrap of silk cut into a triangle at the apex of her thighs kept her from total nakedness.

Had he a mouth, Rafe knew it would have watered.

He had to look away or douse the room in darkness to preserve the privacy she had no idea she did not have. Suddenly, the lanterns she'd lit upon entering the room flickered, then went out.

"Strike me, what now?" she shouted, frustrated.

She stumbled away and then a light from a smaller room behind her flicked on. Backlit, her body tortured him anew. She was lithe and slim, yet muscled. Her skin glistened as if she'd spent her whole life in the sun.

Despite the wrongness, he wanted to see all of her.

The lights in the room came back on. She gasped,

eyed the stone warily again, then whispered something to herself that he could not hear, though her uncertainty rang loud and clear. She closed the door to the smaller room with a decisive bang.

Moments later he heard water, as if a rainstorm had started inside the tiny room where Mariah had disappeared. After a while, steam seeped from a gap between the door and the floor. Water? Inside? And how had it heated so quickly? He sensed no fire. Saw no maid to draw a bath.

This woman brought him nothing but confusion and conflict. He had not wanted to leave Valoren. He'd never wanted to know the world outside of his homeland. Unlike his brothers, Rafe had been born in the Gypsy colony, and unlike his sister, who longed to explore, Rafe had never entertained any desire to leave. Now, trapped within Rogan's magical stone, he had no choice but to go wherever this woman took him.

And added to his torture now was Mariah Hunter herself. She moved with the same sensuality as the wind in a storm, possessing all the same flashes of emotion, the same thunderous desires. Her tempestuous emotions wreaked havoc on his long-dormant abilities to care about the world outside. Long ago, he'd come to terms with his fate—or at the very least, he'd forgotten how to rage against it. What point did fighting serve? No matter how he'd once tried, no matter what he'd lost, he could not free himself from his magical prison.

And yet, until he'd crossed paths with Mariah Hunter, he'd never experienced the incredible pull he suspected would lead him to the outside. All he had to do was surrender. Give in. Trust that submitting would not result in something worse than perpetual imprisonment.

Suddenly, the memory of his first hours trapped inside Rogan's marker rushed back at him. Pain slashed at his nonexistent innards. He tried to push the images away, but he had nowhere to hide from the anguish, nowhere to run from the guilt.

He remembered little of what happened to him immediately after he'd drawn his dagger to destroy Rogan's mark on the gemstone embedded in the unfinished gate. He recalled a flash of light, intense pain—and then nothing. Only at daybreak had he determined that he'd been magically sucked inside the stone he'd attempted to destroy, unable to free himself or communicate with anyone who passed.

Unfortunately, the only people entering the village through the unfinished gate were the soldiers. They'd marched in just after dawn, as he'd learned they would when he'd ridden reconnaisance for his brothers the night before. The mercenary army had carried swords and bayonets and shields, as if the tiny community of peaceful Romani would offer resistance. He heard the paid fighters curse the emptiness of the village, endured the sound of the leaders ordering the scouts into the mountains to search the caves. Trapped inside the stone, he could not warn his people—he could not help his wife.

And then she appeared.

Irika.

As if he'd conjured her with Rogan's black magic—the same way he'd saved Mariah from falling off the cliff—his wife had appeared.

Had he magically summoned Irika to her death? Though his memory was untested, he recalled hearing his wife desperately shout his name before she'd crossed into his line of vision. Why had his beloved, strong-willed wife left the safety of the caves? To search for him? Had she mistaken the marauding army for allies of his father, the former governor, instead of enemies of the Romani clan?

He'd never know. Her calls for him had nonetheless sealed her fate. In seconds, a soldier had captured her, slammed her to her knees and held a blade to her throat while he shouted for his superior. Quickly surrounded, Irika was assailed by questions about the whereabouts of Rogan and the Gypsy inhabitants of the village.

She refused to speak another word, so they killed her.

And there was nothing Rafe could do to stop them.

Suddenly, the thick blackness of the memory pressed in on him like the smoke of a lethal fire. He choked on his rage, on his powerlessness. Irika had died trying to find him. He'd wanted to emerge from the stone and save her from the murdering soldiers, but he'd been unable to move. Squeezed tight inside black magic, he'd pounded against the invisible walls for hours, to no avail.

And then, he'd simply . . . faded.

His existence since that night had been as uncertain as it was unending. At first, he marked the change of seasons as the snow fell or melted around him, as the birds nested and sang or abandoned the cold climes for warmer weather to the south. But after decades of watching the world go on around him, watching the stain of Irika's blood fade into the soil, he stopped caring. He slept, unconcerned about the world outside.

Now a strange woman had touched the stone for the briefest instant, and he had to employ all his strength to remain within.

A greater torture did not exist.

A sound from outside the rented room suddenly cleared the darkness. Rafe sensed someone coming near—someone who fed on vile emotions such as hatred, disgust and the kind of frenzied anger that resulted in bloodshed. The rainlike sound from the smaller room had stopped. Mariah emerged, swathed in only a towel, her hair dripping wet, when the door from the hallway burst open. Two men charged inside. Dressed entirely in black, one grabbed Mariah roughly. Her towel dropped in the struggle. Rafe hardly noticed until he saw a silver blade flash against her moist and vulnerable neck.

"Where is it?" the assailant demanded.

Mariah, like Irika, refused to speak. The second man grabbed the stone from the bed and held it against Mariah's cheek until the gem bit into her skin. Only her anger overrode her terror.

"Thought you could steal from us, did you?" the man asked.

Despite her nudity, Mariah's topaz eyes flashed with defiance. "I found it fair and square."

The man with the stone laughed while the other ran his free hand roughly over Mariah's breasts, then down her belly. Rafe shouted for them to release her. Both men flew away from her, pushed by the magic that entrapped him, by the dark essence that instantly constricted around his soul.

The man holding the stone scrambled to his feet. He stretched the rock away from him, but did not let go. Rafe sensed his conflict. He was terrified of the voice he'd just heard and the force that had pushed him aside, but he was equally fearful of what would happen to him if he did not complete his mission.

The man with the knife climbed to his feet just as quickly, too dazed to recapture her. She slammed her fisted hand against his nose, then doubled him over with a well-placed elbow to the gut. She grabbed his wrist and twisted until his knife flew from his grip, unaware that his partner had raised the stone above her head.

Rafe could not allow another woman to die. He surrendered to the pull. Pressure attacked him from all sides, as if his entire body were being squeezed through the eye of a needle. He couldn't contain a furious roar when he finally broke free.

He ignored the dizzying pain and struck out at Mariah's attacker, throwing the man backward over the bed. His eyes, visible only through slits in a covering knotted tightly over his face, widened with terror.

"Who the hell—"

Rafe turned and watched Mariah crumple the second assailant with a well-placed punch to the jaw.

"Dress yourself," Rafe ordered, forcing his gaze away from her.

For a second, he anticipated that she might argue, but her nudity demanded attention more than did her shock. She tugged her shirt over her wet skin and jumped into the breeches, then pointed at the dumbfounded man on the other side of her bed.

"That rock is mine," she insisted.

"He will not take the stone," Rafe replied, holding out his palm, knowing, somehow, that he could summon his prison back to him with a thought. "Return to me."

The man cursed as the stone jumped in his grasp. He threw his other hand over it and attempted to pull the rock tight to his chest.

Rafe took a bold step forward and repeated the command.

The stone flew from the thief's grip and thudded into Rafe's outstretched palm. The heavy heat against his flesh was unlike anything he'd experienced. In his moment of hesitation, the thief rushed toward him. Rafe waved his other arm and, instead of landing atop him, the attacker flew through the air, crashed against the wall and fell, motionless, to the ground.

Rafe moved to examine the stone again, but his palm was empty. Mariah had reclaimed the marker with amazing swiftness.

"I don't know who you are," she said to him, her eyes wide and apprehension rolling off her body, "or what you are, but I think we'd both be better off if we got the hell out of here."

As she spoke, she scooped her belongings into her bag and tossed her boots over her shoulder.

"Where are you going?" he asked.

She pulled up short, her eyebrows arched high above her wide, amber eyes. She swallowed deeply, then gave the now-splintered door a cursory glance. "I'm leaving. Thanks for your, um, help, but I suggest you do the same."

She had no idea where he'd come from; of this Rafe was certain. And she'd either not seen him summon the stone from the thief's grasp, or else she was ignoring what her eyes told her was true. After a split second's hesitation, she left.

Rafe remained behind.

Though the man nearest to him stirred with a moan, Rafe ignored him, focusing instead on the shape of his own hands. Then his arms and legs and chest. He still wore the leather breeches he'd worn that night. His shirt, nearly as dark as his boots, felt damp against his skin and smelled of rain and horse and sweat. He spotted a mirror near the window. Stepping over the unconscious attacker, he stared into the looking glass, shocked at how little he'd changed.

His hair was still black and long. His skin untouched by time.

But before he could form another thought about the resilience of his youth, the stone's pull yanked him yet again. He flew from the room like bait on a fisherman's hook and, a split second of darkness later, he was beside Mariah, sitting on a seat inside a carriage made entirely of leather, metal and glass.

"Strike me," she cursed.

He spied the stone instantly, nestled between her legs. Her left hand gripped an odd wheel while her right twisted a key into a tiny lock just below it. A roar erupted, and he tensed in response.

"What is that sound?" he asked.

"Your cue to get the hell out of my car," she replied. "Look, thanks for helping me out back there, but I can handle myself from here on out."

Rafe took a chance and grabbed her wrist.

"Hey," she protested.

"I cannot leave you, my lady."

"Wanna bet?"

From beneath the seat, she withdrew a pistol. He'd never seen such a design before, but he had no doubt the weapon was deadly. He released her and held his hands up in surrender.

"I have no wish to harm you," he said.

"I have no wish to be harmed, so this should go real easy. Get out of my car."

He glanced around. So, this thing was called a car.

She used the gun to gesture toward a handle in the door. "Now. I don't know who those guys were in my room or how they found me, but I'd like to avoid tangling with them again."

"A wise plan of action," he agreed.

"But I don't know you, either. So if you don't mind . . ."

With an indulgent grin, he attempted to twist the handle, then figured out that pulling it toward him released the latch. He pushed open the door and climbed out. He had no desire to be shot, though he highly suspected that while she possessed Rogan's stone, leaving her was not an option.

His theory was tested immediately. The moment he was out of her car, she somehow made the wheeled contraption move. A screech not unlike the caw of a massive hawk echoed against the walls of the odd stone building. Red lights blinked from the back of the vehicle, which drove down a ramp and disappeared.

He looked around. The structure housed rows and rows of these so-called cars, though none of them seemed engaged at the moment. How amazing these modes of transportation were, requiring no horse to pull them, as far as he could see. Just as he was about to investigate a nearby vehicle, the blackness captured him once again, and this time, when he opened his eyes, he was not unprepared to find himself beside Mariah as she sped down the road.

She, however, swerved in surprise, initiating a spin that convinced Rafe that if he hadn't died centuries ago, he might soon enough.

5

Mariah squeezed her thighs together, determined not to lose her hold on the damned stone even if she crashed into the telephone pole she was using all of her driving skills to avoid. She eased off the brake and allowed the car's momentum to carry it through a full rotation before she applied measured pressure to the pedal and counterbalanced the steering so that they went off-road, but missed hitting anything.

Once she had the ignition off, she scrambled for her gun again. Unfortunately, the spin had dislodged it from under her seat. She was unarmed and vulnerable to someone who'd just appeared out of the ether.

Maybe he wasn't the crazy one?

"Who are you?" she demanded. "How did you get back in the car? What do you want with me?"

For all his swarthy good looks, her mysterious rescuer suddenly looked a bit green around the gills.

"Is this how men travel now? In devices that make one ill? I much prefer a horse."

"Typical Texan," she muttered, reaching farther beneath her seat for the gun, finding nothing but a fast-food wrapper that was likely over a year old. The last time she'd used this car—a getaway vehicle she'd kept stashed near the airport in case she needed a quick set of wheels—her main ride had been in the shop.

She gave up trying to find the gun. She had a strong suspicion the weapon wasn't going to deter him. She could no longer deny that he had arrived from nowhere. For the third time. The first two times she'd written off his sudden appearance as a product of her attention being diverted elsewhere. This time, that explanation did not apply.

"Damn it, who are you?" she asked again.

He swallowed thickly, and when he turned, the nauseated look on his face had disappeared. His skin tone had returned to a healthy, sun-kissed complexion reminiscent of the men she'd met in Egypt—though not quite as dark. Set in perfect balance beneath thick lashes, his eyes were a startling gray. His mouth curved into a smile that might have stolen her breath under other circumstances.

"Rafe," he replied. "My name is Rafe."

She cursed inwardly as his mellifluous voice rode roughshod over her frazzled nerves. This Rafe was utterly hypnotic—like a living, breathing pendulum.

"Rafe what?" she snapped, determined to ward off any attraction. So what if he'd come to her rescue in the hotel room? Another minute or so and she would have taken control of the situation—though she had to admit that without his intervention, she might not have gotten a spare minute at all.

He eyed her quizzically before finally replying. "You require a surname? Forsyth. Rafe Forsyth, son of John, Earl of Hereford."

"You don't sound British," she decided. Though the

inflections of an accent tinged his words, his manner of speaking was more exotic.

"You do," he said. "Sound British, that is. Only . . . not."

"I'm Aussie by birth," she explained. "American by living arrangements."

"Aussie? American? I do not understand. Where am I?"

"Don't you know?"

He leveled an impatient glare at her. "If I knew, would I ask?"

"You're in Texas, in my car, where I did not invite you. In fact, this is the third time you've shown up, and I don't even know . . ."

As she stared at him, she realized she'd seen this man before. In her dreams. On the plane. Kissing her.

"You need to leave now," she insisted.

"I cannot," he replied. "You have tried twice to rid yourself of me, but I am bound to you for as long as you possess that cursed stone."

She glanced down at the rock, still clutched between her legs. "What are you talking about? Look, I don't have time for this."

"Time is not your problem, my lady."

"What's up with the 'my lady' crap? This isn't the seventeenth century."

"I should hope not, as I was born in the century following. But the fact of the matter is, that bauble you retrieved from Valoren has possessed my soul for quite some time, and from what I can tell by the events of this evening, as long as you have it with you, you have me as well."

He crossed his arms over his chest—a rather impressive chest, she could tell, as the ties on his midnight shirt had come undone, allowing her a generous sampling of his tanned muscles beneath. With squared shoulders and forearms whose lean tendons were obvious even through his sleeves, the man looked like no stranger to physical activity. And while Mariah was no slouch when it came to self-defense, this guy could probably break her in two with very little effort.

Only, his eyes betrayed not a single violent tendency. He seemed perfectly content to sit in her car and tell her some wild tale about how they were connected to each other through a magical stone.

At that moment, she blinked, then fully processed what he'd said.

He was from the eighteenth century.

The stone possessed his soul.

She swallowed, her tongue suddenly thick and dry. "Come again?"

His impressive lips quirked up at one corner. "Which part shall I repeat? The fact that I was born in 1722, or the bit about the stone you appropriated from the forest of Valoren actually being a magical prison to which I am inexorably tethered?"

She wasn't exactly an expert on history, but she wasn't a novice, either. She'd studied archeology with her mother at the Jasper Museum in Sydney before taking off with Ben to steal treasures rather than catalog them. Rafe's manner of speech, while odd, definitely didn't fit in her century. Neither did his clothes.

Ben's warning suddenly rang in Mariah's ears. He'd cautioned her that the stone was an object of black magic. And Rafe, with his dark hair, liquid silver eyes, sweeping pirate shirt, leather pants and boots, looked every inch a man out of time. Still, this had to be some kind of elaborate joke, right? Some plan cooked up by the endlessly duplicitous and undeniably clever Ben Rousseau to trick her into surrendering the stone?

And yet, how the hell had this Rafe Forsyth materialized inside her moving car?

She leaned forward and banged her head gently on the steering wheel, hoping to knock some sense into her malfunctioning brain. Maybe she hadn't used her considerable driving skills to avoid an accident. Maybe she'd crashed and Rafe Forsyth was a delusion spawned by a serious head injury.

Her temple pressed to the wheel, she turned and gazed into Rafe's increasingly concerned eyes. "Am I dead?"

He did not smile, but reached out and pushed a stray hair off her cheek. As his fingers trailed across her face, her skin heated. She was blushing? She never blushed. Of course, she never saw gorgeous men who popped in out of nowhere, either.

"You do not feel dead," he replied.

"Are you dead?"

He ran his hands down his chest, something she suddenly considered doing herself. Just to hear if he had a heartbeat, of course.

"I do not believe so. I have a body. According to the teachings of my people, spirits do not take physical form."

She whimpered and banged her head one more time, a little harder than she intended. "Your people? Tell me you're not in some wild cult that worships rocks."

"I am Romani."

Her gaze locked with his again. Of course he was Romani. He looked the part in every way—from his swarthy skin to his dark hair and clever eyes. But if there was one thing she'd learned in her extensive travels, it was never to trust a Gypsy.

"I don't believe you," she said.

"That I am Romani or that I am tied to the stone?"

"Take your pick," she replied.

His frown indicated deep thought more than displeasure. "I cannot deny that my story is hard to accept, but you must at least believe this—until tonight, I *was* trapped within the stone you took from Valoren. I had been in that state for hundreds of years and must be tied to that abominable rock still. Each time you've attempted to leave me behind, I've joined you shortly thereafter, through no actions of my own."

He wasn't lying. She knew this, not only from the sincerity in his gaze—and she had a high-quality bullshit detector—but because, weird as it was, his explanation fit with what she knew to be true. She'd left him behind in the hotel room, but she'd taken the stone. All the way down to the parking garage, she'd listened for footsteps behind her and had heard none. He might have taken the elevator, she supposed, but that didn't explain how she'd abandoned him shortly thereafter and he'd appeared, miraculously, inside her locked and speeding car.

"I don't understand how this could be possible," she admitted.

He sighed, but the sound held no impatience. "Of course you don't. No sane person would. But when it comes to magic, I've found it best to put sanity aside."

Mariah listened intently as he told a tale that would have made a fabulous bedtime story with an angry king, a vile wizard, a love-struck girl and a collection of Gypsies imbued with magic. She found herself so utterly caught up in the drama that the pounding in her head receded. She gasped when he told her how he'd driven his dagger into the stone, only to find himself trapped within the gem itself. He was sketchy on what happened afterward, but she supposed that was natural. As natural as any story of one enslaved by the unexplainable could be.

"Until you touched the gem," he said, with a clipped edge to his voice that told her his story was finished, "I could not venture outside the stone. Now that you have touched it, I can't seem to stay within."

Mariah gulped, then, operating on automatic, restarted the car and drove in calm silence off the shoulder and into the nearest empty parking lot. Neon lights advertising a big, blowout furniture sale threw a funky red glare into the car as she shoved the gear into park. She looked behind her. The street was full of cars. The breeze from their passing tossed the branches of the scrawny trees in the median. Overgrown weeds sprang from cracks in the pavement, which glittered with brown shards of broken beer bottles. She wasn't dead. She might not believe in heaven, but if she did she wouldn't imagine the place looked like this.

Which left only one scenario to believe—Ben hadn't been lying. The stone was magical. She'd seen so many strange and unusual things over the course of the years, but nothing that had made her believe that Rafe's story could be true. Only, he was the proof, wasn't he? There was no other explanation for how he could have materialized inside her car. She'd locked the doors. She'd driven away. She'd remembered catching sight of him in her rearview mirror. She had no doubt that she'd left him behind in the parking garage, and yet here he was.

"Remarkable," he said, bracing his hands on the dash. He gazed out through the windshield, then spun around in his seat to watch the cars speeding by on the street behind them. "This is how everyone travels now? By . . . what did you call it? A car?"

She ignored his question. "You're really from the eighteenth century?"

He nodded. The movement of his head was swift and decisive.

"And a curse trapped you in the stone?"

She'd heard his story, but the realization that he wasn't making up some elaborate tale required her to verify some of the details.

He reached toward her crotch. Instantly, she grabbed his wrist and twisted.

"You are quite quick," he said with a chuckle.

"If you're being condescending, I can break your wrist to show you I don't appreciate it."

He relaxed his arm, which she pushed away.

"I apologize," he said. "May I have the stone, please?"

She looked around. Even if he grabbed the mysterious rock and tried to make a break for it, she could run him over with the car before he got fifty feet away. Because, cursed or not, she suddenly understood the full breadth of this stone's value. She had no idea what she was going to do with the damned thing, but she certainly wasn't about to let it out of her sight. She placed the rock in his hand, then flicked on the map light.

His eyes rounded in surprise, but he made no comment. He merely raised the rock to the light and turned the stone over in his palm. Mariah gasped when she saw that the red gemstone embedded within had started to glow.

"What is that?"

He leaned closer to her, and she couldn't resist inhaling the scents of leather and man that clung to his skin, along with a moist, clean fragrance, as if he'd just stepped out of a shower or a rainstorm.

"See here." He traced an etched image with his fingertip. She hadn't had any time to give the rock a decent cleaning. Dirt still smudged the surface. He used his sleeve to brush some of the filth aside, but the image etched into the stone was still hard to see.

"This is a hawk," he explained. "The hawk was Rogan's symbol, though I know not why. He never, to my knowledge, owned one. He preferred the company of a rather damnable cat, if I remember correctly."

"This isn't a ruby, either," Mariah said, putting the stone as close to the dim map light as possible. "It's too orange. It's a fire opal. They were mined in my country at one time."

"Rogan had an impressive collection. He embedded them into many items. Goblets. Weapon handles. Even a brooch he wore on his cloak."

In her line of work, Mariah had come to know quite a bit about rare and expensive gemstones, which made her wonder how an eighteenth-century European had come into possession of so many. While they could be found on the continent, they were mostly mined in ancient Persia and India. But that wasn't what had her hackles up.

The fact was that fire opals were most often found in Mexico. The ancient Mayans called the stone *quetzalitzlipyollitli*, for the native bird of paradise. Only in the last decade had Mariah started specializing in retrieving Mayan, Incan and Aztec treasure for deep-pocketed collectors, but she'd seen enough of the stone to know, even in the insufficient light, that this one was of extraordinary quality and size. Could it be a coincidence that this rock she'd found in some godforsaken corner of Germany might have ties to the native people who'd forged the coins she'd stolen and lost?

She restarted the ignition. Her brain was on overload. She needed to get someplace where she could think straight, and she supposed, for the moment, she'd have to take Rafe Forsyth, son of the Earl of Hereford, with her. Whether she liked it or not.

"This is a lot to swallow," she said, "but I can't forget that someone broke into my hotel room and tried to steal the stone. Someone who thought the stone belonged to them. Any idea who they were?"

Rafe shrugged noncommittally. "This is your world, my lady, not mine. I have no enemies here. Can you say the same?"

She snorted. "Lately, I've got more enemies than a croc has teeth."

After showing him how to use a seat belt, Mariah shifted into reverse, executed a rather tight turn that had Rafe clutching the dashboard again, then headed toward the one place she knew they'd be safe—the sky.

6

Rafe pressed his hands to the contraption Mariah Hunter had strapped over his ears before she'd announced that they were about to rise into the air. They'd transferred from the car to an elaborate mechanical wonder she called a helicopter. It had taken her hours to prepare the odd vehicle, and as she did, she'd explained precisely how it worked. He was amazed. Never in his life had he imagined such things as internal combustion engines, or crude oil that could be refined into a fuel that would power them safely into the air. She'd spared little time answering the myriad questions pummeling his brain, but he'd learned enough to know that his expectation of adjusting to this new time and place with ease had been wholly fanciful.

With each moment that passed, Rafe realized that he'd possessed no true conception of how fully society had changed. Mariah was born in a land that had not existed in his time, and now lived in another country. He'd heard his father speak once of the colonies in the Americas, but he'd never given the community much thought. He'd been concerned with only one colony—that in Valoren, home of the Gypsies.

As if to fully illustrate just how out of time he was, Mariah had buckled him into a machine with giant blades that chopped the air, drawing them into and across the sky. Magic in this time, called technology, knew no bounds.

He shifted in his seat, nearly dislodging the bag Mariah had given him to safely hide and transport the stone. More than once, he considered the consequences of simply tossing the cursed rock into the darkness that surrounded them. Would he fall after it? Would he then die?

And was that what he wanted?

His Romani beliefs allowed for an afterlife. The *Chovihano* himself had taught Rafe how, after death, a Gypsy spirit either returned to Grandmother Earth or risked entrapment in obscure realms from which they could not escape. Was this what had happened to him? Was he dead, yet trapped in the living world because he had not been burned with his belongings, as was Romani custom? But if he was but a specter, why, after all these years, did he feel so incredibly alive?

"You doing okay?" Mariah asked, her voice invading his ears through the device she'd called headphones.

He nodded.

She reached across and adjusted a small arm so that a round piece she'd told him was a microphone crossed his lips. "Go ahead and talk," she instructed. "It'll be a long, boring ride otherwise. You must have a million more questions, now that we're in the air."

He bowed his head again, but she tapped the microphone, indicating she wanted to hear his reply.

"I hardly know where to begin," he said.

"Well, feel free to start anywhere," she said, making adjustments to the various instruments in front of and above her. "Because if it weren't for hearing your voice, and the fact that these jeans are pinching my naked arse, I'd think I was mad as a cut snake and dreaming this whole night."

He could translate only every other word of what she'd said, but the sentiment came through. Rafe had long ago accepted magic as a real and powerful force. Despite her ability to fly, Mariah had insisted that magic did not exist in her world—just technology based on invention and science.

While he was not knowledgeable in the subject, he at least understood the concept, thanks to his educated father and brothers.

Still, there was so much he did not know, particularly why they were running from the men who had tried to capture the stone. Rafe did not believe in fighting, but turning tail from a blatant attack seemed cowardly and unwise. They knew nothing of their enemy. What would save them from falling prey to yet another offensive assault?

"Who do you think attempted to steal the stone?" he asked.

She shrugged. "I wish I knew. I'd suspect Hector Velez sent them, but he didn't have the time. I'd only just gotten off the phone with him. Unless he was having me followed or tracked, which, I suppose, is a distinct possibility."

"Who is Hector Velez?"

"A collector I pissed off."

"A collector of what?"

She kept her vision trained through the glass windows of the helicopter, her mouth turned downward in a frown. She did not like his question.

"Antiquities. Coins, usually, but statues and jewelry and tools—anything associated with the Mayan empire. Or Incan. Or Aztec. I, um, acquired a collection of rare gold coins for him a month ago, but through absolutely no fault of my own," she said, sarcasm tingeing her tone, "I had to dump them in a Mexican jungle. When I went back for them, the GPS device I'd attached to the package would not work. I couldn't find them, and he's not happy about it."

Rafe spent the next hour asking her questions that would lead him to understand what she'd just said. She explained about a place called Mexico, about Spanish exploration and invasion against the native people, about the value of artifacts from this era, about her talent as a pilot of various aircraft and the basics behind a system of electronic tracking . . . and then electricity.

"There is so much I don't understand," he admitted.

She reached over and patted his hand. The minute their skin made contact, Rafe pulled back. Now that she'd explained the concept of electricity, he finally appreciated the sensation of her flesh on his. So much like lightning, yet more deliberate. More controlled.

And yet as wild as the open sea.

Her frown returned.

"So you think this Hector Velez sent his men to take the stone to replace the gold you lost?" he asked, hoping an increase in conversation would make up for his unfriendly reaction to her touch.

"It's a theory, but it doesn't quite add up. I told him I might give him something else willingly, after I found out what it was worth. But I never told him what it was. Those men who attacked me knew what they were looking for."

Yes, they'd known about the stone. Had Rogan sent them? Had he also found a way to cheat death and was now seeking Rafe out? To what end?

He gazed out of the windows, marveling at the glow of a city beneath him. With miracles like electricity and air travel at the disposal of so many, a man like Rogan might never have risen to power. Despite the fact that Rafe had only hours ago fought against his release from Rogan's cursed stone, his curiosity and natural need to understand the world around him fueled his desire to remain free.

If he had to battle the rogue in this century, he had to be prepared, though having Mariah Hunter as his guide in this new and fascinating world posed both problems and solutions. From her description of her profession, she was undoubtedly untrustworthy, and wily as a fox. He'd once believed his sister to be headstrong and resourceful, but Mariah's actions thus far made Sarina look every bit the child she'd been. Even his wife, Irika, who possessed the wisdom of centuries, had not known how to fight like a man or how to protect herself against attackers intent on doing her harm.

Mariah navigated this strange world with a confidence he'd never seen before in a woman and a sensuality he believed she greatly underestimated or, perhaps, ignored completely.

"What will you do now that you know that I am still tied to the stone?" he asked.

She spared him a sidelong glance. "You've certainly complicated my plans."

"I apologize," he said, wholly unrepentant. "Of course, I might point out that I did not ask you to remove the stone from the forest of Valoren, nor did I request that you take me away from the man who seemed to know what Rogan's marker was really about."

"Those blokes were trying to kill me."

"I mean the man you shot at in Valoren."

"Ben?" she said with a laugh that was neither flippant nor funny. "He was bluffing."

Rafe turned to face her as fully as he could, restrained as he was by the straps she insisted would assure his safety. "And how, precisely, do you hold to that judgment? He warned you that the stone was cursed by black magic. On this point, he was entirely correct."

She scoffed at him, waving away his assessment. "I know Ben," she insisted. "Intimately. Every so often, he makes a good guess. That's all that happened."

Rafe arched a brow. "You were married to him?" he asked.

She grimaced. "Crikey, no. But I wasted several years thinking he might pony up at some point. Suffice it to say I do know him well, and he was after the rock for profit and for profit only. His ramblings about black magic were meant only to scare me."

Rafe focused again on the sky outside. Streaks of red and purple shot up from the horizon in the east, lightening the blackness to a dusky gray. Though sunrises remained constant, the world had truly changed more than he imagined if a woman could confess relations with a man outside of marriage with no shame. Even if she were not herself Romani, the conventions of his era precluded a woman speaking of such intimacies. Although the female servants in his father's British household did not hold to such lofty ideals, coupling regularly with whatever soldiers had been sent to man the small garrison outside the valley, Rafe followed the customs of his mother and her Romani kin.

In the village of Umgeben, marriages were arranged by the elders and blessed by the *puri* or the *Chovihano*, as Rafe's had been. His father, who had taken a Gypsy wife long after he'd been made a widower by Rafe's brothers' British mother, had tacitly approved. John Forsyth, Earl of Hereford, was a great many things that Rafe had not approved of, but he'd never been a hypocrite.

Nor was Rafe. He'd made love to only one woman in his lifetime, and she had been his Irika. And yet, the idea that Mariah had experienced the pleasures of lovemaking freely and without disgrace spawned an interest he had no right to feel.

"Did I shock you?" she asked, a smile tugging at the corner of her mouth.

"Yes," he admitted.

"Then our next discussion needs to be about the society's changed attitudes toward sex."

Rafe had no idea whether he was prepared for what he was about to learn, but he knew without a doubt that if Mariah Hunter had decided to impart this knowledge, he would not have a choice but to listen.

That was, until a bright light broke through the windows to his right. He had only a moment to recognize the full sunrise before his world went dark. The last thing he heard was Mariah shouting his name.

7

"This doesn't look good," Cat said, eyeing the destruction that had once been Mariah Hunter's hotel room. When they'd lost her in Europe, Ben had insisted they travel to Texas, where he'd guessed—correctly—that she'd pick up a getaway car she kept stashed near the airport and then would register in a hotel under an assumed name, paying with cash. They'd been calling around to low-cost car-rental companies when the police scanner had given them their first solid, albeit disturbing lead—an assault of some sort in a hotel room rented to a woman using one of Mariah's noms de plume.

Again, Ben had anticipated his ex's actions to the letter. Either Mariah Hunter was a terrible creature of habit, or Ben had seriously underrated the intimacy of an affair that ended a decade ago. Either way, Cat found herself inexplicably miffed. She was too self-confident to be jealous, but she copped to annoyance, which wasn't lessened by the concerned look on Ben's face while he knelt over a patch of dried blood on the carpet.

"You think she's hurt?" he asked.

Cat pushed away her exasperation and fingered the

watch she'd slid into the pocket of her slacks. Rugged in condition and techie in design, the slim and feminine timepiece she'd found near the stairs matched Mariah's psychic signature. But that's all she could sense. If Mariah wanted to be found, Cat's special gift with objects might have allowed her to key into her location. But as it was, the last thing the woman wanted was for anyone to know her whereabouts.

With a sigh, she closed her eyes and concentrated, trying to at least get a bead on the state of her health. Enough people had gotten hurt in this quest to reunite the Forsyth brothers and stop the K'vr from possessing the magic of the formidable Lord Rogan. Mariah didn't deserve to die just because she'd been greedy in stealing the stone when Ben had warned her to leave it alone.

Truth was, if Ben had been Cat's ex-lover rather than her current one, she might have ignored his advice, too.

"She's fine," Cat replied.

Ben glanced at her with wary eyes. "You're certain?"

She gave a noncommittal shrug. "Well, you know her better than I do, but she's proved resourceful so far. I don't think you need to worry about her too much."

Ben blinked, as if shocked by her suggestion. "I'm not worried about her."

Cat turned and headed into the bathroom. She and Ben didn't need to have this conversation now, especially when she knew that confronting Ben's residual feelings for Mariah meant she'd have to confess her own growing sense of insecurity. Best just to focus on the task at hand.

After paying a hefty bribe to the night clerk, they'd learned that the police had found one man unconscious after the people in nearby rooms had called the front desk to report a loud disturbance. Another witness reported seeing a woman matching Mariah's description tearing out of the parking garage, alone but in a damned big hurry. Though the cops had taped the room off, Cat's donation to the bored employee manning the front desk gained them ten minutes to look around. And they were running out of time.

Cat couldn't help but wonder if following Mariah was worth the trouble. She'd beaten them to an artifact in that dank and dense forest of Valoren, but neither Cat nor Ben knew exactly what she had. For the past six months, they'd been trying to find artifacts associated with Valoren, Lord Rogan or the Forsyth family. Ben had checked with some of his old contacts and, to his surprise, learned that his former partner in crime had flown to the exact part of Germany where the little-known Gypsy enclave had once been. Convinced this was no coincidence, they'd followed. They still didn't know how or why Mariah had come to learn about Valoren, unless, as Cat suspected, she'd been tracing Ben's reemergence in archeological circles and had simply tried to beat him to an important find.

Which she had.

Unfortunately, the item she'd nabbed for profit meant much more to Ben than financial gain. It could contain a connection to his family—a family he didn't even know he had until a year and a half ago.

Suddenly, Ben's hands slid over Cat's shoulders, his fingers kneading into the knotted muscles at the base of her neck. "What's wrong?"

"Men shouldn't ask that question unless they really want to know the answer," she replied. "Don't expect a coy 'nothing' from me."

Despite her mild annoyance, his chuckle did more to alleviate the stress in her body than his increasingly delicious massage.

"Only an idiot would associate the word 'coy' with you, sweetheart."

"True," she conceded. "Maybe it bothers me a bit that we're spending all our time tracking down your ex."

"She has something we need," he replied simply.

"And she's your ex."

"With very good reason," Ben said, with more laughter in his voice than she appreciated at the moment. "You met her, Cat. She's not exactly pining after me. She nearly shot my foot off."

Mariah's pining for Ben wasn't her worry. Ben's unresolved feelings for his ex were. The thought of losing him, either emotionally or physically, was quickly becoming a major concern. And Cat didn't like it one bit.

She pulled away from Ben's amazing hands and the solace they imparted, and went back into the bedroom. She'd come to depend on him too much. Her life and his had been inexorably intertwined by both their professional interests and their personal attraction for too long. But now, over a year since they'd first met, they were still in the same place—hunting down artifacts, making love when it suited them and never planning for any future that focused on only the two of them.

"So," she said, needing to change the subject, "what do we do next?"

Ben shoved his hands into his pockets, and Cat watched a disappointed look skitter across his face, then disappear. "We keep looking for Mariah."

"What about your father?"

"What about him?" he asked sharply. "Does he still not want to be found?"

Cat slipped her hand into Ben's back pocket, taking a split second to revel in the fine muscles of his glutes, and retrieved the photograph of Ben's mother that he'd been carrying around for months.

"Hey," he protested, his expression somewhat abashed.

"I knew you had it with you," she replied.

"That's the danger of living with a psychic."

"That's the danger of living with someone who pays attention," she countered.

After Paschal had disappeared, purportedly on some sort of mission with outcast K'vr princess Gemma Von Roan, she and Ben had searched his Texas home for clues to his whereabouts. Of all the items in his house, she'd gotten the strongest psychic vibrations from this tiny picture. He'd kept the locket-size photo with him ever since.

"I didn't want you to think I was a mama's boy," he said.

She laughed. "Your mother's been dead a long time. I don't have to compete with her, too, do I?"

"You don't have to compete with anyone," he assured her, but Cat ignored his obvious attempt to alleviate her insecurity and focused on the photograph. Unlike Paschal, who used psychometric power to connect items to specific events in the past, Cat's ability allowed her to zero in on the owner's emotions and, with extreme effort, their current location. *If* they wished to be found. From touching the picture, she knew that Paschal had loved his wife deeply and had been committed to her happiness until the day she died. But that was all she got.

"Still nothing."

Ben pressed his lips together. "But he's alive, right?"

Cat blew out an anxious breath. Paschal wasn't a young man, a fact both Ben and she accepted but rarely discussed. That he went willingly with Gemma—a known enemy—was disturbing enough. Factoring in his advanced age made it hard to remain optimistic.

"I'm not sure," Cat admitted, "but I think if something happened to him, we would know. Besides, Gemma needs him, for whatever reason. She won't let anything happen to him until she has what she wants."

He snorted, but without humor. "That's the problem. We don't know what she wants. She might already have it. My father could already be—"

"He's not. You know he's not."

Ben didn't reply, and his eyes, gray like his father's, were stormy with his unspoken fear. She couldn't blame him for worrying. The danger to Paschal was very real, just as was the danger to Mariah. Anyone connected with the Valoren curse put their lives on the line, which made Cat feel all the more like a stupid girl for concerning herself with the state of her relationship with Ben when his elderly father had run off with a woman of dubious alliances, and Mariah had disappeared from a trashed hotel room with blood on the floor.

"Where do we go next?" Cat asked.

Ben ran his hands roughly through his thick, dark hair, breaking Cat's heart with the sense of loss that surrounded him.

"We go back to the beginning," he answered.

"Back to Valoren?"

He grabbed her hand, reeled her in and kissed her with such passion, Cat decided to let her doubts about their future melt away with the heat. "No, back to my office at the university, where we first met."

The light in his eyes was one she knew well. He wanted to make love, and far be it from her to deny such a request. "The university still considers you an employee?"

He shrugged. "Last I heard, they haven't moved our stuff out yet. Officially, Dad and I have applied for a sabbatical to do research on the Romani culture that will be the stuff of legend, or so I told the department chair. And I think it's time to put some truth behind that statement. Until Mariah tips her hand. She's smart, but she can be sloppy when she's under a lot of pressure."

"You mean that business with Hector Velez? You still don't want to contact him, maybe find out what he knows?"

By his immediate frown, she knew he wasn't yet willing to poke that sleeping dog. "Men like Velez don't give up information on the cheap. I'd rather not tangle with him if we can avoid it."

"And if we can't avoid it?"

"Then once again, we're in big trouble."

Morning did not bring the answers Gemma had sought. She and Paschal had spent most of the night on the floor of the repository, sleeping off a fatigue Gemma hadn't experienced since she'd battled the flu. By four o'clock a.m., she'd regained enough energy to drag herself and a barely conscious Paschal up to the first-floor bedroom. She dropped him on the bed, covered him with a blanket, then grabbed a quilt and cuddled into a ball on a chair at his bedside. When the sun defied the drawn wooden blinds at sunrise and flooded the room with light, she awoke with a start.

Paschal was watching her, a hint of a smile on his still-pale lips.

"What are you looking at?" she asked, instantly defensive.

"You snore," he replied, implying that he'd been awake and watching her sleep for quite some time. His skin still looked as thin as paper, and the circles under his eyes made him resemble a raccoon.

She sat up, yanking at the blanket that had tightened around her. "Yeah, well, so do you."

"I'm sure I don't sound quite so cute when I'm doing it, though."

"Cute is for puppies."

"Yes, and so are food and water, if you get my meaning."

She did. She struggled to her feet, and though she still felt as if she had not slept in a few days, she pushed herself out of the room and raided the kitchen. She found a wheel of cheese still encased in wax, some whole-grain crackers and a bottle of cabernet sauvignon. Wasn't exactly the food of champions, but it would have to do.

Paschal didn't complain. Several bites into their repast, his color seemed to return.

"I suppose you have a lot of questions," he ventured.

"You have a talent for understatement," she replied, sipping gingerly from her wine and then taking a hearty bite of the cheese. The shakes were still threading through her system. So much had changed since yesterday, but she couldn't even begin to process it all until Paschal told her what he knew. *Everything* he knew.

"Why could I see what you saw?" she asked.

Paschal grinned. "Why am I not surprised that the first question you ask is about yourself?"

Gemma grabbed the blanket again and pulled it around her. The house wasn't particularly chilly, having been closed up for days, but she didn't like Paschal's implication, even if it was true. "What else do you want to tell me about?"

"Aren't you still curious about Rafe Forsyth?"

"Not particularly," she replied. "You already told me he was an enemy of Lord Rogan. Something horrible happened to him. Serves him right."

A flash of something close to anger played across Paschal's eyes, but he covered by sipping his wine. "You do realize, then, that your ancestor was not a well-loved man."

"He was feared," she shot back. "To me, that means he was formidable."

"He was that," Paschal replied. "He was also ruthless and charming and determined to act on his own private agenda, no matter whom he hurt in the process."

A chill shot up Gemma's spine. "That's the second time you've sounded like you knew him."

"I've been studying him for years," Paschal replied, a little too quickly. "I know him as well as any man can."

She eyed him curiously, aware that Paschal's attempt to meet her eyes boldly belied the truth. He knew more about Rogan than would just some researcher. She'd been through all the documentation on her infamous ancestor, and even she didn't have much of an idea of what kind of man he was.

"To the K'vr, he's always been something of an enigma."

"Curious," Paschal replied.

Gemma finished off the last of her wine, then draped the blanket over her shoulders and walked to the window. The light that had woken her less than an hour ago was already starting to fade from clouds rolling into the area. With so many shade trees huddled around the house, the atmosphere outside took on a quality of night even at the break of day.

Unbidden memories of her childhood suddenly struck her hard. She'd spent so much time here in this gloominess, surrounded by things that looked and smelled of age and decay. She rubbed her cheeks unconsciously, wondering for the first time how this place had infected her young psyche. She'd been the daughter of a man who ran what amounted to a cult, the eldest child denied her right to ascend to the leadership simply because she was a girl.

"Rogan's life was never the concern of the K'vr," she said finally. It was easier to talk about the group than to sort out her conflicted feelings about her family. "All we ever wanted was his magic, the power promised to his followers by his brother."

Paschal slid the plate of cheese onto the bedside table. "And did anyone ever consider the fact that Lukyan Roganov might have been full of shit? That he lorded this reputed magic over uneducated farmers in order to control every aspect of their lives and incomes?"

"Of course," she answered. "At least, I did. But the magic *is* real. Why didn't Rafe Forsyth die when he tried to strike down Rogan's mark? He was hit by powerful magic."

"Magic you want for yourself," he concluded.

She lifted her chin higher. "Of course I do. It's my birthright."

"Not according to the K'vr council."

Gemma bristled. She'd scale that treacherous wall

at some point, but for now, she concentrated on deconstructing the vision. Unlike the shortsighted elders who kept her from the leadership solely on the basis of her gender, she knew women had always been important to Rogan. Or at least, one had.

"So, then, tell me about her," she requested.

"About whom?"

"Sarina, of course. Who was she, other than this Rafe Forsyth's sister and Rogan's obsession?"

"Obsession," he repeated with a snort. "How intuitive you are, my dear. Yes, he was fixated on her. She was young and impulsive and passionate. And the sister not just to Rafe, but to five British brothers who never quite appreciated the fire in her blood. Each one of them put his life on the line to save her from your glorified goon of a great-great-uncle."

Gemma went back to the chair and plopped down. Her own brother wouldn't have risked breaking a sweat on her behalf, much less put his life in danger. "The stories claim Rogan loved her deeply, but that she betrayed him."

"They would," Paschal replied. "Women have never been valued much in your line."

She didn't reply. The truth was self-evident.

"Sarina was a young girl who'd grown up in a particularly closed society," Paschal continued. "What do you know about Valoren?"

"It was a Gypsy colony set up by the king of England to rid London of the Romani."

"Yes, and the governor of this colony was a rather unusual nobleman named John Forsyth, Earl of Hereford."

"I've never heard of him before," she said.

"Seems in his later years, he went to great lengths to keep his own name and the names of his children out of the history books," Paschal noted. "But he loved the Gypsies, even married one after his first wife died. She gave him both a son and a daughter. The son he named Rafe. The daughter, Sarina."

"What about the other brothers? In the vision, Rafe thought about a soldier named Aiden and, um, the oldest one . . ."

"Damon."

"Wait," Gemma said, her memory clicking. "Damon Forsyth! That's the man who's taken up with Alexa Chandler, the man who fought my brother at Isla de Fantasmas. Are you telling me he's from the past? That he's over two hundred years old and alive and well?"

Paschal did not acknowledge her supposition, but his steady stare confessed the truth.

"How can that be possible?"

"Rafe did not die that night; nor did his brothers. They were trapped by magic of Lord Rogan's design."

Gemma threw off the blanket, feeling suddenly overheated. She jammed her fingers through her hair and considered the unlikely chance that this could be true. "But if Damon is back, does that mean . . ."

She thought about the name Aiden Forsyth. She'd heard it. Read it, maybe. Without explaining to Paschal, she ran downstairs to the bag she'd brought with her when she and Paschal broke into her childhood home. She retrieved a magazine she'd bought at the convenience store while they'd waited for the last of the K'vr to abandon the house.

Back in the bedroom, Paschal now sat with his legs over the side of the bed, as if he were attempting to stand.

"Sit down," she ordered. "You're not strong enough to move yet, and I'd appreciate your not falling down and breaking a hip while I'm the only one around to pick your ass up."

He muttered several obscenities, but did as she requested, remaining in place while she tore through the magazine and finally found an article about the upcoming final film in the very popular Athena series, starring Lauren Cole. There, in a steamy clench with the international superstar, was a new and previously unheard-of actor named Aiden Forsyth.

"This is why you're looking for the objects associated with Rogan," she replied. "You're looking for these brothers."

When she glanced up at Paschal, she gasped. He'd moved into the light, and for the first time, she noticed that his eyes were nearly identical to those of the man in the picture.

"Not just these brothers," he answered. "*My* brothers. And you are going to help me find them."

8

"Rafe!"

Instinctively, Mariah strained against her seat belt to grab at the space where Rafe had just been sitting. Dawn had broken over the eastern horizon, and the moment the light had touched the helicopter, Rafe had vanished. She moved back into her seat and made a course correction, then scanned the land below for a place to touch down. If she was going to lose her mind completely, she'd rather not do it while hovering in midair.

After twenty minutes of searching for friendly terrain, Mariah put the bird down and tore out of her bindings. Above her, the rotors slowed to a steady, visible chop. She grabbed the bag holding the Valoren stone and searched until the rock was tight in her hands. The gem in the center retained its ghostly glow.

"Rafe? Where are you?"

Nowhere. Everywhere.

The intimate whisper spawned a wildfire of gooseflesh across her skin. He was here. She had so many questions. Odd how, just hours ago, she'd been wondering about the advisability of stealing the stone out from under Ben. But now that Rafe had been with her for a few hours, she wasn't ready to let him go.

She inhaled deeply and calmed her rapid breathing. "I can't see you."

I am here, Mariah.

She leaned toward his seat, her hand lingering on the spot that might have still been warm from his body heat if she'd landed sooner. She snatched the stone from atop the leather dilly bag and stared into the heart of the fire opal, which glinted from the rising sun.

She swallowed thickly. "What . . . what happened?"

I do not know.

His voice was like a lover's murmur, caressing her skin with an unexpected intimacy. Images of their dream kiss sneaked back into her consciousness, taunting her.

"Are you inside the stone again?" she asked.

The tether to the stone has tightened, Rafe replied, *but I do not feel trapped. It is as if I am one with the air inside this machine. The sensation is not unlike flying.*

"Oh," she said, placing the stone gently back into the bag, then burying her head in her hands. Okay, half an hour ago, she'd been talking to a man who'd claimed to be from the eighteenth century and who had appeared out of nowhere inside her hotel room. Now she was talking to the freaking air. How could she cling any longer to the impossibility that she was still in her right mind? Owing so much money to Velez, meeting up with Ben and fending off an attack by unknown assailants had caused her to lose her mind.

"What do I do?" she asked.

Continue on. I am with you as long as you have the stone.

Somehow, his claim gave her comfort. She had a time-traveling ghost of sorts attached to her . . . and she found it reassuring?

But continue on she did, though she did not attempt to communicate with Rafe any further. The sun had risen fully. She made a stop at a friendly airstrip outside of Abilene and refueled, paying with the last of her emergency cash. She considered using the old rotary pay phone to call Ben Rousseau and find out exactly what he'd gotten her into, but resisted tipping him off to her whereabouts. It had been her own poor choices that had led her to this madness.

She'd had a bad feeling about Hector Velez from the beginning, but she'd ignored her instincts in favor of money. The coins had been sitting in the basement of a government official who'd taken them as a bribe. The jerk had been completely clueless about what he'd had. Tossed in a pile with the other valuables he'd taken from the people in his region to keep him from arresting their sons or forcing their daughters into workhouses, the coins had been an easy snatch.

She'd retrieved a valuable national resource and given it to a man who would, at the very least, appreciate the value. At least, that was how she'd justified the job at the time. For the past three years, Mariah had worked almost exclusively as a private pilot and flight instructor. For the first time in her life, she had a relatively normal job, a home and a group of friends. But she also had a schedule, bills and stress headaches. She'd become domestic and ordinary and had craved the excitement of her past. She couldn't have turned down Velez's offer without huge regrets.

Now she was up to her eyeballs in regrets that could get her killed.

She flew three more hours in silence, considering how she was going to pay for the next load of fuel. She made an inventory of the items of value she had with her and decided she was going to have to make a few calls. At the next stop in Amarillo, she charmed an old acquaintance in order to use his cell phone and called her home base—an airstrip outside of Austin run by the Barketts, a friendly couple who'd taken a liking to Mariah since she'd first berthed her plane in their hangar.

"Jan, I need a favor," Mariah said.

"Where've you been, girl?" the Texas native drawled. "People been looking for you."

"People?" Mariah asked, trying to keep her voice steady and casual. "What people?"

"Some guys. Rough types."

Mariah realized her decision to take her chopper out instead of the Cessna had been a wise one. She'd figured that if Velez were looking for her, he'd stake out the hangar where she kept her plane, leaving her free to escape via other means. "Were they Hispanic?"

"Who isn't around here?" Jan said with a laugh. "They wanted to know where you lived, where you kept your gear or if Ken and I had heard from you."

Mariah silently cursed. She didn't want to bring any trouble down on Ken and Jan. They were good people. Ken was a former army pilot who'd avoided being shot down during Vietnam, and his wife, a more than adequate pilot who'd bucked the Texas old-boys network to start her own successful airstrip, had opened her heart to Mariah, even when they knew damned well that the Aussie transplant was usually up to no good.

"What did you tell them?" she asked.

The older woman snorted derisively. "Nothin' true,

what do you think? Said you'd cleared out two weeks ago and we hadn't heard from you since. Told 'em we'd confiscated everything to pay your bills, including your plane."

"Unfortunately, that's not entirely fiction," Mariah muttered.

"We know you're good for the money. Besides, we do have your Cessna as collateral."

"I'm glad to hear you say that," Mariah started, then explained her dilemma in the vaguest terms possible. She didn't need her friends dragged into her drama, but she needed money. Less than an hour after the call, the Barketts had sent her enough cash to get her to her cabin in Colorado.

She'd bought the place only a year ago and had visited only once. Accessible only by helo, since the one and only road had washed out from a landslide two years before she bought it, the place had been extraordinarily cheap. Two hours outside Denver, the cabin on Butler's Mountain was the perfect hideout. She'd registered the property in the name of an old pilot friend who'd since died, but had left her as executor of his will. Velez wouldn't be able to track her to the cabin. At least, not easily.

Mariah made one last stop in Colorado Springs for fuel, and then finished the ride up to the cabin, which had just enough land in a northwest clearing for her to put the bird down. Dark clouds hovered just above her as she made her approach, forcing her to fight through turbulence to set down easy.

Sunset wasn't the glorious event she'd craved. The clouds and mist muted the oranges and reds until they were shadows that faded into night. She'd had just enough time to secure her gear when the blackness of the mountain night swallowed her whole and the rumbling of thunder echoed nearby.

She took out a flashlight and directed the beam at the cabin. It looked untouched since her last visit, when she'd stocked the freezer and pantry for emergencies just like this. If only she could remember precisely where she'd tucked the spare key.

"Do you need assistance?"

Mariah screamed. The sound ricocheted off the cliff and bounced down into the valley below. Instinctively, she spun and kicked toward the voice. Rafe caught her foot just seconds before it connected with his chin.

"You can't just jump out at me like that!" she insisted, tugging her foot from his grasp and losing her balance for her trouble. The flashlight tumbled a few feet away, but Rafe retrieved it, eyeing it with interest even as he held out his other hand to her.

"I'm afraid I have little control over the matter," he replied, tugging her up with such force, she smacked flat against his chest.

The temperature on the mountain had been dropping until that moment. Ghost or not, Rafe Forsyth put off a kind of magnetic heat. Mariah allowed herself to lean against him. With the flashlight directed upward toward their faces, she caught sight of his full lips and wondered if he'd taste as spicy and elemental as he had in her dream.

Rafe, however, stepped away. "I awoke with the sunset, as if from a deep and powerful sleep. I wished to be with you again . . . and here I am."

Her heart was beating the hell out of her insides. From the shock of his appearance, of course. And nothing more.

"You wished to be . . ."

She let the words die on her lips. Whom else would he want to be with? She did, after all, have the stone. He could have wished to be in the presence of the bloody queen of England, and still she was the best he'd get.

"Remarkable," he said, turning the flashlight over in his hands, the beam shining around them like a beacon. Which, under the circumstances, wasn't a good thing.

She threw out her hand to stop him. "We don't need to broadcast that we're up here, okay? It's bad enough that the chopper is so noisy. I have no idea what neighbors I might have, but I'd prefer not to let anyone know where we are."

He nodded, then followed her toward the cabin. "I understand, but tell me about this fireless torch. What's it called?"

"In Australia, a torch," she noted with a snicker. "In America, where we are, it's a flashlight."

"Australia?"

"My homeland. You might know it as . . ." she started, trying to remember the history of her native country, "New South Wales."

He stared at her blankly.

"Aren't you British?" she asked.

His lip curled and his nose twitched, as if a skunk had discharged a warning directly in their path. "I am Romani."

"Half Romani," she said, remembering that his father had been a British earl.

He merely sniffed in response. "In my world, the Romani half was all that mattered."

"Probably not to your father," she said.

"Especially to my father," he replied curtly.

Mariah let the matter drop. She understood better than most how relations with parents could be complicated and contentious. She loved her own father deeply, but he'd been a bush pilot in the Northern Territory who considered rough living to be the ultimate test of his manliness. He'd raised two sons the same way. He'd never exactly been sure what to do with his daughter.

Her mother hadn't been any more insightful. When she'd abandoned the family to move to Sydney, she'd left Mariah behind, taking her in only after Mariah had reached puberty and Bert Hunter had left his ex-wife no choice. When Mariah wasn't rebelling against high expectations and responsibility, she'd gotten on pretty well with her mum once they were reunited. Unfortunately, the damage to their relationship had been done. Mariah was still fending off the demons born of a childhood of not fitting in, and she didn't want to stir up those memories tonight.

"We should get inside," she said, pointing the beam of the flashlight toward the door just as a cloud opened up and dumped a flood of rain on top of them.

Lightning followed. Mariah cursed as sheets of cold rain doused her, ruining her chances of remembering under which clay pot she'd buried the key. Suddenly, Rafe took her arm and pulled her inside, shutting the wide-open door firmly behind them.

"How'd you do that?" she asked, swiping water from her face. "Wasn't it locked?"

He did not reply. Mariah lit the kerosene lantern she kept on the table beside the door, then darted to the supply closet, where she pulled out a couple of towels. She handed one to Rafe, then dried her face and hair so that water didn't drip down her back. Still, she was shivering, and if there was one thing Mariah hated, it was being cold. She longed to strip out of her soaking wet clothes, but realized she'd left her only change of wardrobe back in the chopper.

She wrapped the towel around her shoulders and tried to keep her teeth from chattering by whistling. Under the dim golden glow, she scanned the room, frowning at the layer of mountain dust clinging to every surface, and especially at the empty wood box beside the fireplace.

The previous owners had sold the place fully furnished, if you could call an old, scarred table with four chairs, a bookshelf filled with Reader's Digest Condensed Books and a stack of *National Geographic* magazines, a tattered sofa that pulled out to a sleeper, and a butt-ugly but comfortable recliner "furnished." Not that she needed much. Mariah had often lived with less. She could do rustic. What she preferred not to do was dirty.

With a sigh, she started yanking the sheets off the furniture, coughing when the dust flew into her nose. Rafe, on the other hand, stood frozen near the door with his arms crossed over his chest, as if waiting for her to finish.

She tossed a sheet onto the floor. "You could help," she suggested, shivering when an icy drop slid off her hair and down the front of her shirt.

"I suppose I should," he said reluctantly.

"I know that men of your birth didn't often do heavy lifting when it came to housework, but like it or not, you're in the twenty-first century now. In our day and age, the men help."

He arched a brow. "I'm not averse to assisting you, but what do you wish me to do?"

She smiled. She liked a man who could take direction. "Well, we need to make this place habitable. We're stuck here for a few days while I figure out where to go next."

He nodded, then rubbed his hands together as if about to lift something heavy. Then he closed his eyes.

She was about to comment that a standing nap wasn't going to make the cabin any warmer when the pop and crackle of a fire caught her attention. She stared at the fireplace. Flames licked at a thick cord of wood cradled inside. The smell of smoke instantly reminded her that in closing up the cabin, she'd likely shut the flue.

Darting forward, she wrapped her hand in a kitchen towel and reached just above the flames to work the mechanism. She coughed and turned to ask Rafe how he'd lit the fire when what she saw nearly knocked her off her feet.

The entire interior had changed. Besides the warm fire, a dozen sconces magically placed throughout the cabin flickered with the light of thick candles. The walls, once rustic pine paneling, were now covered by draping tapestries that blocked out the windy cracks and made the space immediately warm and cozy. Even the furniture had been transformed. Dozens of tasseled cushions covered the couch, the bare floor was now hidden beneath a half dozen animal skins and the rickety table was now made of mahogany and burgeoning with fresh berries, steaming meat and a large carafe of wine.

"What . . . ?" she said with a gasp. "What did you do? How did you—"

He held out his hand to silence her, his eyes still closed. The tension in his face, in his entire body, was palpable. She took a tentative step nearer and saw that he was shaking.

"Rafe, what's wrong?"

His eyes flashed open. His pupils had expanded so that his irises were a slim silver circle around total blackness. His stare was unfocused, but penetrating.

The hair along the back of her neck, which had dried from her nearness to the fire, stood on chilled ends. Something was very, very wrong.

"Rafe?" she asked, taking a tentative step toward him.

He turned to her, stabbing her with his sharp gaze. "You must make love to me. Now."

"Excuse me?"

She blinked, and he was standing directly in front of her. He grabbed her shoulders, his fingers digging into them. "Make love to me, Mariah, or we shall both die."

9

The demand ripped from a crack in Rafe's soul he'd thought long sealed. Lust tore through the weakened fissure, hard and hot, tensing every muscle in his body, making his head rush as blood flooded to his loins. Never in his life had he made such a crass demand to a woman, not even to his own wife.

But the impulse to mate, to feel his hard sex buried deep within Mariah's softness, overwhelmed him. The tips of his extremities prickled with fire. His eyes burned. The storm now raging outside mirrored the tempest brewing within his body. On impulse, he slammed out of the cabin and dashed into the rain. He threw out his arms and shouted at the wind, howling like a man who'd lost his mind, praying the water would cool this inexplicable heat.

He sensed rather than saw Mariah come out after him.

"Go!" he ordered, not daring to look at her.

"What's happening?"

He wished he could tell her. He had no words to convey the madness crashing through him—a crazed blackness that burbled from deep within him like a foul and viscous sludge. He needed to purge the hot pitch from his insides, and he knew, somehow, that the only way to stem the flow of darkness was to make love with Mariah. To surround himself with her light. To bathe in her powerful strength and beauty.

He dropped to his knees. Icy water sluiced down his face, shirt and breeches, cooling only the outer layer of his skin and doing nothing to alleviate the burning deep inside. Lightning flashed above him, and with the thunder he wailed in anguish, the sound echoing against the tumult of the night.

"Rafe?"

Her voice was soft. Concerned. She'd come nearer. Too near. Had the woman no sense? He'd thought her so unlike Irika, yet here she was, looking for him in the dark night when she should be running in the opposite direction.

He took her by the wrist and dragged her to him until their lips smashed together. Instantly his heart lightened. The infusion from her mouth gave him enough self-control to push her away.

"I'm sorry," he said.

She'd skidded across the wet ground, but pulled herself to her knees and swiped the back of her arm over her mouth.

"Look, I don't know what kind of women you hung out with in your century, but I'm not hot for men who manhandle."

He buried his face in his hands. The kiss had lightened the darkness inside him, but the living shadow still remained. Tied, he suspected, to the magic he'd wrought inside the cabin. He'd wanted only to provide comfortable quarters, but he should have known that using Rogan's powers came with a bitter price.

As he looked up at her, he dragged his fingers down his face. "I would never force myself on you. It's the magic. It has infected me."

"What are you talking about?"

He flew to his feet, took her by the hand and attempted to throw her into the cabin, to remind her of the handiwork that had brought him down this path, but she was ready for him this time and countered his touch, flinging him to the ground. He fell to the sodden dirt with a painful thud, his breath stolen. She'd backed away, but stood at the ready, prepared to battle him again.

"Explain," she demanded.

He closed his eyes, willed his lungs to obey him and attempted to comply. "The magic that imprisoned me within the stone is evil, and it is at my disposal. When I used it to make the cabin habitable, the darkness overwhelmed me. I feel it now, slogging through my veins like tar. But I know," he said, looking up and blinking against the rain, "I know that touching you, kissing you, will purge the madness."

She glanced back into the cabin, where the door remained open and the inside glowed with comfortable warmth. She stepped closer to him, then, shockingly, placed her hands on his shoulders.

"That's the craziest pickup line I've ever heard," she said. Her tone told him the comment should elicit humor, but he could feel nothing at the moment but the darkness and, thanks to her nearness, the renewed ache of desire.

"You should leave," he said.

She smirked. "Which one is it? Do you want me to leave or do you want to kiss me?"

He couldn't answer. The war raging within him between honor and insanity was too much for any mortal man to fight. Only, he wasn't a mortal man anymore. He was something else—something evil and magical and trapped, and yet free. Mariah's touch had released him, even as he'd fought against the pull she had awakened.

Swallowing thickly, he looked up into her eyes. The calm amber of her irises spiked his need.

"Kiss me," he begged.

He saw the hesitation in her eyes, just as he saw the moment when her gaze narrowed in determination. She placed her hands firmly on either side of his cheeks and pulled him close. Their lips met with a clash. He hardly trusted himself to respond, terrified that the magic would force him to take too much, too fast, but she proved as deliberate and strong in intimacy as she was with the attackers who'd attempted to steal the stone.

He fought to give quarter to her hungry lips, to yield to her gentle coaxing. When he opened his mouth to thrust his tongue against hers, she stopped him, rubbing her thumbs along the edges of his lips until he relaxed. Then, slowly, she dipped her tongue into his mouth and, with slow, deliberate swirls, diminished the anger surging within him.

But it wasn't enough. Concentrated in his center like a single beam from the white-hot sun, his lust did not abate. He mimicked her position, hands splayed across the sweet flesh of her face, and sucked from the kiss all the dizzying light he could take. But even as the darkness receded, his need for her increased. Not because of the magic within him, but because he was a man.

Her flesh was like satin. She tasted of rain and smoke from the fire. He moved his mouth so he could drink in the rivulets of rain flooding down her face, tasting her skin with renewed hunger. His shirt clung to him so tightly he could hardly move, so he ripped it off and allowed the deluge to soak him completely.

She pulled away, but in her eyes now, where there had been both fear and anger, he now saw blatant desire.

"Better?" she asked.

Had he incentive to tell the truth, he might have said they could stop—that her kiss had broken the dark spell. Her wide, round pupils and softly panting breaths convinced him to stay the course.

"Not quite yet," he replied.

This time, he kissed her. Immediately, she slid her hands down his chest, sighing against his mouth as her fingertips grazed his skin, tangling her fingers in the hairs on his chest and tugging until he groaned in grateful appreciation. She pressed closer, and her nipples, taut with need beneath her blouse, grazed his heated flesh.

The kiss was slow and deliberate and thorough. He licked her lips, prying them open with soft, gentle flicks, working his hands down her back as he progressed to a full mating of mouths. He curved his fingers over her backside, enraptured by the groan of pleasure she pressed from her lips into his. She wanted him as much as he wanted her—and she had no magic to blame.

"We should go inside," he said.

"Why?" she asked.

"It's cold," he replied, though the chill had utterly surrendered to the heat of their embrace.

"Then let's get warm."

*   *   *

Mariah took Rafe's hand in hers and led him to the cabin, unsure about what was happening. Over the course of the last forty-eight hours, she'd gone on the run from her ex-lover, nearly fallen to her death off an isolated cliff, flown back to the States while dreaming of a swarthy man whose kisses made her dizzy, and escaped an attack in her hotel room with the help of that same dark stranger.

She could no more deny that he possessed a real and powerful magic than she could refute the fact that she wanted him with the kind of desperate need she hadn't felt in years.

That alone had pushed her over the edge into recklessness. Whether or not she believed that the dark magic he'd used to conjure the now beautiful interior of the cabin stoked him to lust no longer mattered. She wanted him. And Mariah was nothing if not indulgent of her desires.

Once inside, the storm shut out by the locked door, Mariah silently stripped out of her clothes. She neared the fire, loving how the heat evaporated the wet chill clinging to her skin, wondering how far Rafe would go to warm her through and through.

When she turned, her backside growing hot so near the fireplace, she was surprised to see him still standing by the door.

"I thought you wanted to make love?"

He opened his mouth to speak, but no sound came out until after he'd cleared his throat. "You are . . . beautiful."

She attempted a smile, afraid her jaded attitude might have turned the genuine curve into more of a smirk. "You say that as if you've never seen a naked woman before."

"It has been centuries," he admitted.

Mariah brushed aside the weight of his confession. "But you haven't forgotten how this works, have you?"

His stride made the cabin seem instantly minuscule. He took her hands and, as he dropped to his knees, tugged her to the ground with him. "I have not forgotten."

She glanced down at his pants and boots. "You sure?"

An instant later, they were gone. She had only a split second to register the aroused length of him when his mouth descended on hers. The magic seemed to fire his lust, and as her mind swirled with the intense pleasure of his lips on hers, she decided the aftereffect was a definite perk.

His hands played across her flesh with a gentle urgency that reminded Mariah how long it had been since she'd had a lover. That was, she surmised, the reason she'd given in so easily. Never one to guard her sexuality, she indulged her needs whenever the mood struck her. And damn, but the vibes were slapping her hard now.

She learned his body with her palms and fingers, marveling at the power in the musculature of a man who claimed to be a ghost. And he was responsive to her touch, groaning with pleasure as she ran her fingers down his spine, rounded them over his strong backside and teased the crevice between his buttocks. He responded in kind, though he tugged her forward so that his full erection pressed against her belly.

Her sex quivered and wept with anticipation. When he skimmed around her belly and then stretched his thumbs upward to tease her breasts, she nearly cried out.

"You are . . ." he started, but he dropped his lips to

her neck, and whatever words he'd begun to say died as his mouth found more delicious pursuits.

"I am hot to feel your mouth all over me," she said, filling in the blanks for him.

He stopped long enough to look her in the eye.

"All over?" he asked.

She licked her lips. "English hasn't changed that much over two hundred years, has it?"

"No," he said with a grin, "but women have."

"It's all for the better," she assured him.

"Undeniably."

Locking her hands around his neck, she tugged him down so that her back was nestled in the warmth of the furry bearskin and her chest was pressed against his. She speared her fingers into his hair as he restarted his downward exploration. He ran his tongue along her collarbone, nipping at her shoulders with just enough pressure to spawn a raging wildfire of gooseflesh across her skin. When he swiped his tongue across her nipple, she felt sure she'd combust from the inside out.

"Yes," she goaded. "Right there. Just like—"

He needed no more instruction, plying her sensitive flesh with lips and tongue and teeth until she nearly came undone. As he stroked and laved and teased, he murmured foreign words against her skin that fired her further. By the time he licked around the edge of her belly button, she was convinced she was losing her mind.

When his breath teased the soft curls at the base of her thighs, she tensed, anticipating the feel of his tongue parting her pulsing flesh. But he stopped.

She pushed hungrily against his cheeks. "Please, Rafe."

He dipped his nose against her and inhaled deeply. "The temptation is great."

She chuckled, not so subtly scooting beneath him so that his mouth was closer to her sex. "Then why stop?"

His eyes darkened, not from the magic, she was certain, but from what she wanted him to do. Had he never? She racked her desire-fuddled brain for some explanation, but remembered that he'd been married in his past. Surely he and his wife had explored all manner of sensual pleasures.

"Try it," she encouraged. "I'll like it."

He shifted lower. She widened her legs. He did not move.

"Give me your hand," she instructed.

He did so. She took his fingers in hers and guided him around her vulva, smearing the natural moisture of her arousal against his hand. She pointed him to her clit, cooing when he found the tiny trigger to her orgasm. "Do that with your hand," she told him. "With your tongue. It's a pleasure you've never—"

His mouth stopped whatever thoughts she might have had after that. He took her at her word and feasted on her until she orgasmed. But even then, he did not stop. He'd developed a taste for her, and he continued to lap and suckle until she teetered again on the edge between desire and utter madness. She held on to the side of his face, unsure whether she could stand any more.

He took the choice from her, kissing a hot and desperate path up her body. The minute his mouth met hers, the flavor of her need clinging to his lips, he pressed inside her.

The thickness of his arousal stretched her to glorious limits. Unable to stem the tide he'd so skillfully stirred, she wrapped her legs around his waist and let him ride her to the brink. He pushed up on one arm, and the muscles in his biceps strained under his weight. She wanted to ply her teeth to the rigid tendons, but he increased his tempo until she could think of nothing more than following him to complete ecstasy.

Once spent, he collapsed atop her. She slid her hands into his dark locks and suddenly remembered how much she loved men who wore their hair past their shoulders. She explored the angles and curves of his shoulders while he pulled in great gulps of air, attempting to regain his ability to breathe.

"So," she asked, wanting to break what was becoming an odd silence. "How do you find sex in the twenty-first century?"

He pulled back and looked surprised to find her smiling. "Confusing. And wonderful. And intriguing. And—"

She placed two fingers across his lips. "Enough adjectives. Suffice it to say you're feeling better?"

He scooted away from her, stopping only when she wrapped her hand around his wrist.

"I took advantage of you," he said.

"Yes," she agreed. "But believe me, I got something out of the deal, too."

His smile barely curved his lips. "I am glad you experienced pleasure, Mariah, but I must make one thing clear." Any trace of humor disappeared. "I cannot use Rogan's magic ever again."

"That could be a problem," she replied.

10

Rafe had never met a more confounding woman, though considering the circumstances, he shouldn't have been surprised. Centuries of time had wrought many changes to the world, and he'd only begun to scratch the surface of the differences between his time and hers.

But they'd found common ground in their lovemaking. His body still thrummed from the aftereffects. So many times, he'd wondered about the flavor of a woman, about the pleasurable effects of exploring every crevice and sweet, soft curve of his wife's body, but his traditions waylaid him. Perhaps if they'd had more time? He and Irika had experienced great joy in their marriage bed, but he'd never fully delved into his deep, instinctual needs as he had with this woman he hardly knew and surely did not love. Irika had been shy about what pleased her and timid about discovering what pleased him. Mariah, on the other hand, had shown him precisely what to do.

In the deluge of such sexual elation, the repercussions of using Rogan's magic had ebbed completely. Rafe was himself again. He had no more excuses for wanting Mariah, for using her body to sate his needs. And yet, the familiar thrum of arousal sizzled over and through his skin.

"I see no problem," Rafe insisted, ignoring how his nostrils flared in search of her scent. "Your world already contains flying machines and flameless torches. The magic imposed on me may bring fleeting comfort, but the price is steep. You need not this evil thing that lives within me."

"How do you know it's evil?"

He pulled himself into a sitting position, which she did as well. With the firelight dancing across her skin and dappling her burnished brown hair with sparks of ruby fire, he was nearly too overwhelmed by her easy sensuality to form a response. She'd folded herself into a position that shielded her naked body, but her modesty did little to slake his desire. Her curves evoked fantasies he had no business entertaining when they'd just indulged in such sweet reality. He wanted Mariah again. Not because of unbidden lust brought on by Rogan's curse, but for himself.

"Lord Rogan was evil," he explained, denying his selfish instincts. "This magic that brought us together is his."

"Maybe," she said, somewhat doubtfully. "But the magic is in you now. You aren't evil. Or were you? Back then? When Rogan trapped you?"

Rafe possessed a fair amount of shortcomings, but wickedness had not been his sin. Not until tonight.

"I was but a simple Romani man hoping to find happiness and peace for my family."

"Tell me about them. Tell me about her." She laid her cheek against her knee, and Rafe was struck by the gentility of her voice.

He stood, and though he risked reawakening the intense consequences of utilizing Rogan's magic, he conjured clean, dry clothes. She *tsk*ed in disappointment.

"The past no longer matters," he said, unwilling to dredge up the memories. He'd been plagued by flashes of bloody images from his last night among the living since his reawakening. To share the details of his previous life now would result in more darkness for his soul than Rogan could ever have forced on him.

Mariah frowned. "The past might be the key to freeing you from the stone."

"I am free," he insisted.

"Only during the night, right?" She patted the rug beside her. He considered the risk of sitting beside her while she remained unclothed and scented with their lovemaking and decided instead to sit upon the couch.

"Yes," he concurred. "During the daylight hours, I am naught but a spirit."

"A phantom," she decided.

"A what?"

She sat up and twisted so that her bare breasts taunted him mercilessly. "A phantom. It's a being . . ."

Rafe closed his eyes and wished Mariah did not torture him so. When she yelped, he opened his eyes. She was now swathed in a pale silk robe.

"Hey!" she protested.

"You could catch your death," he warned.

She smirked, but thrust herself to her feet and joined him on the sofa. "Is it safe for me to sit beside you now that I'm not naked?"

"Safe enough," he replied, though he wondered. The storm within him had abated just as the squall had outside, and yet, the sexual connection he shared with

Mariah had strengthened. Now that he knew the intensity of making love to her, he could not imagine denying himself the experience again, should the chance arise. He supposed he'd simply have to ensure that the opportunity did not present itself.

He scooted a few inches to the side.

She rolled her eyes. "Whatever," she said. "Back to phantoms. Thanks to my mother, I know a great deal about the legends and lore of the magical and paranormal."

"Your mother?"

Mariah leaned forward, eyeing the wine Rafe had conjured earlier. Rafe took the hint and poured a goblet for each of them, and delivered the bowl of fruit, which she cradled in her lap. "She is a curator at a museum."

"A curator? Of a . . . ?"

She pressed her lips together, thinking hard before she explained. "A curator is someone who catalogs and researches the items that museums put in their collections for the public to see. That rock, for instance."

She nodded toward her dilly bag. "A museum that specializes in Romani history would probably pay a lot of money to have that stone. If museums that specialized in Romani history had a lot of money, which they generally don't."

He nodded, but he had no idea what she was talking about. She seemed to intuit this, because she patted his knee encouragingly. "Don't worry. You'll catch on soon enough. Suffice it to say that in her line of work, my mother encounters many items of mysterious, even magical origin. She reads and hears lots, too. When I was a teenager, I went to live with her, so I heard the stories, as well."

"You did not live with your mother previously?"

"I don't want to spit the dummy," she said, taking a long sip of wine.

He arched an eyebrow.

"Sorry," she said. "I've lived in the States for a decade, but I forget sometimes and revert to Aussie slang. Means I don't want to lose my temper, so let's pick another topic—unless you have another two hundred years for me to adequately explain the weirdness that was my childhood."

Rafe suspected he did not have another two centuries for discourse, but he found that he wanted to know more about Mariah and what circumstances had pushed her to the life she now led. She was, at the core, a thief—one who cared little for ownership and more for survival. He'd known her for only a few days, but he'd gathered that she followed a nomadic existence not unlike that of his people, and not unlike the life he might have lived if not for the accident of his paternity.

He loved his father, but they'd had nothing in common. As much as the earl claimed to love the Gypsies, he had done little to plead for his people's release from the king's banishment. His father had argued that colonization was the best solution and that the Gypsies in Valoren were honest artisans with always enough to eat, but Rafe never could abide his imperialist attitude.

He shifted so that his back leaned against the armrest. "And a phantom?"

She mirrored his position, but pulled her legs onto the cushions, crossing them as one might when sitting around the village fire. He was thankful when she adjusted her robe modestly. "Well, there are lots of stories about them, but there's no definitive definition. Some cultures equate phantoms with ghosts. Others view them as spirits of people sent to the other realms before their time, but who long to return to the earthly plane."

Rafe nodded. "Sounds accurate."

"But it doesn't really matter what you're called," Mariah said, popping a grape into her mouth, chewing and then chasing the fruit with the wine. "The facts are thus: You possess magic, and I need some if I'm going to find those missing coins and get my arse out of Hector Velez's sling."

Rafe remained silent. Without Mariah, he would not have found freedom from Rogan's marker, even if only during the night. Despite his aversion to the idea of utilizing the dark magic again, he could not help but consider her situation. Mariah had proved herself clever and resourceful. He had no doubt that if anyone could figure out how to free him entirely from the stone, it was her.

"I am listening," he said.

Her grin could have lit up the entire room. She wiggled in her seat as she laid out the details of her situation, unable to contain her enthusiasm. "After I stole the coins for Velez, I had to fly over the jungle in Chiapas to rendezvous with him at Villahermosa. I got word the Mexican authorities were waiting for me there, tipped off that I'd taken the coins from a dusty basement in Chajul, which I had. I put the coins in a padded bag, equipped it with a locating device called a GPS monitor, flew low over the jungle and dropped it. After I landed, I was boarded and searched, but the police found nothing, so they had to let me go, warning me to get the hell out of their country and not come back."

"But you defied their orders," Rafe guessed.

"Of course," she said with a quirk of a smile. "I waited a bit, then trekked back into the jungle on foot, thinking I'd be able to retrieve the coins and get out before anyone noticed me. But the coins dropped in a remote area and the signals from the locator were imprecise. I heard the authorities were coming after me again, so I lit out. Now I'm in debt to Velez, and he's on my trail."

"Those men in the hotel room?" he asked.

She frowned. "I don't know; it really doesn't fit that those men worked for Velez. Whoever attacked me in the hotel definitely knew I'd taken Rogan's stone. Velez wouldn't know anything about Rogan."

"What about the man who chased you in Valoren?"

"Ben?" She shook her head. "He'd never hire anyone to retrieve the stone from me. He'd do it himself."

Rafe crossed his arms. He'd never met a woman who could get herself in more trouble with more dangerous men—except, perhaps, his sister.

She scooted closer. "Look, let's deal with one problem at a time. No matter who is after your stone, I have to retrieve the coins before Velez has me killed. And trust me, that's what he'll do. If you could use your magic to give the GPS a boost, find those coins for me, then I can stop looking over my shoulder and concentrate on freeing you—permanently—before someone tries to steal the stone again, too. And you, since you're a package deal."

As he took a long draft of wine, Rafe considered her proposal. He did not have to comprehend all of the details to find the simplest thread—she needed his help and he needed hers. The only thing holding him back from immediately agreeing to her plan was the fact that utilizing Rogan's magic on such a scale was dangerous. Two women he'd loved deeply, Sarina and Irika, had died because of Rogan's insatiable lust for power. And as wondrous as the sorcerer's magic might have been when wielded by its master, it had not saved his sister from becoming a casualty to the man's inherent evil. Nor, despite Rogan's claims to want to protect the Gypsies, had it saved Irika from a mercenary's knife.

He shook his head. "There must be another way," he concluded.

Mariah slid closer to him and pressed her hand directly over his heart. "If it's the madness you're afraid of," she said, her voice low and husky, "we know the antidote."

He opened his mouth to protest, but she covered his lips with her fingers.

"Don't say it. You're not taking advantage of me any more than I'm taking advantage of you. I need your magic, and in return, you get hot sex with a willing woman. In this century, we call this a win-win proposition."

They remained in the cabin until their supplies ran low three days later, and still, Rafe had neither agreed to nor denied her request. She'd stopped asking. The man might be a phantom, but he wasn't stupid. He needed time to consider the ramifications of and advantages to using the magic to help her out of a jam.

During the nights, Mariah spent most of her time teaching Rafe Forsyth everything he'd need to know about the twenty-first century. Without a computer to check her facts, she focused mostly on the basics in areas such as world history, politics and religion. On the subjects she knew by rote—human nature, the sexual revolution and flying—they talked for hours, down to the most trivial detail.

Well, on flying, Rafe mostly listened, though the wonderment in his gaze never faltered, even when she knew he was utterly scandalized by her treasure-hunting exploits. She'd shared a few of her more exciting stories about operations she'd pulled off in Egypt, Eritrea and the Sudan. Only when the subject had turned to Ben Rousseau had she'd skimped on the particulars. She didn't like the way Rafe's eyes darkened when her former lover's name came up.

On most topics, Rafe proved a serious student, listening intently, asking pointed questions and trying to draw comparisons with his Romani society, which wasn't always easy to do. And yet, she couldn't help admire how open-minded he was. He had had the advantage of having been tutored by his formally educated brothers, but he'd lived in such a remote part of the world, with no opportunity to see more than one tiny corner of the universe, which, even in two hundred and sixty years, hadn't changed. At least, not from the little she'd seen of it.

Had she stayed with her father in the Northern Territory rather than moving to Sydney to thrust herself on her mother, her life might have been more like Rafe's, only she didn't have brothers who would have spared her the time to teach her anything beyond how to play a brutal game of rugby or the best way to skin a roo.

They had not made love again, something that vexed Mariah just as much as it relieved her. Rafe was sexy and sensitive, smart and mysterious, but she accepted that making love for him was something more than just surrendering to physical urges. She couldn't remember being with a man who ascribed any real importance to the act beyond satisfying pent-up needs. Not at least since Ben—and even then, what she'd believed to be the seedlings of true commitment for Ben had turned out to be nothing more than the stupid weeds of youth.

During the day, Rafe slipped back into the stone to rest, not out of choice, but necessity. Mariah tried to sleep, but despite her cut-and-dried plan to exploit Rafe's magic in order to solve her Velez problem, she tossed and turned until only sheer exhaustion overrode her whirling mind.

And then, dreams plagued her. She watched Rafe morph from a light-eyed Gypsy who quirked one eyebrow when a modern attitude or expression amused him to a shadowed, black-hooded figure whose eyes gleamed orange-red like the center of the fire opal that contained him. She ran from him, slicing through thick jungle vines, pursued, terrified, until the ground dropped from beneath her feet and she fell into the nothingness, screaming Rafe's name.

11

"Mariah?"

She bolted upright. She took several seconds to realize she was lying on the plush couch in the cabin and not dead and broken at the bottom of some rocky cliff. She blinked, rubbing her eyes until the pink light from outside the window no longer blinded her.

"I'm awake," she replied gratefully. "I'm awake now."

A whisper of a touch smoothed her cheek. It was not yet sundown, but Rafe was awake and toying with the state between phantom and man. Exhausted and unnerved by her dream, she couldn't resist leaning into the sensation. Degree by degree, Rafe's warmth washed away the terrifying images of her nightmare.

"Your sleep was fitful," he said.

"Were you watching me sleep?"

"How could I resist?"

His invisible caress curled around her chin and lifted. Drowsy, she anticipated a press of lips. But like the ground in her dream, it never came.

She tossed aside the soft blanket she couldn't remember drawing over her body and shivered against the chill. Even in early summer, the mountains could be cold. Especially right before nightfall. She glanced longingly at the fireplace, but knew they'd stayed at the cabin long enough. Rafe hadn't exactly agreed to use Rogan's evil magic to help her find the coins, but he hadn't denied her, either. If she was going to get out from under Velez's threats, she needed to act.

Besides, the sooner she paid back the collector, the sooner she could find a way to release Rafe from his cursed tether to the stone. Not that she didn't enjoy having a man around who could make things appear out of nowhere and who needed hot sex to remain sane, but the situation was already hugely complicated. And if there was anything Mariah hated, it was complications.

Ever since her breakup with Ben, she'd striven to keep things simple. Her business. Her attitudes. Her relationships. And though she hadn't known Rafe Forsyth for long, she had more than enough evidence to conclude that he was the epitome of complexity.

"Ready to go?" she asked, standing and shaking off the last of her lethargy.

"Have I a choice?"

"Good point," she said. She'd already packed the stone in her bag the night before. Still, she'd like to think she wasn't technically forcing him to help her. He had, after all, agreed to go to the jungle with her before he determined whether or not he would call upon Rogan's cursed magic to find the coins.

No matter his decision, she knew she'd do what she could to free him, perhaps help him regain the life cut short by magic. Not that carrying around her own personal sex slave wasn't tempting, but she was a thief, not a psycho.

"We're both better off if we get out of here," she continued. "Staying in one place too long is never wise when you're being hunted."

"Tell me about your dream," he said, his voice caressing her neck.

Instinctively, she curled her hair back behind her ear before shaking away the intimate sensation. "Sometimes people dream when they sleep. Not a big deal," she replied curtly. Grabbing her jacket, she shrugged into the worn leather and headed toward the kitchen to gather the last of the rations.

"Your dreams disturbed you. What did you see?"

Determined to ignore the images still lingering on the edges of her consciousness, she shoved the beef jerky into a Baggie. "Nothing important."

"Then why did you call my name?"

She spun in the direction of his voice, suddenly frustrated by his invisibility. Had she shouted out to him in her sleep? Even as she questioned herself, the echo of the desperate cry reverberated in her brain like a giant Chau gong.

"I don't know. I don't remember."

"You lie," he accused.

Since he was right, she did not respond, but stuffed the last of the apples he'd conjured into a plastic bin.

Luckily, he did not press further.

His presence lingered around her while she locked down the shutters on the windows, collected a few of the soft pillows and blankets, then made sure that the fireplace was emptied of ash and embers. His scent, as fresh and invigorating as the forest outside, teased her nostrils until she found herself smiling again, despite her disturbing dream and his probing questions.

Once the chopper was ready for takeoff, darkness had descended and her mood had lightened. Rafe materialized and, as planned, had altered his appearance so that he no longer wore clothes that were centuries out of style. His hair swept his shoulders and his boots gleamed, but now jeans of butter-soft denim hugged his lean hips, and an equally supple blue shirt did amazing things to his silver eyes. He silently buckled into the seat beside her in the cockpit as they'd practiced, then stared at her expectantly, his mouth curved in an anticipatory smile that almost made her check to see if her blouse had come undone.

"Something amiss?" he asked.

The humorous lilt in his voice reminded her that he had a wicked talent for reading her emotions, which was only one step away from reading her mind. Mentally shaking off her libido, she concentrated on getting them into the air. Fifteen minutes later, they were headed at top speed to an abandoned airstrip outside of Boulder, where they'd initiate the first part of her plan. In the interest of her sanity, she concentrated on her scheme to get them out of the country and into Mexico unnoticed rather than on the way the blue instrument lights played against the jet-black shine of his hair.

As a result, they did not talk. Out of the corner of her eye, however, she caught sight of Rafe staring out into the night, one hand pressed against the glass, as if he had to brace himself for the world outside. She tried to imagine what was going on in his mind as they flew over a landscape so foreign to him. Bright lights. Imposing buildings. The blur of cars darting down the highway. If she managed to pull this salvage operation off, he'd have a wondrous world to explore. And she'd be alive to show it to him.

As the general concern of organizations like Homeland Security and border patrols tended to focus on keeping foreigners out of the United States rather than keeping their own citizens in, she figured it wouldn't be too hard for her and Rafe to slip into Mexico unnoticed, especially by air. Until her screwup with Velez, the Mexican authorities had believed Mariah Hunter was the name of a tourist exploring the decadence of Cabo San Lucas or the real estate possibilities in the Yucatán peninsula. After her plane had been boarded and searched for the missing Mayan coins, however, the police had told her to never darken their doorstep again and her passport had been flagged. Well, she'd heard worse threats from more corrupt governments. She was probably still a wanted woman in parts of the Middle East and northern Africa. She wasn't about to be frightened off now.

At the airstrip, Ken and Jan Barkett met them with her Cessna. On the spot, they paid a fair cash price for her chopper, giving her more than enough money to finance this excursion. During the course of the transaction, they eyed Rafe suspiciously, but asked no questions. Mariah didn't offer introductions. If Velez's men accosted the Barketts again, she didn't want them to know anything.

From Boulder, she flew to Elsa, Texas, a town not too far from the Mexican border, where she knew of a guy who would help her and Rafe with forged documents, including passports, for two brand-new identities, just in case. A half hour before sunrise, she and Rafe snuggled together on a futon in the back room of the forger's house to wait for the man to work his own brand of magic.

Exhausted, she could not fight the contentedness that

drifted over her when Rafe's hand slipped across her belly.

"The sun rises soon," he said.

Another entire night had passed, and they'd wasted his solid form by not making love. They'd refrained since the one time in the cabin, just as Rafe had refused to use any magic since then. Magic led to darkness, which led to sex. Rafe held fast to his pledge not to take advantage of Mariah to cleanse his soul, and Mariah, though not averse to being used in such a delicious way, had respected his choice. She had to keep her eyes on the prize—convincing Rafe to call on Rogan's sorcery to help her find the coins.

She'd acted in many more mercenary ways in the span of her lifetime, but for some reason, this situation cut more deeply.

And yet, she was tempted. Oh, so tempted. He was warm. His scent, no longer reminiscent of horses or leather, but of fresh-chopped wood and a hint of mountain rain, was instant aromatherapy. Her eyes closed; she tried not to imagine Rafe's hand, settled possessively across her middle, moving either higher to her breasts or lower to her suddenly pulsing sex. Both ways led to decadence—and regrets. At least, on his part.

"We should sleep," she murmured.

He shifted closer. His erection pressed against her back. Along with his muscled thighs, strong arms and rock-hard chest, she was surrounded by a solid wall of man that made her want to do nothing less than melt against him.

"Is this natural?" he asked.

The question, so unexpected, made her turn toward him. "Is what natural?"

Languidly, he ran his hand from her stomach to her side, denying her fantasy, and yet firing her desire to nearly unbearable levels.

"This attraction we share."

"It's certainly not unnatural," she replied. "You're a very handsome man, Rafe. And I'm not unattractive—"

"You're beautiful," he countered.

She smiled, despite her natural inclination to modesty when it came to her physical appearance. Mariah knew she could turn heads. She knew she could flirt or seduce men in the name of manipulation. A pretty face and decent-size breasts made this a common reality for women everywhere. But as much as she needed Rafe's help and craved his touch, she couldn't imagine operating that way with him. Something about him engendered honesty.

"Thank you," she replied. "I'm not sure what you're asking, then."

His fingers toyed with the edge of her blouse. "I met Irika when I was a child. I knew from the first moment I laid eyes on her that I would marry her."

"Really?" she asked, genuinely surprised. "I've never met a man I thought I could marry, especially not when I was six."

"Not even Ben Rousseau?"

She smirked. She'd walked right into that one.

"Maybe for a brief moment, I thought it would be possible," she admitted. "He came into my life when I was seventeen, but I looked older, and I conveniently neglected to tell him I was still underage. He was supposedly an archeological intern studying at my mother's museum. He was sexy and smart and unattainable, though he flirted with me shamelessly. And I ate it up and found a million excuses to follow him around. Anyway, when it turned out that he wasn't actually at the museum to study the artifacts but to steal them, my constant presence became a liability. I could have ratted him out. Luckily for him, I was so enamored, I not only helped him take the pieces he wanted, I ran off with him. He taught me the ropes of the treasure-hunting game. By the time I was nineteen, we were lovers. I didn't want marriage or a family—I wanted adventure and risk and excitement. And he gave me those things in spades."

"And as a husband, he could not do the same?"

She chuckled. "Honest to God, Rafe, I never even thought about it. My parents divorced when I was five. Neither one of them married again. Even my brothers are still single. Marriage simply has never been on my list of things to do."

As she'd hoped, Rafe's fingers had drifted beneath her shirt. His touch skimmed up and down her sides, always stopping just shy of the curve beneath her breast and the low-slung waistline of her jeans.

"Such a shame." His eyes were liquid silver, sharp and hot. His touch finally slipped beneath the lacy edges of her bra. "Imagine having someone to make love with each and every night. Sharing your secrets with them. Learning their bodies and having them learn yours until pleasure is both unspoken and yet assured."

At that moment, he tweaked her nipple. She gasped as an orgasmic spike shot straight down to her clit, which suddenly needed his touch so much more. She snuggled against his erection, and yet he denied her. He remained utterly still, his only movement continuous sharp circles around her areola, softly scratching her skin until the itch became unbearable.

"You don't have to be married to connect with some-one that closely," she said.

"How do you know?"

She bit her bottom lip, trying to answer quickly so that he'd continue his sweet assault on her senses. With Ben, Mariah had had a hot sex life. That much was un-deniable. But she didn't fool herself that they'd ever shared any real connection. What they'd enjoyed had been simple and direct, with none of the nuance that might have come with time and real commitment.

"I don't," she answered.

"I do," he replied. "And I am the one who was married."

"Does it hurt to talk about her?" she asked, un-surprised when his hand stilled. She would have been sorely disappointed if he'd been able to continue arous-ing her when he was talking about his wife. And as much as she wanted him to use his last minutes of solid form to soothe her sexual ache, she couldn't resist learning more about what made him tick.

"Yes," he replied.

A single syllable, fraught with the deepest of emo-tions, cut straight through her. She pressed her forehead against his chest. "Then don't say another word. I'm sorry I asked."

For a long minute, she heard nothing but his steady breathing, commingled with a heartbeat. The sound wasn't strong and seemed almost hollow, but phantom or not, Rafe Forsyth lived. He witnessed the new world with fresh eyes, and he mourned the woman he'd loved with an honest heart. She suddenly felt very inadequate, and she didn't like the emotion one bit.

She forced a yawn. Rafe pressed his arm possessively around her back and whispered, "You are exhausted."

She murmured her agreement, and then closed her eyes. In her entire adult life, she never remembered wanting a man to hold her until she fell asleep. This was certainly one for the record books, she thought, before the soft stroke of Rafe's hand along her spine lulled her into dreamless sleep.

"If there's one thing I love about thieves and reprobates, it's that they don't ask a lot of questions," Mariah replied to Rafe's inquiry the next evening about how she'd explained his disappearance to the man who forged their new passports. "By the time I took possession of our papers and paid him, he had a whole new set of customers."

Rafe nodded, looking out into the inky black night and wondering how Mariah knew where she was going when there were no landmarks visible from this height and night was too cloudy to use the stars for navigation. He simply had to trust that she knew what she was doing, a task he found increasingly difficult since their talk just before dawn, when he'd learned how little she understood about something as elemental as relations between men and women.

In her century, sex no longer had the same importance that it had in his—but the basics had not changed. Attraction led to pursuit, which often led to pleasure. His study to become the next village shaman after his father-in-law, Belthezor, made him keenly aware of how sexual relations rooted not only a marriage, but families and, therefore, the clan. Only after he'd spoken vows to his wife had he taken Irika to bed.

He'd not been unknowledgeable of the mechanics of coupling, but he and Irika had discovered together what brought them the most pleasure. Skin to skin and heart to heart, they had shared dreams and wishes for their future and had created the life that had become their son.

Once Irika had been with child, they'd made love more gently. Even as a girl, Irika had never been robust. The *puri* women of the tribe predicted trouble for her and the baby if she did not rest. She obeyed them, drinking the herbal remedies they cooked up for her over the open flames in the center of the village, while Rafe learned to do without the comfort of his wife's body.

After Stefan's birth, Irika had taken a long time to heal. Then, just when the sparks of their passion had reignited, the mercenary threat arrived, Rafe had been cursed and Irika had died. Rafe could not help regretting all he'd lost. His wife. His son. His future.

What could Mariah offer him, other than his freedom?

Or, more telling, what could he offer her?

Naught but the magic.

"How will you land this airplane in the dark?" he asked, knowing that the shadowy shapes beneath them were mountains and hills and thick treetops.

"Very carefully."

She flicked on an instrument to her right, igniting a glowing green line that moved in a circular motion over a dark surface, blipping and beeping.

"Here we go," Mariah said, pointing into the darkness.

Rafe saw only more shadows.

"I see nothing."

"See that light? To the west, just there."

He squinted and thought perhaps he saw a flicker of orange.

"It's a bonfire. The locals keep it burning for the rangers who patrol this area, part of which is a preserve. It's right on the edge of an airstrip the drug runners once used before the *federales* commandeered it. I've flown in here before. Rain and wind sometimes shift the path, but if I can touch down without breaking us up, we can hide the plane in a hut where *narcotraficantes* used to store their stashes before deliveries. Yeah, this will work. This will work perfectly."

Rafe ignored the fact that her claims seemed more intended to convince herself than him. He braced himself, enduring the rocking of the airplane and the sudden, unexpected bounce that made her whoop with excitement. Just when he thought the experience of landing in the dark could not possibly get worse, the tires bounced hard on the ground, jarring him from his teeth to his toes.

She squealed with glee once the plane began to slow, though it tossed them from side to side until finally stopping abruptly. Rafe exited the aircraft quickly. When his boots touched the earth, he had to fight hard not to fall prostrate and kiss the unmoving soil.

Mariah tossed a bag onto the dirt beside him before she exited the airplane. "A little airsick?"

"Is that what you call it?" he asked.

She laughed and continued to unload. "Not everyone loves a bumpy ride. But we need to make this quick. Take our supplies over to that trail," she said, pointing toward a thick line of trees. "I'll take the plane into that hut of a hangar and get her secured."

Rafe did as she instructed. The weight of the packs

tempted him to use Rogan's magic, but he resisted. After the second trip to the forest edge, hauling the supplies Mariah had insisted they'd need to reach the remote area where she'd dropped the coins, the sweat that soaked down his back and the pulling pain in his arms and neck invigorated him even as the effort exhausted him.

"Ready for another adventure?" she asked, carrying two bags on either shoulder when she joined him.

The moon overhead, a crescent of incredible brightness, threw a silver glow over the field and the adjacent forest. Rafe took a moment to breathe in the unfamiliar air and register the scents of verdant trees. The sunbaked earth beneath his boots seemed to drink in the moisture of the night. While the sensations of this place were completely unlike Valoren, they seeped into his blood and immediately became part of who he was.

He was Romani.

Gypsy.

One with the earth.

"Rafe?" she asked.

"This place has magic," he decided.

"This place has you," she replied, patting the bag where she kept Rogan's marker. "And the stone. Where you go, magic goes."

"No," he said, taking her by the shoulders and pulling her close. "This is a new magic. One that may make Rogan's evil sorcery utterly useless."

12

Rafe intended to explain to Mariah what he meant, but angry voices from the south spurred them to grab their things and thrash into the forest for cover. The trees and thick foliage provided an instant blind of shadow, blocking them from a half dozen men, dressed in what appeared to be nightclothes, running toward them with crude but still dangerous weapons. Long blades and thick broom handles. A rusted old rifle. They cursed and spat in a language Rafe had never heard before, but judging by the way Mariah curved tighter into an invisible ball and grabbed his hand to encourage him to do the same, they were not spouting salutations.

Only twenty paces into the brush, he and Mariah were invisible to their pursuers. Rafe caught his breath and squeezed Mariah's hand tighter, not surprised that her anxiety matched his own. He would use the magic if necessary, but he could not allow the constant pull of the evil sorcery to become second nature. His soul was already infected. Willful command of the dark powers would send him down a path more perilous than any in this foreign jungle.

Mariah remained perfectly still beside him. The slice
and chop of the swords against the leaves and branches
that surrounded them sent them scurrying farther into
the foliage, abandoning their belongings. They ducked
low to avoid exposure from flashlights, but after a quarter of an hour of searching, the incensed group seemed
satisfied with their disappearance and went back in the
direction they came.

He and Mariah waited another ten minutes just in
case. Once the silence was filled with the buzzing, cawing and rustling of what Rafe assumed were the native
animals, they retrieved their belongings and eased back
onto the path.

"What language were they speaking?" he asked.

"Spanish, mostly," she said, moving their packs
around to equally distribute the load. Rafe grabbed a
haversack she'd intended to take herself and slung it
over his shoulder. "The dialect was hard to place, though.
Around here, there are quite a few natives, descendants
of the Mayans, whose coins I'm after. The plane is probably walkabout," she grumbled. "There's an outpost
of sorts not too far from here. I bought supplies from
them last time, and I paid a more than fair price, so they
should be somewhat happy to see me."

Clicking on the light she'd attached to her shoulder, she illuminated the narrow dirt alley that would
lead them to their first destination. She started walking
with surprising speed. Despite having flown for hours
on very little sleep, despite the danger and uncertainty
she'd faced over the past several days, Mariah's voice
hitched higher with excitement the deeper they went
into the jungle. She was in her element—the uncertain
and unknown.

Though the atmosphere quickly grew steamy and sweaty, Mariah kept up a steady pace. Unlike the dry forests of Valoren, this jungle hung on to moisture like a sponge, then dripped it onto his skin. They'd hiked for what Rafe guessed was over two miles when she finally declared they should stop for a rest and a drink.

She pulled out a canteen filled with cool water and offered him the first swig, which he declined. She drank greedily, swiped her mouth with her sleeve and then pressed the container into his hands. They did not speak. Between quenching their thirst and attempting to regulate their breathing, there wasn't much energy left for chitchat.

At least, not for her. Rafe sat still, closed his eyes and listened to a heartbeat in the jungle that had nothing to do with the pounding in his chest. This place overflowed with magic. The farther into the wildness they wandered, the stronger it became. The sensation was familiar and yet utterly foreign. He had no idea whether proceeding would make Rogan's dark magic stronger or, perhaps, defeat it altogether.

"The outpost is just down that slope," she said, packing the water again and slugging it back into her bags.

Rafe grunted his understanding. It had been many years since he'd worked this hard. If, however, the slope proved farther than she thought, he'd call upon Rogan's magic to, at the very least, conjure up a cart and horse.

As promised, the outpost, which consisted of a single thatch-roofed hut surrounded by a ramshackle fence that somehow managed to contain several asses, a half dozen snorting and snuffling pigs, nesting chickens and one loud, barking dog, was less than a ten-minute walk from where they'd rested. Mariah motioned for him to remain at the edge of the jungle. She draped the bag that contained the Valoren marker around his neck, and then proceeded toward the dwelling alone.

Only he knew that she had a pistol hidden in the waistband of her jeans, covered by the hem of a loose, long-sleeved shirt.

From the hut, a woman armed with a rifle emerged from behind the blanket that served as the door. Mariah held a stack of what she'd told him were twenty-dollar bills and spoke in the woman's native tongue. The woman shouted over her shoulder for a compatriot, who came out and shone a light in Mariah's face.

Seconds later, the rifle disappeared, the man whistled for the dog to quiet and the woman came out beyond the gate to talk with Mariah for a solid five minutes before money was exchanged and Mariah returned.

"Okay, we've got us a burro."

"A what?"

She pointed to one of the asses. "We'll move faster if we don't have to carry all this stuff ourselves."

"We keep traveling tonight?"

Mariah started arranging their bags so that the heavier items, like a supply of bottled water, would go with the beast. "There's a river about a kilometer northeast of here. We'll follow it until we're safely away from any civilization, then set up camp. With old Pedro to do the heavy lifting, I can do most of the hiking tomorrow. Now that we're here, it's safer to travel in daylight. This jungle is on the edge of a preserve, so there's a lot of wildlife. Not to mention natives who'd rather not be bothered by outsiders."

In less than an hour, they were hiking down a slightly more traveled path. The deeper and denser the jungle

became, the more invigorated Rafe was by his surround-
ings. Several times, he thought he caught glimpses of curious spirits trailing beside them, watching them, but by
the time he turned his head, they were gone. As they
walked, Mariah told him a bit about the natives of this
area and their Mayan ancestors. His visions began to
make sense.

"They understood magic," he concluded, after hearing about their attitudes and rituals in regard to the land.
Like his Gypsy forebears, the Mayans communed with
the land they lived on, and in return, the earth showed
them her secrets. Unlike the Romani, the Mayans did
not wander. They did not comprehend the true nature
of the conquistadors and were, therefore, destroyed. Of
course, Gypsies never trusted the *gadje*, and the people
of his village were just as dead.

"I don't know much about Mayan beliefs about
magic," Mariah replied. "But I do know that while the
people were highly advanced, they were also brutal and
uncivilized."

"Were they uncivilized or simply uncivil to their
invaders?"

She chuckled. "Touché. Don't get me wrong. I find
the whole Mayan culture fascinating. I don't know much
about them beyond what Velez told me, though."

"And yet you steal their ... what is the word?
Artifacts?"

"They're not exactly around anymore to protest, are
they?"

He held his tongue. They were here. And closer than
she believed.

"I was just doing my job," she continued.

"A job that is not legal," he pointed out.

With a snicker, she hacked away at what must have been a particularly thick vine. "I can't believe I'm getting an ethics lesson from a Gypsy," she muttered.

Rafe smiled. "So my people still have a negative reputation among the *gadje*?"

"Mostly earned," she insisted. "I've known quite a few Gypsies in my lifetime, and I couldn't trust a single one."

He adjusted one of the straps that had been digging painfully into his shoulder. "There aren't many people you trust, Mariah Hunter. I doubt Gypsy blood makes any difference."

She stopped. The ass—or burro, as she called it— halted and shook his head in protest of the break in his steady pace. She quieted the animal with a gentle hand on his neck.

She then turned on him with those guarded amber eyes.

"I trust you," she said.

He stepped nearer to her. "Have you any choice? As long as you continue to possess the stone, you possess me. Our interactions are inescapable."

"Nothing is inescapable," she countered. "You've told me yourself that you have this evil entity inside of you because of the magic that traps you. Just a few nights ago, you went bonkers in a thunderstorm, but I didn't run from you, did I? I ran to you. I helped you. If that doesn't say trust, then I don't know what does."

The burro shuffled impatiently. Mariah turned and, with the animal's bridle in her hand, continued to press forward.

Rafe lagged behind, mulling over her words and considering how, yet again, Mariah Hunter had utterly surprised him. Though cagey and suspicious by nature, she'd taken him and his wild story as truth. By coming here with him, she was risking her livelihood—her very life—on the belief that his story was true. And yet, she still erected walls around her emotions like no other woman he'd ever met—walls he suddenly wanted very much to scale.

As she'd predicted, they came upon a river soon afterward. Mariah bent down and took a sniff of the water before splashing her face, hands and neck. Rafe joined her. The night was hot and the air sultry. He was surprised when the ass refused to drink, and he tried to coax the animal to the water's edge.

"He'll drink when he's thirsty," she told him. "Burros are accustomed to this heat and humidity. We're going to stay near the water for a while. He'll be okay."

"We'll camp here?"

Mariah focused her light up the path and frowned. "This is a little too exposed for my tastes. If we go upstream about"—she consulted her map—"a quarter mile, I think we'll be better off. Up for more hiking?"

Rafe readjusted the pack. "Lead the way."

The river rushing beside them provided a natural music like none Rafe had ever heard. The water in Valoren had come from a spring in the mountains, which flowed down into slim streams that swelled only with the winter melt. He'd never seen a body of water quite as large as this, and upon admitting this to Mariah, she told him about the nearby Gulf of Mexico.

"Like an ocean," he said. "My brothers were all born in England. They loved the ocean and often spoke of its hypnotic ebb and flow."

"What about you?"

"I've never seen any body of water beyond the springs of Valoren."

"You've missed out." They'd left the path, and now Mariah hacked through undergrowth with a sword much like the ones carried by the villagers who'd greeted them at the airstrip, which she called a machete. "The gulf is warm, not cold like the Atlantic, which is what your brothers would have known. And the beaches here in Mexico and Florida—they can be as white as snow, with not a rock in sight. And the color—I don't even know if I can describe it. It can be the most amazing shade of aquamarine, somewhere between a blue and a green, depending on its mood."

Rafe stilled her hand when she moved to chop through another layer of thick, verdant leaves. The longing in her voice spawned an emotional rush he could not resist. He needed to touch her, if only for a moment, to gauge whether he alone experienced a renewed pull of attraction.

"Sounds amazing," he said.

Entirely aware of the state of them—tired, hungry, smelling of sweat, donkey and something she'd called bug spray—Rafe couldn't resist the instantaneous sizzle of his skin against hers. For a fleeting moment, an irrepressible yearning coursed through her. Was it from her description of the Gulf of Mexico or from his touch?

"Don't," she said.

"Don't what?"

"Touch me," she said, though she made no move to jerk out of the contact.

"Why?"

"My hands are dirty."

"Your entire body is dirty, as is mine."

The moon broke through the branches laced above their heads. Rafe spotted a smudge of dirt across Mariah's nose. He'd have wiped it clean if his hands weren't just as covered by dark grime and perspiration. And yet, the thought of not touching her simply because of the filth of a long and tiring night seemed vain and superficial. He'd gone so long without so much as accidentally brushing against her. He had not realized until now how his body ached for contact with hers.

"We'll wash once we make camp," she said, pulling out of his reach.

Her gaze dipped to the ground as her tongue swiped softly over her lips. A sudden breeze, ripe with attraction, blew off her body.

"You've labored long enough," he said, taking the long-bladed knife from her grasp. "Allow me."

Their hands touched, and just before she pulled away, he experienced a hint of hunger emanating from her skin. She wanted him as he wanted her—with no magic driving them except the natural allure of the dark and dangerous jungle.

He chopped down with the machete, amazed at how the sharp blade sliced through thick branches as if cutting through a single sheet of parchment. He led the way, entirely aware of Mariah following close behind, not from the muffled clop of the donkey's hooves on the loamy ground, but from the wave of trepidation following behind him.

Mariah was not fearful of the jungle or the darkness. The man who'd threatened her life did not intimidate her, and the thieves who'd stolen into her hotel room barely gave her pause.

But Rafe—he frightened her to the core.

13

The sound of the rushing water was too irresistible to ignore.

"This way," Mariah said, grabbing the machete from Rafe's hand. A jolt of desire shot through her the minute their skin made contact. If she didn't know how his reluctance to use Rogan's magic had resulted in his carrying heavy bags far into the Mexican jungle, she might have suspected that he was using the sorcerer's powers to enchant her.

But he wasn't. She knew it, just as she knew that she would not be able to go another night without making love with him, especially out here in the hot, sticky wilderness after she'd removed her clothes and bathed in the freshwater of the Usumacinta River, which ran through this corner of Chiapas. Fed by mountain springs of the Sierra Madres, the waterway mingled with the flow from the Pasíon River in nearby Guatemala.

The irony did not escape her.

With one determined slice, she opened a wall of vines that led into a small clearing. She stepped aside so that Rafe could get the full effect.

His gasp broke through the night sounds of the jungle. She dropped the bag and unhooked the light she'd attached to her shoulder, her entire body drinking in the unmapped waterfall.

It wasn't high. The rock formation was only about a story or two above them, but the water flow was intense down the center, causing a delicious mist of freshwater to float in the soft jungle breeze. Along the edges, the tide was stemmed by a tangle of vines popping with bright pink night-blooming buds that swelled under the constant current. Under the light of the half-moon, the water sparkled as if the crests were embellished with diamonds. The effect stole her breath, as it had his.

Mariah stepped to the edge and peered into the pool that cradled the waterfall's offering before the rapid churning pushed the water into the river. To the left, however, the water was calm, trapped still by an outcropping of rocks. She flashed her light into the tranquil water. Rocks worn round by erosion sparkled up at her. Kneeling, she slipped her hand into the billabong and cooed at the cool sensation against her skin.

Unable to resist, she ripped off her shirt and tossed it aside. She heeled out of her boots, yanked off her jeans and then touched one bare foot into the water. The rocks were slippery, and she might have lost her footing if Rafe hadn't steadied her.

"Careful," he said warningly, cupping her elbows.

She glanced over her shoulder. His dark, long hair curtained eyes that sparkled with hunger. His chest heaved even as his strong hands braced her against a fall.

"You have a habit of saving me from falling," she said.

"'Tis my pleasure, my lady," he answered huskily. "Gives me reason to touch you."

She swallowed, the moisture in her mouth catching in her dry throat. "You don't need a reason."

The burro had wandered over. With his nose, he nudged them out of the way, nearly sending them both into the river. Laughing, Mariah moved aside, then balanced on a flat stone, with her hands in Rafe's.

"Hand me the light."

After a second's hesitation, he released her and retrieved her flashlight from underneath her clothes. She explored the water and the nearby bank for any sign of wildlife that might not like humans in their little corner of jungle heaven. This particular area was known as home to a wild array of snakes, lizards, parrots, monkeys and the occasional jaguar. And crocodiles were not unheard-of in the Usumacinta, though they were relatively rare. Still, it wouldn't hurt to take some precautions against the indigenous wildlife.

"We should start a—"

By the time she turned, a campfire burned within a circle of stones, and the burro had been relieved of his load. Rafe had not moved, but still stared down at her, his expression unreadable, but his eyes broadcasting the torture of watching her in the water.

"I thought you did not want to use his magic," she said.

Slowly, button by button, he undid his shirt.

"I had no choice," he said. "I cannot wait another moment."

He stripped down to nothing, and she couldn't help but watch, willing her body to remain still even as the combination of the chilly water and hot desire made her limbs weak. He stepped boldly into the water, took her hands and washed them thoroughly, rubbing over her palms, down her fingers and along her wrists. When he lifted her hand to his mouth and kissed the sensitive center, slightly reddened and blistered from wielding the machete, electricity chased away any apprehension she might have had about making love with Rafe again. This time, it would be different. This time, she didn't have to make love with him to save his soul. She was simply surrendering to a need that was too powerful to resist.

Something, likely a fish, swam past her leg. She jumped and landed flush against his chest. Suddenly, her decision to keep her bra and panties on seemed utterly ridiculous.

"You're trembling," he said.

"Something touched me."

"I'm envious," he replied, his voice husky. "But nothing in this water will harm you."

"You don't know what's in here."

"I don't need to know," he assured her. "But you're safe. Trust me. You said you did."

Though surrounded by crisp, clean water, Mariah couldn't muster enough moisture in her mouth to speak. As if he could read her mind, he cupped his hands into the pool and then raised them to her lips, inviting her to drink. As she did, the sweet water dribbled down, wetting her bra until it was translucent.

"The water is cold," he said.

She glanced down at her nipples, fully visible and erect beneath the thin swath of lace. And before she could protest, he'd grabbed her shoulders and leaned sideways so that they crashed beneath the surface together.

The water wasn't deep, but their splashing caused a

raucous cawing from the treetops and a loud flutter of wings. Doused completely, Mariah dropped all pretense of modesty by tearing off her lingerie, wadding it up and tossing it near the fire.

Silence descended on the jungle as she swam through the pool and into the mist kicked up by the falls. She could feel Rafe's eyes on her as she slid away from him, swimming a head-up breaststroke when the depth changed, kicking out her legs in a wide, circular motion she knew would reveal glimpses of bare backside. With every layer of dust and sweat and dirt that washed from her body, she wanted Rafe's mouth and hands and sex to replace them.

Seconds later, he splashed into the water behind her, but stopped his forward motion when the pool bottomed out.

She climbed the rocks just in front of the falls and turned.

"What are you waiting for?" she shouted.

"I do not swim," he replied, treading the water with his hands.

She looked at him questioningly, then pushed aside her libido long enough to consider reality. Rafe had grown up exclusively in Valoren. The place wasn't exactly overrun by mountain lakes of a temperature made for frolic and play.

"Shame," she said, and then stepped beneath the falls.

Leaning her head back, she allowed the water to rush over her hair. She worked out the leaves and twigs that had tangled there before stepping completely underneath the flow so the water sluiced sensually over her every curve. Hard and cold, the pounding flow aroused her even as it cleansed her, a sensation that increased when she opened her eyes and saw that, despite his inability to swim, Rafe had somehow managed to cross the chasm and was now standing just out of range, the whitecapped swirls of water rotating around his waist.

Intermittent glimpses of his erect penis made her mouth water. She held her hand out to him, and wordlessly he took it.

After he stepped beneath the showering water, Mariah washed away the remnants of their jungle trek. She relearned how his shoulders were wide and muscled. How his stomach tapered to hard thighs and buttocks. How the small of his back drew her like a hunter to treasure. She kissed a path down his spine and spotted a birthmark in the shape of a half-moon not unlike the one that gleamed above them.

The water was loud, so speaking was impossible. Mariah was glad. She wasn't sure what needed to be said. They circled each other, touching, kissing, arousing, bathing in the water and their mutual desire. Rafe grabbed her hips and moved her beneath the falls again so that, with his hand possessively holding her steady, she arched her back and the water splashed across her breasts. Coupled with his mouth and tongue and teeth, the conglomeration of sensation left her gasping for breath.

She hooked a leg around his waist. Twirling out of the rush of the water, they slammed against the wall of rock hidden by the falls and kissed until they couldn't breathe. He pressed against her, but the water made her tight. Skillfully, he used his fingers to coax a sweet rush of moisture from within, and she cried out as her body responded. Lifting her bottom, Rafe filled her. She felt sure he murmured her name when he could press no deeper, but the rush of water muffled any sound.

The wall she leaned against was slippery, yet Rafe never stumbled and she never slid. He drove into her wildly, freeing her with every thrust, pushing her closer and closer to the orgasmic edge she so desperately wanted.

Their kisses were wild and flavored by the water, which was cold and sweet and fresh—a perfect contrast to the sultry night. She wrapped her arms around his neck, pushing herself higher, shifting so that he struck her precisely in the spot that caused her climax. She clung to him, allowing her entire body to rejoice in the explosion of sensation. Seconds later, she felt the hot injection of his sperm and suddenly, she wanted nothing more than to make love with him again.

"Don't stop," she begged directly into his ear.

He kissed her long and hard, and she mewled with disappointment when his sex softened. He set her down, took her hand and then guided her beneath the falls, where they rinsed simultaneously beneath the rushing water, caressing and cuddling and speaking with only their eyes.

The feel of the water dripping down into her sex only reinvigorated her. One time in such a perfect setting could not be enough. At the cabin, they'd made love out of necessity. Tonight, they'd surrendered to desire that hadn't been spawned by evil magic—and this need was harder to sate.

She led him to the calmer side of the pool. He pushed himself up onto a rock, his lax penis cradled on his lap, the water covering him from the knees down. He moved to pull her up beside him, but instead, she slid between his legs, kissed his nipples and chest and toyed with the smattering of hair that lent another touch of darkness to his swarthy, irresistible body.

"Mariah," he breathed.

"I'm not done," she said, blazing a path with her lips across his pecs, lapping at the water that dripped from his skin.

"Were you not satisfied?"

"Do you mean did I come?" she asked. "Yes, yes, I did. But once isn't enough. Not tonight. Not out here. Under the stars and the moon, in this perfect slice of heaven. I don't want to waste a single minute of this. Not. A. Single. Minute," she said, emphasizing each word with a nip of teeth or a soothing kiss.

"I am spent," he declared, though he managed to run his fingers sensually through her hair.

She smoothed a hand up his thigh, then across his penis, which quivered in response. "Not for long, you're not."

Again her mouth watered for a taste of him, and this time she indulged. She dipped down into the water and tugged him forward, not caring if she scraped his delicious backside against the rocks. After a long lick that spanned the entire length of him, she took the head of his penis into her mouth.

In seconds, his sex hardened. She stroked him rhythmically, patiently, laving him with her tongue until the flesh and muscle thickened and stretched to the length she now knew was the perfect fit for her body. Underneath his silky skin, hot blood pulsed. The sounds of his amazed pleasure spurred her to be bolder. She ringed her thumb and forefinger at the base of his cock; then she suckled him completely until he needed release nearly as much as she needed him inside her.

"Mariah," he gasped.

When a salty taste met her tongue, she released him, dropped below the surface, swished her mouth with water and then emerged. Her lips and tongue now cooled, she gave him one last, long lick before easing up his body, kissing him from his abs to his chin along the way; then she straddled him and pressed her now-throbbing sex against him.

"Ready for me again?" she asked.

"You know I am," he said simply. "But you . . . I must."

She knew what he wanted by the way he licked his lips and gazed down into the water. And boy, oh, boy, did she want the same. They switched places and, seconds later, she was leaning back on her elbows and slipping into delirium from the feel of his tongue inside her. He parted her with his fingers, exploring her, pleasuring her, chuckling into her flesh when she cried out for mercy. Seconds from climax, he drew her legs around his waist and pulled her forward until they were once again joined.

The heat of desperate need abated, they made love slowly this time, twirling around in the water as they mated. Mariah closed her eyes tightly and concentrated solely on the feel of his body, so slick, so hard, joined with hers. When he spilled them onto the riverbank and brought her to orgasm with long, slow strokes milked from the deepest part of her body, she could not help but cry out his name in sheer ecstasy.

He grabbed her hands and drew them high above her head. She tucked her knees against his chest and shifted. The new position created the last sensation he needed to press deeper and longer until he came again, wonder on his face and her name on his lips.

Rafe rolled beside her and drew her tight against him.

Mariah suspected she could have fallen instantly asleep, but she struggled to remain awake, if for no other reason than to get dressed. By morning, Rafe would be gone. She didn't want to be shocked awake by some ecotourist who'd taken a wrong turn.

Rafe, who'd laid his hand across her belly, drew his touch away as if burned.

"What?" she asked, barely energetic enough to manage that simple syllable.

"We just made love," he said.

Though his words bordered on matter-of-fact, she heard the distinct sound of incredulity in them.

"I'm well aware of that," she said, attempting to snuggle back against him. "Is there some Gypsy afterglow ritual I'm missing?"

He stared at her, his eyes narrowed and his jaw set in an expression that bordered on angry.

"What's wrong?" she asked.

His scowl caused a flutter in her belly. He was furious, but she had no idea why.

"Nothing I should not have been prepared for," he replied. He glanced up at the sky, then around at the bags. He retrieved the clothing she'd purchased for him and donned the undergarment and jeans without a word.

She was too frozen by his icy demeanor to move. When he finally spoke, she was almost afraid of what she might hear.

"Get some sleep, Mariah," he said. "My decision is made. In the morning, I will use Rogan's magic to find your coins."

14

"Really?"

The excitement in her voice was unmistakable, particularly when paired with the wave of enthusiasm that rolled off her skin with the force of a rock slide. He'd given her a great gift in agreeing to her plan—but at what cost to him?

He'd already paid so much. He'd lost Sarina. He'd lost Irika. He'd lost his son, Stefan, long before he'd had a chance to know whether his child shared his mother's gentle nature or his father's spiritual gifts.

Rafe suddenly hated what he could do. A person's emotions should be private. The intimacy of sex with Mariah had made him foolish, made him believe, if only for a blissful moment, that she cared as deeply for him as he did for her. But he'd sensed her laissez-faire feelings. He couldn't deny that her inability to match his emotions cut with more precision than the machete she'd used on the jungle vines.

In her unguarded moments, he'd experienced her intense passion, her kindness and her irrepressible sense of fun. She lived to take chances. She loved to defy convention. She deeply desired him and wanted to introduce him to pleasures he'd never known with any other woman. But the moment her needs had ebbed and she had control of her thoughts again, her vulnerabilities vanished.

Her emotions snapped shut like the heavy lid of an iron chest, locking out anyone who might steal what she'd hidden inside.

"I see no reason to delay the inevitable. I will use whatever means necessary, as long as you pledge that once your debt is paid to Hector Velez, all of your resources and time will focus on breaking my bond to Rogan's curse."

She tilted her head to the side, her amber eyes questioning. "Of course," she said softly. "I'd help you even if you didn't help me, Rafe. You need to know that."

He swallowed thickly. He stood at least five long paces from her, yet he knew she was sincere. And confused. Had he really thought she was the type to abandon him? Had she possessed true mercenary tendencies, would he have come this far?

He did not know the answer. She was, after all, the only person he'd had contact with in over two centuries. As much as Rafe wanted to believe his ideals would keep him from falling into bed with a woman unworthy of his emotional loyalty, he was still a man. Rogan's curse had fired his lust the first night in the cabin, and since then, the blaze had not truly been extinguished. The embers even now, after their quenching swim, smoldered. While he was still tied to the marker, he could not distinguish between true attraction and magical hunger. And until he knew, he would keep his heart at a distance from this woman. His body—while she possessed the stone—he had little control over.

"At daylight, we begin," he said.

"But you're not solid in the light," she argued.

"This will work to our advantage." He struggled to remain as cool and forthright as he guessed Mariah would if their roles were reversed. "When I am in the phantom state, I can expand my senses further than I can when I am corporeal. I will rely only upon my own gifts of the earth."

"Don't you need to rest?"

"There is time enough. I will be fine."

"You feel stronger in this jungle, don't you?"

He nodded. He'd known from his first step into the wild environment that he was home—or at least as close to home as he could be while thousands of miles away. This place was not Valoren. The topography, the climate and the rhythm were as different from his homeland as night was to day. But as in the Gypsy enclave, the spirits of the earth roamed freely here. They had not been shunted aside by civilization and the creations of man. The native people—the Mayans and their progeny— borrowed the land and treated it with awe. Like the Romani, he sensed that the people of this region had not claimed the land to conquer it, but to live on it for as long as the spirits allowed.

"This land calls to me," he admitted. "The magic is strong. We will find your coins."

"But you told me that your . . . ability . . . is about feelings," she countered. "Last time I checked, coins don't have emotions."

"Do you?" he snapped. "Or perhaps you only choose to deny them."

Cruelly, he'd cut straight to the heart of her most vulnerable weakness, and he could feel the battle brewing within her. The war between indignation and denial raged like cannon fire.

As he buttoned his shirt, she cleared her throat and stood, her emotions suddenly as naked and raw to him as her luscious body. She was hurt. Deeply hurt. And he'd caused her pain.

"I don't deny anything," she said. "I'm about the most honest woman you'll ever meet."

"Honest with me?" he asked. "To the extent that you can be, yes, you are very forthright. But until you learn to be completely honest with yourself, you'll never share your heart with anyone."

She lifted her chin defiantly. "Maybe I don't need to share my heart with some man in order to be happy."

"Maybe if you stopped considering me as simply 'some man,' your life would bring you more joy."

Rafe grabbed a few dead branches from nearby, fed them to the fire, and then unrolled the bag she'd explained earlier would be used for sleeping. Though flimsy and light, the cushioned fabric might add comfort to the mossy jungle floor, so he tossed it flat on the ground beside the fire, stretched out and folded his arm over his head to block out the orange glow from the flames.

He breathed in and concentrated, evoking the old tricks he'd learned from his mother and from the *Chovihano* to prevent the emotions of others from overwhelming him. He'd never experienced the full upheaval and conflict of someone he wasn't touching, but he supposed his increased intimacy with Mariah, the magic that connected him to the stone and the enchantments in the jungle all around them had amplified his abilities. Slowly, brick by brick, he constructed a barrier that restored the silence inside his head.

Mariah stood still as the night for a long time before he heard the rustle of her movements. He peeked one eye open and watched her slip into fresh lingerie, soft slacks and a snug, long-sleeved shirt. She retrieved a sleeping bag, but did not settle down. Instead, she stood just outside the glimmer of the fire, as if she couldn't decide whether to stretch out near him or retreat to the other side.

With a sigh, he patted the grassy ground beside him. She frowned.

He shrugged, put his arm back over his eyes, crossed his feet at the ankles and tried, yet again, to sleep. Yes, his muscles and joints protested against the long tramp through the jungle—not to mention the vigorous exercise of making love—but his mind whirled with the realization that while Mariah might have saved him from an eternity buried beneath Valoren soil, she would never be part of his future.

If he had a future. At the moment, he had nothing—no homeland, no family. Nothing to compel him to find a way out of Rogan's curse except the curse itself.

Exhaustion finally began to overtake him by the time he heard the snap of Mariah unrolling her sleeping bag. She found a spot as close to him as possible, but without intruding on his space. The scent of her fresh, clean skin taunted him, made him regret invading her emotions and causing the rift between them that left her so confused. Mariah wasn't uncaring, but just as he was unaccustomed to the technology and changes in the twenty-first century, so was she unfamiliar with the act of opening her heart.

Of course, for him to teach her fully about the pleasures of sharing a spirit with another, he'd have to first become human again. And to do that, he'd have to use Rogan's black magic to find the coins.

He'd simply have to deal with the repercussions as best he knew how.

"Summon the coins again," he said.

Mariah pressed the activation code into the global positioning system yet again. Standing under a break in the jungle canopy so that a single beam of sunlight seared the back of her neck, she wiped the sweat pooling above her lips while the mechanism searched for its companion.

This had been the strangest day in her entire life. She'd marched for hours, tossing aside maps and following Rafe's instincts regarding which paths to follow— even when no paths existed. Her hands burned from wielding the machete, and she wouldn't be surprised if her feet had swelled to twice their size inside her boots. Eventually, the path had become so treacherous, she'd left the burro and the bulk of their belongings in a clearing about a half mile back. With both food and water nearby, she'd removed Pedro's bridle and hoped that if a predator came near, the animal could escape. Of course, for all she knew, the donkey would use his wicked sense of direction and find his way home the moment her scent faded from the breeze.

Didn't much matter if she lost her stuff. She expected that the plane had already been confiscated by the villagers or the *federales*. Besides, if she didn't find the coins, a couple of bottles of water, a few changes of clothes and dehydrated food weren't going to make any difference. Velez would have her killed.

In his increasingly silent way, Rafe had assured her

they were safe, protected by the spirits of the jungle. During their tedious journey, he told her about the other entities haunting the jungle—dark eyed and dark skinned like him, yet native to the land in the way he was foreign. They greeted him with gentle nods and pointed the way. She couldn't believe that ghosts of the ancient Mayans would help her recover coins that had once been theirs, but she couldn't worry about supernatural ownership rights right now. She'd been awakened this morning by the sound of a helicopter buzzing not too far from where they'd slept beside the billabong. Someone either knew she was here—or would soon.

Thing was, it made no sense for Velez to come after her. He'd hired her to find the coins. She was in the jungle to recover his treasure—on her own dime. Why would he put out more capital to retrieve what she was pursuing on his behalf? In her entire career, Mariah had never cheated a single client out of what they'd paid her to retrieve.

She wondered about Ben and Cat, but she'd made very quiet inquiries before she'd left the States, and her intel placed her ex and his lover at the university where Ben worked. He'd have no way of tracking her here.

That left the people who'd attacked her in the hotel back in Texas. All morning, she'd racked her brain for exactly what the thug had said to her.

Thought you could steal from us, did you?

Those words could come only from someone hired by the government official she'd lifted the coins from—except . . . the guy wasn't rich. He wasn't even influential outside of his tiny corner of the world. And if he had enough money to hire muscle in the States to track her down, why had he left the coins so vulnerable in the first place? The man lived high on the hog by some standards, but he hadn't spent a single penny on security. Mariah was certain he had no idea of the true value of the stash.

Was there, then, a fourth player in this increasingly dangerous game?

The instruments on her tracking system beeped impotently. The range on the device was supposed to pinpoint the item with the matching frequency within one mile. Though the signal had grown stronger in the past fifteen minutes, it was nowhere near specific enough for her to know how to proceed.

"This isn't working," she groused.

A whisper of a touch pressed at the small of her back, propelling her a few feet forward until she fell under the cool shadows of the treetops.

"Rest, Mariah. I shall return."

"Return? Where are you . . . ?"

But a second later, she could feel that he was gone. Instinctively, she reached into the dilly bag and took out Rogan's marker, clutching it between her hands. The warmth she associated with Rafe still buzzed against her skin, and the fire opal, when held up to the dappled sunlight, glowed with the fire that had won it its name.

Assured that Rafe hadn't somehow left her for good, she unscrewed the top of her canteen and drank. The cool water reminded her of the river, of the falls and of the lovemaking she and Rafe had shared under the silver moonlight. She'd never been one to fall for romantic clichés, but damned if she didn't totally understand the appeal now. The sensations of the humid air, the churning pool and Rafe's amazing body had her antsy all over again. She was suddenly very aware of the sweat pooling between her breasts and the nearly imperceptible breeze tickling the hairs at the back of her neck. She removed the hat she'd donned against the strong Mexican sun and waved the wide brim in front of herself, ignoring the buzz of mosquitoes that flitted nearby, confused by the intermingled scents of human flesh and bug repellent.

She took another swig of water, then splashed some across her neck, moaning appreciatively at the refreshing trickle of coolness down her shirt. They had to find the coins soon, if for no other reason than to save her from melting. Not just physically, but emotionally. Like it or not (and she decidedly did *not*), Rafe Forsyth was starting to get to her.

"Mariah."

His voice made her jump. She twisted around but saw, appropriately, nothing. Rafe sounded distant, as if he were only marginally tethered to the stone she'd dropped into her lap.

"Where are you?" she asked.

"Follow me."

The stone rocked against her thighs. Knowing somehow that the GPS tracker was no longer necessary, she shoved it and Rogan's marker into the bag and marched toward the northwest, wielding the machete with renewed vigor. She must have hiked a half mile before she felt Rafe's invisible hand on her elbow, tugging her deeper into the jungle than she thought one measly blade could penetrate.

Amazingly, the thick wall of leaves began to rustle, undulate and part. A tremor vibrated through her—whether from the excess of magic or something else, she didn't know. Machete at her side and the dilly bag with the stone and extra water and supplies on her shoulder, she walked into the utter darkness, propelled by Rafe's continued assurances that she was moving in the right direction.

When a break finally came, the trees behind her folded inward and trapped her in a scene that might have come straight out of an archaeologist's dream.

A flat-topped pyramid rose up to the top of the jungle canopy. The apex was just shy of the height of the tallest branches, as if the jungle itself wished to keep this amazing find hidden from the outside world. Thick vines crept up the tall, thick blocks of sun-baked limestone, and the carvings, though darkened by moss, remained visible.

What she saw next made her stumble.

Rafe emerged from a doorway that had been hidden by an illusion of the stone.

He shimmered. He was not solid as he was in the night, but his body was outlined in light that did not come from the sun, which barely mottled the overgrown clearing with specks of golden light. The colors that surrounded him—vivid greens and deep blues and warm coppers—nearly hurt her eyes.

"What . . . ?"

His smile stole her breath.

"The magic here is powerful," he said, and his voice shook the leaves around her, as if imbued with command equal to the supernatural forces. "From the land, the sky, the jungle itself."

She chanced a step forward.

"How are you doing this? I can see you."

He raised his chin, bathing his face in the light that came from within rather than from above. "I'm drawing on the native magic. Tenuous threads weave together the spirits in this jungle with the structures they built centuries ago. Civilization has broken some of the connections, but the path here was strong. I simply followed the strands. Use your device now, Mariah. See what you find."

Device? The splendor of Rafe's appearance stunned her. More than anything, she wanted to touch him and be touched by him. Almost absentmindedly, she slipped her hand into the bag as she walked up the stone steps of the pyramid, which had alcoves and indentations at many different levels, as if statues had once stood as sentinels for this ancient place of worship. Or perhaps hid soldiers from the tribes, caked with limestone mud so that they blended in. Her hand brushed against Rogan's marker, which, while still warm, had cooled considerably. She found the GPS tracker, but could barely muster the energy to hold it in her hand.

She approached him cautiously. She raised her fingers to his face, but did not touch him.

"May I?" she asked, unsure why she sought permission.

Even amid the wash of light, his eyes glowed with his need to be touched by her.

"Please," he responded.

His flesh was not solid, but he wasn't ethereal, either. His skin reverberated with warmth, and the vibrations traveled across her nerve endings until she was nearly engulfed in the magic. He took her moment of surprise to wrap her in his translucent arms, pull her tight against his chest and kiss her.

In that instant, Mariah experienced sensations beyond her wildest imagination. He was against her, inside her, behind her, above her—all at the same time. Heat flooded through her, and her senses exploded so that she could smell not only the musk of his skin, but the scent of the flowers blooming on a vine hanging yards above them. She tasted his tongue against hers with the same deliciousness as the flavors of the moist jungle wind. Unbidden and unexplained, tears filled her eyes from the conflagration of emotions she couldn't begin to process—euphoria, deep despair, intense need and complete surrender.

"What . . . what was that?" she asked. "What are you doing to me?"

His lips turned downward in a frown, and the colors that surrounded him seemed to darken, as if a shadow had passed overhead.

"Do not be afraid," he said softly.

"I'm not afraid. I'm confused. I'm . . ." Overwhelmed. Intrigued. Tempted. Oh, so tempted. "What do I do?"

He reached toward her. Involuntarily, she stepped back. Only when she felt the tug on the GPS did she remember to check the device for new readings.

The screech was unmistakable—the coins were close. She scuttled around the pyramid and then determined that, in order to find her missing treasure, she had to go up. As with so many Mayan temples, slivers of stairs had been carved on all four sides. She took them three and four at a time, using her hands to ensure her balance, until she reached the very top.

She found the package she'd dropped out of her airplane nearly dead center, as if it were an offering to the Mayan gods. She snatched the pack, gave it a cursory kiss, then climbed back down slowly, attempting to keep her occasional bout with vertigo at bay. Once she was six or seven feet from the ground, she leaped the rest of the way, fell to her knees and unzipped the case to make sure she'd finally found the treasure.

Mariah couldn't contain a whoop of triumph as the coins spilled from the packaging into her palms, perfectly asymmetrical, chunky and, since she'd polished them for delivery shortly after she'd stolen them, iridescent gold. She turned to show them to Rafe when a loud crack exploded from behind her, and the unmistakable sound of a bullet sliced by her ear.

15

Bullets tore through Gemma's body, ripping her from her neck to her groin. She gasped and clutched at her stomach, expecting blood and pain.

There was nothing.

She scrambled to her feet. The flute she'd rested on her chest what seemed like seconds ago clattered on the hardwood floor and rolled away.

Paschal's chair scraped as he pushed back from the table. "Gemma?"

She blinked rapidly, trying to make sense of the images she'd just witnessed. She must have fallen asleep. Or had she? Somewhere between dreams and reality, someone had shot at her. No, wait. Not at her. At a woman with a straw hat dangling across her back, dressed in khakis that rode low on her hips and a long-sleeved T-shirt, crouching beside Rafe Forsyth, who'd been engulfed by an eerie, otherworldly glow.

"How is that possible?" she whispered.

She dropped back onto the love seat, still staring at her uninjured chest and stomach. Rafe must have been hit. But in his insubstantial state, he was unharmed. Like her.

Paschal abandoned the collection of books he'd spread across the dining room table and limped over to her.

"What did you see?" Paschal asked.

Gemma concentrated, trying to reconstruct what had happened before she'd had the vision. Bored with watching Paschal work, she'd snuggled onto a love seat in the adjacent sitting room, twirling the flute in her fingers like a truncated baton. She'd watched the instrument roll over her knuckles, the tiny holes spinning, the ivory mouthpiece flashing white against an increasingly dark room. She had not drifted to sleep, but into a trance, and she'd seen Rafe Forsyth, the man Paschal claimed to be his brother, in some distant jungle with a woman who was not from the past.

Gemma glared at Paschal, suddenly realizing that there was much more to this story than the old man had told her. Much, much more.

"I just had a vision of your brother," she snapped.

"Where? Where is he?" he asked, reaching for the flute on the ground.

Gemma kicked it away. "You weren't anywhere near me. I wasn't piggybacking on your power. I saw that scene on my own."

Paschal's mouth flattened into a thin line. After a long second regarding her with surprisingly hard eyes, he nodded. "I suspected this would happen."

"Suspected *what* would happen?" She grabbed him by the shirt, balled the soft knit in her fist and dragged him up close. "What aren't you telling me, old man? What have you done to me?"

He seemed utterly impervious to her attempt at intimidation. He merely arched a brow and gave her grip on his person a cursory glance. "There's no need to beat the information out of me, my dear. You asked a valid question. I am fully prepared to give you an adequate answer."

Rage and frustration shook her, not to mention fear. All the cool detachment she'd worked so hard to perfect peeled away from her body, sliced off by the magic she'd always believed belonged to others. Her grandfather. Her great-uncle. Her father. But never her. Never, ever her.

She released him. "Start talking."

He pursed his lips. "Where to begin?"

"I'd say at the beginning, but I don't have all day while you recount more nonsense about the eighteenth century. Start with what just happened and work your way back."

"I hear suspicion in your voice," he noted.

"Do you blame me?"

Up until now, Gemma had accepted Paschal's story. She'd been raised on the possibility of a great magic that could transcend time and space, so his claims to be an eighteenth-century member of the British peerage seemed, comparatively speaking, reasonable. According to Paschal, a powerful curse set forth by her ancestor had trapped him in an enchanted mirror until the end of World War II and had since then given him the excessive vigor he now enjoyed despite his advanced age.

Even the fact that he could mentally travel into the past had not entirely surprised her. What shocked her, from the start, was her ability to experience his vision.

But this time, she'd had a psychic episode on her own, and she wanted to know why. And how.

"Sit down," he instructed.

She glared, prepared to argue, but he gave her shoulder a shove, and she teetered back into the love seat.

"You are a mimic," he said.

She leaned forward, assuming she'd misheard. "A what?"

"A mimic. It's a rare psychic ability. It allows you to absorb the preternatural skill of someone you come into close contact with."

"That's ridiculous."

"Is it? Tell me about your father."

"He was an asshole who ignored me because I was a girl. What else do you need to know?"

"You are certain your gender alone explains why he continually kept you at arm's length?"

She attempted to stand, but he pushed her down again.

"What do you know about him?" she demanded.

"Nothing more than what you've told me. But you've left out the more relevant details. From what I've been reading," he said, gesturing toward the stacks of papers on the dining room table, "the grand apprentices of the K'vr all possessed some psychic powers. Clairvoyants, mostly. Or at the very least, clever con men. What could your father do?"

Gemma frowned until her face hurt, not really wanting to remember the man she'd called Father—a man she barely knew. When he was home—which wasn't often—he expected a cursory visit from her in the morning to give his instructions for the day to her nanny, and a sometimes longer audience during dinner, particularly when they had guests. Even then, she sat at the opposite side of the table in the space normally reserved for her mother—at the farthest distance from the man she both admired and hated with all her soul.

Outside these scheduled interactions, Gemma saw her father only when she secretly watched him from one of the many hidey-holes in this house. And as Paschal suspected, she'd seen and heard a great deal during that time. Secrets she'd told no one—not even Farrow. Particularly not Farrow.

"Lies," she answered begrudgingly. "He had the uncanny ability to root out lies. Neither Keith nor I could ever get away with anything. Never mind the people he worked with every day. He just knew when people weren't telling the truth."

Paschal arched a brow. "How did he use this to increase his wealth? That is one of the key tenets of the K'vr, yes?"

She nodded. The search for the source of Rogan's magic wasn't cheap, and descendents of Lukyan Roganov had never lost the taste for living high on the hog. "Blackmail. He'd watch politicians and public figures on television or would meet them in person at black-tie affairs in New York or Washington. When he sensed a lie, he'd do some digging. Invariably, he'd find the truth and exploit it. He made millions."

"And how long have you shared his talent?"

"Not long enough," she quipped, always suspecting that she had inherited her father's ability, but she was never entirely certain.

Her father had always refused to hear a single question about it. Then he'd died, leaving a permanent wedge between his children and the organization that had been his only legacy. Or had it?

"I certainly had no idea you were nearly three hundred years old," she said.

"Ah, yes. But I never once lied about my age," he countered. "I always claimed to be *more* than ninety . . . and you rarely believed even that much."

"You old dog," she replied, realizing that, despite her gift, he had indeed found a way to fool her.

From the first time she'd met Paschal, she'd known he was keeping a secret. Trouble was, no amount of research on her part into the supposed university professor's life had revealed that he'd been born in the seventeen hundreds and had survived the centuries because of exactly the black magic she'd spent her life searching for.

Her father's ability was not to know the truth—only to recognize the lie. And that much she'd done.

"Big lot of good this gift has done me so far," Gemma said.

"You knew Farrow was going to dump you long before he had a chance to. You were able to make preparations so that you are still in the running for the leadership."

"Only by staying alive."

More and more, Farrow Pryce had teetered toward obsession in his quest to take over the K'vr. He already had mounds of money and, therefore, a shitload of power. She could never understand why he so desperately wanted to be in command. His family had amassed millions simply by working alongside the grand apprentices. Why did he need the title?

"Women know when they're about to get kicked to the curb," she reasoned. "Most just have too many romantic notions to get out before it's too late."

"Explain then," Paschal continued, "how you knew the picture of the chalice you showed me back in my hotel room all those months ago was important to me, even when I claimed at first that it was not? Not to be a braggart, but I'm quite an adept liar. And yet you knew I was not telling you the truth."

Gemma rubbed her cheeks, then her eyes and finally her arms. She'd always thought her talent for ferreting out lies was courtesy of her father, but only because she'd inherited his cynicism, not because she'd stolen some paranormal ability.

"So, being around my father, I just absorbed what he could do?"

"And you've done the same with me. After accompanying me on our little journey, you can now touch the flute and transport yourself into the past."

"No," she corrected, her hand involuntarily going to her stomach—to where she'd almost felt the bullets piercing her skin. "Not the past. The present. The now."

Paschal calmly drew a chair across from her, but she could tell his coolness was as much a lie as any words. "Tell me what you saw."

Gemma considered keeping the story to herself, but she could see no purpose. If she truly possessed a paranormal ability—or two—her chance at the leadership of the K'vr had increased exponentially.

Unlike her, Paschal understood how this shit worked. He could guide her. Teach her. Give her the knowledge she needed to exploit this discovery until she had exactly what she wanted.

"Rafe was there, but he wasn't solid. He was all . . . sparkly."

Paschal's brow furrowed. "I don't know what that means. You're sure it was him?"

"Pretty sure," she replied. It was kind of hard to

tell, since he had been, essentially, see-through. But it wasn't her eyes that told her the being of light was Rafe Forsyth—it was something deeper. "And I saw a woman. Brown hair. Relatively tall. Dressed in khaki and standing in front of what looked like . . ." She searched her memory for a comparison. She'd seen a structure like that before, but not in person. In a book. On television. Maybe a movie. "Chichén Itzá."

"Mexico?" he asked.

She shrugged. "Hell if I know. The place looked Aztec or Inca or Mayan. You know, one of those pyramids with lots of steps up the sides and a flat top. And old. Really, really old."

"Perhaps you did see into the past again," he said, finding the flute and, holding a hand across his lower back as a brace, bending down to retrieve it. "To one of the previous owners, before the K'vr took it back into their possession."

He attempted to hand her the instrument, but she waved it away.

"No, thanks."

"You are not drained," Paschal insisted. "Not like before. You can do it again."

Only a few days ago, their initial contact with the flute in the underground repository and the subsequent witnessing of past events had knocked them both out, though she'd been in decidedly better shape than Paschal. Now, she supposed she felt a little woozy, but nothing in comparison to before. That didn't mean she wanted to take the risk if the payoff wasn't worth it. What more could she see?

"Maybe I bounced back quicker because I'm younger," she teased.

"All the more reason for you to try again," he concluded.

"I wasn't trying to transport myself anywhere. I was just playing with the damned flute. I don't want to do it again."

He continued to stare at her. She wasn't one to back away from a challenge, but she needed a few minutes to come to terms with all she'd learned.

Paschal stood and began to pace, his hands hooked behind him. She watched him go back and forth until she thought he might hypnotize her into agreeing.

"Will you stop that, please?"

Paschal turned sharply on a heel. "Tell me more about the woman."

Gemma cradled her chin in her hands and stared sightlessly at the lines in the floor, trying to re-create the images in her waking mind. "She was definitely from this time. She was wearing pants and had a backpack. She was holding something. A package. Something shiny."

"Did you see her face?" he asked.

Gemma closed her eyes, wincing at the terror that had marred the woman's attractive face. "Yeah, for a split second."

He held the flute out to her again. "Show me."

"I said no," she insisted.

"To find my brother Aiden," he argued, "it was the woman with him who was the key. Maybe this time, I'll know this woman as well. We have to take the chance. There's something about this. Something . . . circular."

Gemma ran her hands roughly through her shorn hair. She couldn't deny Paschal's impression—she'd felt it, too. The Roganovs, the Forsyths, the Gypsies, the K'vr—they'd all been interconnected for centuries.

Nothing in her entire life had ever happened by accident. If she'd caught sight of that woman in Paschal's presence, perhaps there was a reason.

She wanted to unravel this mystery. She wanted to explore the full breadth of her new ability. Could that override her apprehension? And what about Paschal? Could he survive another journey?

A vision of the present—or perhaps the future—might not tax Paschal as their previous journey together had. She supposed she had to try.

"Sit down," she directed him.

He obeyed.

She took a begrudging seat beside him. "Yeah, now you start taking my orders."

He held out his hand. "Let's do this."

She rolled the flute across her palm, gasping when her skin started to tingle. "I have to warn you," she said, leaning back into the cushions and twirling the flute across her knuckles again, trying to re-create the circumstances of her journey. "When I last saw her, someone was shooting at her."

Paschal groaned. "Then she must be with my brother. There's something about Forsyth men that draws women to danger."

She took his hand in hers and closed her eyes tightly. "Tell me about it," she muttered, just before the world began to spin.

16

Unseen, Rafe pushed Mariah to the ground. He huddled over her, as if he could protect her in his insubstantial state. But he couldn't. He'd saved her from a hail of bullets, but as long as he was a phantom, she had to rely on her own street smarts to stay alive.

"Remain down," he ordered.

"No," she argued, punching through him until he burst into a puff of colorful smoke.

With no time to indulge her shock, she clawed for the dilly bag and then crawled for the nearest cover behind a narrow stack of stone that, from a distance, looked to be part of the pyramid. It actually stood about a foot away, giving her just enough room to slide behind. Another gunshot exploded on the ground, sending shards of brittle limestone spiking against her skin.

From behind the obelisk, she grabbed Rogan's marker and shoved it deep into a pocket on her pant leg, which she zipped closed. She also retrieved her 9mm Glock 19, which she'd loaded this morning after the chopper had first appeared. She couldn't believe anyone had managed to track them this deep into the jungle.

Yeah, she'd left some pretty obvious machete marks, but she'd doubled back twice and had forced the donkey to walk on the rockiest of paths in an attempt to hide his hoofprints.

Whoever fired those shots had been determined to find her. She'd have to be just as determined in order to escape.

"Rafe," she whispered, her voice as much a prayer as a plea.

"I'm here," he replied. He'd faded once again into nothingness—and for that, she was very grateful.

"You need to tell me exactly where the shooters are."

"I understand."

She felt his disappearance, and her chest ached from instant loneliness. She concentrated on checking her weapon, loading extra ammunition from her bag into her pockets and wrapping a sheathed knife around her middle and hiding it beneath her shirt.

"Ms. Hunter," an unfamiliar voice called from just beyond the clearing. "I apologize for my associates. There was no need for gunfire. Please come out."

Man. Educated. The accent was urbane, but American. Not the Mexican government official she'd stolen the coins from, though Mr. Friendly could be a mercenary hunter much like herself, hired to steal back what she'd taken for Velez. The rustling and cursing told her there were at least a half dozen men out there, likely all armed and waiting to get a clear shot at her.

Suddenly, Rafe joined her again. He sounded surprisingly out of breath. "Over your shoulder, to the northwest."

She'd gotten turned around during their trek and

barely knew which way was up. "Pretend a clock is behind me. Twelve midnight directly ahead. What time is he at?"

"Ten o'clock," he replied. "And another at three."

She spun out from behind the obelisk and fired four rounds—two in each direction Rafe had indicated. A flash of red and a scream punctuated the volley to her left, and she heard grunts and a crash to her right before she twisted back behind the obelisk. She couldn't take them all out, but she needed to establish that she was just as armed and just as dangerous as they were.

"I'm not coming along quietly, mate," she shouted. "And I'm not giving up my find. Just back off and no one else has to get hurt. Least of all me."

She muttered the last part to herself.

Sounds of boots scraping on limestone alerted her that someone was attempting to come up from the other side of the structure. She was practically out in the open, alone and armed with only two magazines of ammo. She was certain she'd been in worse situations before, but she sure as hell couldn't remember when.

"Rafe, around back. Is there anything you can do?"

If he replied, she didn't hear him, because the man below had called out to her again.

"You've proved yourself an able marksman, Ms. Hunter. Your show of strength is duly noted. But, please, I did not come all this way to harm you. I'm willing to negotiate for what I want."

Mariah's heart slammed against her chest with the force and rhythm of a native drum. A split second later, she heard the descending scream of someone falling off the pyramid on the other side. Rafe had done as she asked.

"That's at least two down," she replied. "Just how many men are you willing to sacrifice to get a bunch of old coins?"

"Coins?"

The man laughed—not exactly the high-pitched cackle of a typical B-movie villain, but damned close.

"I am not after your Mayan coins, Mariah Hunter. Yes, I know who you are. I know about your disagreement with Señor Velez, and I know that you were, less than a week ago, in a hard-to-reach corner of Germany that the locals called Valoren, the land of the lost. I also know that you took a stone from there, centered with a large fire opal that has, shall we say, special properties? I want that stone, Ms. Hunter. And I want it now."

The tall obelisk she'd hidden behind began to shake. Sand and stone rained down as the structure began to break apart. With the dilly bag tight across her chest, she dashed for the nearest opening in the pyramid, only to be stopped by a second cascade of stone.

She spun around. This couldn't be a natural occurrence. Earthquakes could be damned inconvenient, but they certainly didn't happen on cue. The trees and earth around the pyramid were completely still. Amid the falling rocks and vines, she spotted a man in creased khakis standing just at the edge of the forest, holding aloft what looked like a shiny silver sword.

Who was he, He-man?

She raised her gun, but a bullet from the enemy caused the weapon to fly from her hand.

"Run, Mariah. Hide."

With a shove, Rafe sent her flying down the side of the pyramid. She spun, uncontrolled, but while the air was knocked from her lungs, she felt nothing as she bounced against the stone. It was as if Rafe had wrapped her in a sheet of plastic bubbles as she fell.

Once at the bottom, she dove into a forest of plate-size leaves, trudging on her hands and knees until she found a fallen tree. Scuttling quickly, she discovered an opening in the rotted trunk and squeezed inside. She caught her breath and tried to decide what to do. She was armed now with only the knife. And while Rafe's magic would come in handy about now, that pyramid hadn't started to shake on its own. It seemed like the interloper had some major mojo of his own.

"You're safe," Rafe said.

"Not for long," she whispered back. "He had magic, Rafe. Magic like yours."

"Seems so," he concurred.

"You have to fight him. We're outnumbered and outgunned. It's up to you."

"I cannot. Merging with the Mayan magic, making myself solid in the light . . . I am drained. I expended the last of my energy protecting you from the fall. Talking to you now saps me further. I need to rest."

She closed her eyes tightly. It figured that a few seconds of glorious sensation would cost her her life—and his.

The stench of Rogan's magic clung to the air like death. Rafe was not a soldier. He was not a fighter. But he'd lost two women to Rogan's evil. He would not lose a third.

He attempted to yet again weave his way back into the Mayan magic, but he failed. The threads were tenuous before, but now they simply melted away whenever he neared them. Filled with rage and fear for Mariah's

safety, he could not access the enchantments born of
the land. Violence, even in defense of the woman who'd
found him, was Rogan's realm. The only magic he could
use to save Mariah was the same magic that could destroy her.

He returned to the pyramid. Every inch of distance
between him and Mariah—between him and the stone—
stretched his powers thinner and thinner.

Four men gathered at the base of the clearing. One
held a sword and watched while the other two tended to
their fallen colleague. Rafe pushed himself closer.

Had he a body at this moment, the recognition of the
weapon would have turned his heart to stone. The sword
had belonged to Rogan. Rafe, along with so many others
in the village of Umgeben, had watched the blacksmith
forge it, had heard Rogan's specific instructions for its design. The twisting golden handle. The thin, double-edged
blade. The prominent fire opal embedded in the hilt.

Who was this man?

Rafe attempted again to snag one of the magical
threads swirling around him, but it remained out of
reach. The darkness he'd sought to deny burbled within
him, but not with enough power to protect Mariah. And
nightfall was hours away.

"Will he live?" the man with the sword asked his soldiers of the injured man, his tone dismissive.

The men's clothes were mottled in greens and grays
and blacks—shades that camouflaged them in the jungle.
One lay on the floor, writhing, while the others wrapped
his injury in cloth that had soaked through with blood.
Another had a similar cloth around his arm. Mariah had
fired off multiple shots. One man was no longer a threat.
The other was merely incensed.

"Yeah," the man with the injured arm spat. "But Juarez never returned when I sent him around back. Should I find him?"

Rafe's confidence surged. The man named Juarez would not join his compatriots anytime soon. He was still alive, but trussed and gagged with jungle vines and leaves, an action that had cost Rafe a great deal of his energy—perhaps the last of it. That left three enemies to waylay long enough for Mariah to get to safety.

If only he were solid. If only he were not so spent.

The man with the sword stepped away from the cluster of men. He was undoubtedly the leader.

He gave the injured man a cursory glance. "Give him a shot of that whiskey you carry in your pack, Simmons, and get back to looking for the girl. She doesn't have to die. Yet. I want the stone, but I also need to know precisely what she knows about it." He glanced longingly at the sword again. "How to use it."

"Yes, Mr. Pryce."

Simmons dragged the injured man out of sight. The last man stayed beside Pryce. Though dressed like the others, he stood out from the rest. He was younger and wore a cluster of hoops around the top of his ear and another spiky stud in his nose.

"If she knew how to use the magic, she would have by now," the young man insisted.

Pryce merely grinned. "Assumptions, Mr. Pyle, are dangerous. Particularly in light of the fact that Mariah Hunter has eluded us this far. I hired Simmons because he knows the terrain, and he and his men were supposed to be crack shots. And yet he missed."

"I think that weird light blinded him. What was that shit?"

"That *shit*," Pryce responded, his lip curled as if saying the word were the same as tasting it, "was magic. Unlike any I've ever seen, but then"—he lifted the sword and examined the blade as if he'd never truly appreciated the weapon before—"until I found this, magic was nothing more to me than a pipe dream. Now that I have it, I want to know precisely what it is capable of. I made the pyramid shake, but I'm not entirely certain how. I need the girl and that stone."

"You'll have them," the younger man assured him, bowing his head. A flash of black and red at the base of his neck drew Rafe's attention. He wore a brand of some sort.

A hawk, clutching a red stone in its talons.

The mark of Lord Rogan.

Rage nearly undid him. The instinct to strike out—to turn that cursed sword against the man who held it so cavalierly—nearly overtook him. But Rafe had not the power. He could feel the magic pulsing from the sword, as dark and vile as that which contained him.

Rafe returned to Mariah, hidden in the hollow tree. If she attempted to escape, they would find her. While Pryce might not kill her immediately, he did not seem the sort of man to leave loose ends behind.

"Can you remain out of sight until nightfall?"

The sudden sound of their assailants stalking through the underbrush answered the question for her. "I'm too close. It'll be a piece of piss for them to find me here. I need to move."

"Leave the stone," Rafe instructed. "Bury it."

Mariah's eyes widened, but after a moment's hesitation, she complied, twisting as quietly as she could until she could shove it deep into a crevice within the tree trunk, which she covered with rocks and moss and dirt. She maneuvered back to the opening. Though the men had not yet stumbled into this section of the jungle, they were not far away.

"Now what?" she asked quietly.

Rafe hated what he was about to propose, but he could not see any other way.

"I have just enough energy left to distract them. You must come out of this hiding place and circle around to the other side. Then you must allow them to capture you."

17

"He's not dead," Gemma gasped, on the verge of hyperventilating. "God, Paschal. Wake up. Farrow's not dead."

Paschal forced his eyes open and looked down at his chest, expecting to see an anvil pressing down on him. He inhaled and exhaled in a steady rhythm, hoping the tight sensation was merely an aftereffect of seeing Farrow Pryce not only alive, but using the Dresden Sword to wield dark magic.

Despite the pain, Paschal pushed himself up. Gemma was now pacing the room, her fingers jabbing into her hair, mercilessly tugging on black and blond spikes.

"Did you see him?" she said, whirling on him. "He's supposed to be dead. You told me he dove off a cliff in California. You told me he died!"

Slowly, the weight on his chest lifted. He wasn't having a heart attack. Much better news than the fact that Gemma's ex-boyfriend and Paschal's nemesis had survived what should have been a fatal fall.

"Seems I was wrong," he replied.

Gemma slid onto the floor. Not for the first time since

she'd convinced him to join her, she revealed her rare but unmistakable vulnerability. The cool seductress she'd pretended to be as Farrow's mistress had melted away. At this moment, she was raw, authentic—and afraid.

Until he'd proved himself capable of surviving a drop off a California cliff, Farrow Pryce had not scared Gemma. Like every other man in her life, he'd been a means to an end. Now he was a genuine threat.

Neither she nor Paschal had anticipated that Farrow was still alive—and worse, using the Dresden Sword to attack Rafe and, shockingly, Mariah Hunter.

"He can do magic," Gemma said. "Not piddling psychic shit. Real magic. He made that pyramid thing shake."

Paschal closed his eyes again, but the images of potential destruction he saw there left him quaking with nearly as much force as the Mayan temple. If ever there existed a man with no business controlling Rogan's dark magic, it was Farrow Pryce.

"He took the Dresden Sword with him when he went over that cliff six months ago. The police searched and found nothing," he told her. "The magic must have saved his life."

"How?"

Paschal frowned. The possibilities were both endless and terrifying.

"We'll sort that out on our way," he said, hoisting himself to his feet, then reaching out to Gemma to help her off the floor. He glanced longingly at the papers he'd scattered on the dining room table. He'd found references to items the K'vr had listed as missing—items associated with Lord Rogan's legacy that they did not yet possess. He desperately wanted to explore that register more thoroughly, but their time in the manse had just run out.

"Where are we going?" she asked.

"To find my son," Paschal replied, dragging her with him as he assembled what he could afford to take. They were still traveling light. He'd have to choose carefully.

Gemma shook herself free. "No! I told you. I'm co-operating only with you. I don't trust anyone else, especially not your son."

Paschal bit back a curse. "Heard the one about the pot and the kettle lately?"

She narrowed her gaze. "I haven't lied to you. Not once. Can you say the same?"

Their standoff was a waste of time. He shoved the register of lost items into a leather portfolio, then tossed it by the entrance to the secret tunnel they'd planned to use for their escape. "Look, you don't have to trust Ben, and frankly, you don't have to trust me. But I'm going to Texas to find my son."

"Why?"

"Because that woman under attack by Farrow Pryce is Mariah Hunter. She used to love my son, and I'm betting that's the connection that is about to get her killed."

Ben flipped his cell phone shut and glanced at Cat, sleeping soundly amid a tangle of snowy white sheets. As he suspected, Mariah had screwed up, and now he knew, generally speaking, where she was. But as much as Ben and Cat had planned to go after Mariah at some point, riding to her rescue was never a scenario they'd considered.

But his father had been very clear. He was on his

way to Texas, with Gemma Von Roan in tow, but traveling would take them a day at the most. Mariah was in a life-or-death situation in a remote part of the Mexican jungle, which Paschal recognized from markings on a nearby Mayan structure. She could also be in Guatemala or Belize, but Mexico was where she'd lost those coins—and Ben had no doubt that the pressure from Hector Velez had sent her back to Chiapas.

And though he was closer here in Texas, he might already be too late. Paschal hadn't been sure if the vision of Mariah being shot at—or shot—was the past, present or future. But positioned as he was, Ben had to respond. He had his pilot's license and, thanks to Alexa Chandler, a plane. All he needed now was a plan—and for that, he needed Cat's cooperation.

Chiapas was vast and Mariah could be anywhere. But Cat could find her. Cat had Mariah's watch, and while she'd tried and failed to forge a connection and pinpoint Mariah's location before, the situation had changed. If they took to the air over the jungle, closer proximity might help Cat key into his ex's psychic energy.

With a mew of contentment, Cat turned over. Bare breasted and beautiful, she made his mouth water. Her dark skin contrasted against the sheets, enhancing her sweet curves. He knew every rise and indentation intimately, but damn if he didn't want to touch her, taste her, feel her over and over again. His body ached for her— but even more, her very presence made his heart hurt.

Because of the search for his uncles, they'd been together for over a year. She knew him inside and out and she stayed with him anyway. She loved him.

Not that she'd said the words. Neither one of them had crossed that hazardous suspension bridge just yet,

even after all this time. And though Ben liked to think
they didn't need a trite phrase to bind them together, he
knew that just like Mariah in the jungle, Ben was running out of time. He didn't need to share her psychic
power to know Cat craved commitment. He just didn't
know how he could honestly make any promises until
this madness with his family was resolved.

And if Paschal was right, they were close to retrieving
yet another Forsyth brother.

If they hurried.

If Cat would help.

Never one to shy away from danger for long, he slid
onto the bed and woke her from her late-afternoon nap
with a long, languorous kiss.

"Mm," she said, shifting the sheet down so he could
salivate over every inch of her incredible naked body.
"That's certainly better than an alarm clock."

She slid her hand down his arm, took his hand and
guided it toward her sex, which he knew would be wet
and ready for him.

Uttering the strongest oath in his repertoire, he pulled
away. "Sorry, babe. There's no time."

Her lazy eyelids flashed open as she turned to the
clock and groaned. "You have an appointment I don't
know about?"

"Actually," he said, "yes."

She grabbed the sheet and sat bolt upright. "I'm not
going to like this, am I?"

"It's hell living with a psychic," he groused.

"I don't have to be psychic to read the look on your
face. What's wrong?"

"So much, sweetheart, I don't know where to begin."

*   *   *

Rafe fulfilled his promise. Using the last of his energy, he drew the searchers away from the fallen tree trunk, giving Mariah just enough time to sneak out of her hiding place and circle around to the back of the pyramid. She considered taking the chance to really escape, but where would she go? She had no supplies. No flashlight or water or machete. No means to exit the country. And since she couldn't risk carrying the stone with her in case she got caught, she couldn't leave Rafe behind, either. The shaking pyramid proved that Pryce character possessed some means of magic. She had to trust Rafe's instincts and attempt to do as he'd asked.

Fake an escape. Make them look for her. Give them a run for their money. And if she got caught, make sure it wasn't until shortly before sundown.

It wouldn't be easy, but she was certainly going to see what she could do.

Unfortunately, she managed to elude them for only an hour. She'd found a second great hiding place, but a scrambling family of monkeys gave her away. She took off before they'd sighted her, but ... damned wrong turns. They got her every time.

"*Alto!*" a man shouted, punctuating his order by shoving the serious end of a Magnum .357 to her temple. She immediately put her hands up.

"Take me to your leader," she quipped.

Unfortunately, the guy she'd grazed in the arm met them first. He punched her dead on the chin, and by the time she'd regained consciousness, she'd been dragged back to the pyramid, where the man named Pryce sat on the steps, contemplating his sword. His men tossed her to the ground. In addition to seeing stars, she was now also spitting dirt.

"Ah, there you are," he said casually. He set the sword carefully on a stone step and extended his hand. "Farrow Pryce."

She pushed herself up and glared at him, but didn't stand. His men must have found this rude, because they wrenched her to her feet. With each arm held immobile, she gave her jaw a wiggle to make sure it still worked, licked away the blood that had gathered in the corner of her lips and hocked a loogie that just missed the toe of his shoe.

"Wish I could say it was a pleasure," she cracked.

He frowned at her spittle, and then took very little care in grabbing her chin and checking out the damage. "You'll have an ugly bruise. Not to mention a nasty welt. I'm sure that's very painful. You really shouldn't have shot one of my men."

"It was self-defense, remember?" Soil coated the inside of her mouth, but she wasn't sure about spitting again.

He hummed in exaggerated contemplation. "A truly unfortunate way of making first contact, I agree. So let's try again."

After his silent nod, the men let her go. She tumbled to the ground and lights flashed all around her. For a second, she thought that Rafe had finally reappeared, courtesy of his new power, but she had only her injuries to blame. She was going to face off with Farrow Pryce alone, surrounded by three men who looked like they'd love nothing better than to kick the shit out of her.

"What do you want?" she asked, attempting to buy time until sunset.

"I told you before," Pryce said, motioning for one of the men to come forward with her bag so he could rifle through the contents. "I want the stone you stole from the site in Valoren."

"That wasn't a site," she contradicted, pulling herself to her knees and attempting to blink away the stars still blurring her vision. "It was a forest. There wasn't anything there."

He made *tsk*ing noises that made her wonder if he'd studied Villains 101. Haughty, overconfident and sickeningly debonair, Farrow Pryce might have been a good-looking guy if he didn't act like such a caricature of Professor Moriarty.

"One of my men had the stone in his hand briefly in your hotel room," he replied. "So you might as well drop the whole 'I don't have it' scenario and move on to the next phase. Which would be ...?"

She forced a grin. "The 'I don't have it with me' scenario."

"Which I counter with the 'I don't believe you' scenario," he said, tossing first the package of coins and then the GPS onto the ground. Once he had completely emptied the bag, he turned to her with an expression of feigned regret, then smiled.

"Search her."

The experience proved just as awful as Mariah expected. The man with the bandaged arm took great pleasure in describing every curve of her body to his compadres as he groped and manhandled her in his quest to see if she'd shoved Rogan's marker into one of her many pockets, beneath her clothes or in some hidden orifice. Luckily, Pryce assured him that the stone was too large for her most private areas, but by the time he'd gotten his jollies, she was minus her knife and panting with rage. It took all three men to hold her steady—a fact Farrow did not ignore when he ordered her tied to a nearby tree.

This wasn't ending up at all as she and Rafe had planned. If the rat bastard tried to torture the information out of her, she'd . . . what? Scream? Who the hell was going to hear her out here?

"Why would I bring the stone with me?" she asked, fighting against the bindings that pulled hard on the joints in her shoulders and cut off the circulation to her hands. "I came here to look for those Mayan coins. They're worth quite a bit. Why don't you take them instead of some crappy rock I took as a souvenir?"

"And yet, you fought like hell to get it back. Won, too. Thanks to a mysterious man who appeared, if I can quote my man, out of nowhere?"

Farrow retrieved the sword again and was once again toying with the hilt, slipping his hand into the tangle of gold at the handle and turning the blade carelessly this way and that. Some might have assumed his movements were casual, but Mariah knew better. He meant to intimidate her. Wasn't doing a half-bad job, either.

"The guy had great timing," she said, aware of the irony of speaking in the past tense.

"And his name was?" Pryce asked.

Mariah swallowed thickly, wishing she had her canteen. And free hands with which to use it. "I didn't catch it. He was gone before I had the chance to ask."

"But came back in time to accompany you here."

"That's crazy," she insisted. "I haven't seen him since that night in the hotel."

"And yet, the helpful couple at the outpost near the river said he was with you," Pryce contradicted. "They did not meet him. He did not speak. But he was there."

The price of discretion must have gone up in Mexico without her knowledge. "They're lying. Telling you what you want to hear. You tracked me this far. Did you find one set of footprints or two?"

"One," he replied. "But there was a double set leading from the hut where you acquired your donkey to the river where you camped the first night."

Mariah forced a grin and laced her words with as much innuendo as she could. "That was the woman's husband. He wanted to make sure I got to my campsite safely."

Farrow frowned. "He didn't say anything about going anywhere with you. And believe me, he was well compensated for every detail he provided."

She chuckled. "You might have a fat wallet, but his wife carries a damned big gun. There aren't enough pesos in this country to have him admitting his . . . private tour . . . in front of his wife."

She was taking a chance, bluffing like this. But what choice did she have? She glanced at the shadows around her, which had already grown deeper and fainter, fading into the natural darkness created by the thick canopy of trees overhead. She didn't know how much longer she could waylay Farrow Pryce, but she intended to keep up the conversation as long as possible.

Farrow licked his lips, and suddenly, the fact that the top two buttons of her shirt had been ripped off in the struggle made her squirm. His stare wasn't exactly lecherous, but Farrow Pryce was clearly a man who liked women and sex.

"So you seduced Armando by the river, not the mystery man?" he asked.

"His name was Andreas, and let's just say that his

wife isn't the only one in that family with a damned big gun."

The sound of Pryce's men chuckling froze the sweaty hairs on the back of her neck. Despite the pain in her shoulders, she forced herself to lean, relaxed, against the trunk of the tree.

"Although," she said, eyeing his weapon, "what's a gun when you can have a sword?"

He grinned. "You noticed my prize, have you?"

"Hard not to. I'm a treasure hunter, remember? Baby like that could fetch a tidy sum with some of the collectors I know."

"I paid a tidy sum for it," he replied. "Well, at the very least, I offered a fool's ransom. When the owner resisted, I simply took what I wanted."

"Man after my own heart."

He leveled the sword at her, but not in a way meant to threaten. She could see by the adoration in his eyes that he simply wanted her to admire the workmanship. The men who surrounded her started to shuffle uncomfortably. The topic had strayed away from sex, and they weren't happy about it.

"Tell me what you see," he said.

She took a deep breath and blinked, trying to remove some of the sand and grit from her vision. "Double-edged sword. Tempered steel. Spanish-style handle. Hand-forged by a master swordsmith."

"And the gem?"

She met his gaze straight on. "Fire opal. About . . . thirty-five carats."

His eyebrows rose a notch. "Forty. What are the chances, do you think, that this faceted beauty was cut from the same mother stone as the one embedded in the rock you stole from Valoren?"

She pressed her lips together tightly, considering his suggestion with a professional air. "Well, fire opals generally aren't very large, though there have reportedly been some as sizable as a man's fist. The color of yours there is a vivid red in the shade, but in the light," she said, noticing there was very little left, "it's a bright orange?"

He nodded.

She continued, "Well, I didn't get much of a chance to look at the stone back in Texas, but they certainly look the same in terms of color and style of cut. But like I said, I didn't have very long to look at it. My priority was to retrieve the Mayan coins. Velez will have my head if he doesn't get those coins in the next few days."

"How do you know I won't kill you first?" Pryce asked.

"I don't," she replied. "But either way, I'm dead. Now, later—what difference does it make?"

Their stares didn't break, and Mariah realized by the slightest twitch in Pryce's right eyelid that she'd struck a nerve. He wanted her alive.

"After your thugs tried to steal the stone," she continued, "I hid it. You likely searched all the most obvious places before you followed me here or you wouldn't have bothered to come this deep into the jungle. Once I deliver the coins to Velez, I'm willing to negotiate with you for the stone."

Farrow ran his fingers lovingly over the opal on the hilt of the sword, then down the blade, though he was careful not to cut himself.

"You're not exactly in any position to negotiate," he said.

She rolled her eyes. "Why do guys like you always say that? I might be trussed up and beaten up, but you still need me. If you didn't, you wouldn't have followed me here, and you certainly wouldn't have kept me alive this long."

As she waited for Farrow to reply, she noticed something that sent another ripple of chills over her body.

The jungle was silent.

Dead silent.

Not a bird cawed. Not an insect buzzed. Even the wind seemed to have stopped tousling the treetops. In that instant, she realized that while darkness had not yet totally descended, the sun had set. And with it, an instant later, came a black and billowing fog.

It rolled out of the openings in the Mayan pyramid and covered them completely. She heard Pryce yell out, but the beams from the flashlights he'd called for could barely break through the soupy atmosphere. Fearing asphyxiation, she held her breath, but then her bindings suddenly sprang free and a sexy, familiar voice whispered, "Run," in her ear.

Rafe took her hand. In seconds, they'd disappeared into the cover and the air cleared. She caught a brief glimpse of his eyes, watery from the smoke, before he pulled her tight against him, kissed her and caused them both to disappear.

18

The kiss cleansed him. Combined with the elemental magic he drew upon from the threads that weaved through the ancient jungle, Rafe spirited them back to the clearing beside the river where they'd first made love. He held on to Mariah, rubbing his hands all over her, partially to make sure she was not hurt, but mostly to erase the revolting touch of the man who'd searched for the stone.

She pulled away, and her eyes, first wide with shock, suddenly shut tight. She wavered, then pushed him violently, ran to a nearby bush and vomited.

He slid to his knees beside her, gathering her hair from her face as she retched up the contents of her stomach.

"Mariah?"

She shook her head, unable to speak. He waited, smoothing his hand up and down her back until the sickness subsided. She rolled onto her backside, drew her knees up and gasped for calming breaths.

Closing his eyes, he conjured a bouquet of herbs, including one that not only would settle the stomach, but cleanse the mouth.

"Chew this," he ordered.

She took it, but did not obey. "What is it?"

"Mint," he replied. "Do it."

She sniffed. Satisfied, she plucked a few leaves and put them into her mouth, closing her eyes as if bracing herself for another round of heaving. Rafe produced a canteen with fresh water. He held tight to the threads of the jungle as he did this, to ward off the aftereffects of using Rogan's magic, but his grasp to the ancient power here, nearer civilization, was tentative at best. Night had fallen. They needed supplies. But they also needed to get out of the jungle before Farrow Pryce's men backtracked and found them.

She took a sip of water, swished the liquid in her mouth and spat it and the masticated leaves into the bushes. She repeated the process three times, then slipped her hand into his and silently asked for his help to stand. She did so, but wavered until he wrapped her entirely in his arms.

"I'm dizzy," she said.

"The consequence of our magical escape, I fear. We shall not travel that way again."

"Good," she replied. "But we need to get out of here."

She glanced at the waterfall and pool beside them, and if he wasn't mistaken, he caught a look of longing in her eyes.

"Pryce will have men guarding your plane," he said.

She nodded. "More than likely. But we'll have to work around that. There's no faster way out of this jungle."

After taking a tentative step, she shook him off, spanned a few more paces, then nearly lost her footing. He caught her again, this time taking her down to the floor, where he cradled her in his lap.

"They are miles away. You have time to recover."

"All the flying I've done in my lifetime and I've got motion sickness? There's irony in here somewhere, but I'm too light-headed to find it." Despite his impression that she'd rather not, she laid her head on his shoulder and closed her eyes. "Pryce might contact any men he has stationed at the plane. They could come looking for us."

"They have no idea where we are. They have no idea we vanished. 'Tis dark and quiet here. Rest a few minutes. Allow me to hold you. I am so sorry, Mariah. The way that man touched—"

With another kiss, she stopped him from recounting her experience. The flavors of fresh water and mint exploded on his tongue, and the soft warmth of her mouth was a balm to his aching conscience. Even as he'd rested within the stone, accumulating power to fight the man who'd wielded his enemy's sword, he'd been aware of Mariah's plight. They were connected now. Deeply. By the magic, yes, but also by so much more.

"He didn't hurt me," she reassured him. "Humiliated me, yes. Pissed me off, definitely. But I'm okay. I'm with you. You saved me."

He smiled. "We're even."

"Where's the stone?" she asked suddenly.

He removed it from the pocket of his jeans. "I retrieved it before I went into the pyramid and created the cloud that gave us cover to escape."

"That was very clever," she complimented him.

"Gypsies are nothing if not cunning."

She took a moment to run her hand softly over his cheek, and though he thought she might kiss him again, instead she tried to stand.

"I'm better now," she said. "Not that I wouldn't want to stick around here and relive last night, but we've got to move. These are the times I wish I had backup."

"Backup?" he asked.

She made it to her feet on her own this time. "Someone whose job it is to stay behind and ride to the rescue in an emergency. I used to do that for Ben. Or him for me."

"I shall fill that role now," Rafe insisted.

"Yeah," she said with a gentle grin. "You already have."

Rafe experienced the soft wave of emotion rolling off of her before she pulled away. She marched again to the edge of the forest, her energy regained. At the wall of foliage, buzzing with activity from the insects, reptiles and birds that made the jungle their home, she turned and held out her hand.

"Coming?" she asked.

"Not yet," he replied. "But perhaps after we return to Texas."

"She's down there," Cat said, experiencing a surge of sensation not unlike riding the crest of a roller coaster. Since Ben was a fairly good pilot, she knew the phenomenon didn't come from their flight. Mariah's watch was burning in her hand. After two hours en route and another circling above the jungle, Cat had made the connection.

"Is she close?"

For speed, Ben had taken a light, twin-prop jet from the Chandler Enterprises fleet—one that would get them across the border quickly and could land, he claimed, just about anywhere. Yet in this part of the world, a clearing amid thick trees wasn't easy to come by. She wasn't exactly sure how they were going to help Mariah if they couldn't get on the ground.

"Not far," Cat answered. "The vibration I'm getting is weak, but I'm thinking it's the best I can do."

"No," Ben said, consulting a map that looked old and hand-drawn. "This makes sense. There's an airstrip nearby that the drug runners used to use. Treasure hunters, too. I'll put down there and we'll see what you can pick up from the ground."

Cat pressed her lips tightly together and tried, once again, to rein in her jealousy, which had become easier to do now that she knew that Mariah Hunter must be in serious trouble if she was willing to accept help to escape. Cat couldn't imagine that Mariah would be thrilled when her former lover and his new girlfriend flew in to her rescue after what happened in Valoren, but if the vibes she was picking up were any indication, the treasure hunter might not care.

"How long till we get there?" she asked.

"Ten minutes. We're not far. It's a tricky landing. You might want to double-check your seat belt."

If the descent was any indication, this wasn't going to be fun. When a pocket of air sent them flying upward and then dipping until Cat's stomach slapped her toes, she reached out from the copilot's seat and clutched Ben's thigh hard. He didn't complain, but concentrated on leveling out the aircraft and adjusting his instruments for a landing without the benefit of light.

Until an explosion at the end of the dirt runway lit the sky like the Fourth of July.

"Whoa!" he said, pulling up hard as flames shot up directly in front of them.

"What was that?" Cat screamed.

Ben didn't reply. He banked hard right and gained altitude just as the watch in Cat's hand burned against her palm again.

"She's down there," Cat said.

"You're sure?" he questioned.

She closed her eyes, trying to ignore the bounce and roll of the plane as Ben made the maneuvers necessary for a second attempt. They had no choice but to put the plane down. Mariah needed them. Cat could feel her fear, even from a distance.

"She's there, Ben. And she's in trouble."

"What's new?" He cursed, making adjustments as he once again aligned the plane with the strip of dirt some crazy drug runners once called a runway. "As soon as we touch down, get to the hatch. And take this," he said, reaching under the seat to retrieve a gun. "Just in case."

She nodded. She wasn't exactly a crack shot, but she could make a showing if she needed to. First and foremost, they had to land without crashing.

At the southwest end of the runway, they saw a structure ablaze. The flames burned white-hot against the darkness.

"Jet fuel," Ben said as he made his final approach. "But not on the runway. Still, be prepared for anything."

"I'm with you, aren't I?" she quipped. "'Prepared for anything' should be sewn into our underwear."

Their banter stopped when Ben touched down and engaged the brakes, then shouted a warning for her to hold on as he threw the airplane into a controlled spin that had them facing the other direction. They stopped with a jerk and he gave her a quick nod before he started preparing for an instantaneous takeoff.

Cat tore out of her restraints and set to work on unlocking the hatch. She'd strapped Mariah's watch to her own wrist, but while she tried to send out a psychic vibration to the woman the way she had to Paschal during his rescue back in the Texas hill country last year, she doubted the message would get through. Mariah had no particular talents with the paranormal beyond stealing items that possessed the souls and spirits of men who, by all accounts, should have been dead.

And yet, the moment she'd flung open the hatch and dropped the steps, a man appeared, dragging Mariah with him, half in his arms.

"Is she hurt?" Cat asked.

The man shook his head. "Motion sickness."

Ben had ripped off his headphones and seat belt and had a second weapon aimed at the man's heart. "Mariah doesn't get motion sickness!"

"She's changed."

Cat didn't need any psychic powers to read the hidden message in that statement. Whoever this gorgeous hunk of man was—and she had a strong suspicion, even if Ben didn't, that this dark-haired, silver-eyed devil shared genetics with her one and only—he knew Mariah. Biblically.

"Get in," Cat ordered, helping drag Mariah on board even as she groaned in protest. Cat leaned out to retrieve the door when a bullet flared across her path. The unidentified man pulled her back, then completed the procedure on his own and with surprising expertise. While he attended to the latches, she'd pulled Mariah into a seat and started to buckle her in when she realized that Ben hadn't moved.

"Ben!" she shouted.

"What? Oh." He turned back to the cockpit and revved up the idling engines.

"What happened?" Cat asked as the stranger joined her beside Mariah.

After assuring himself that Cat had done an adequate job with Mariah's, he pulled on his own seat belt. Mariah groaned again and her head dropped against his. He reached across and cradled her intimately.

"Just hang on," he encouraged, whispering to Mariah, though she appeared nearly unconscious. "We'll be in the air soon."

Ben yelled to Cat, who realized she was the last one standing. She slid into the copilot's seat and hung on as Ben hit the throttle and they bumped over the uneven runway, gaining speed. Pings and pops sounded on the hull, but they suffered no damage—even after a bullet hit them directly on the windshield.

She turned to see the mystery man sitting, eyes closed and concentrating, his mouth turning deeper and deeper into a frown.

She swallowed thickly. The bullets were ricocheting off them because of magic.

They were airborne. Once they'd achieved the right altitude, Ben engaged the autopilot and turned to face Mariah, who was finally coming to.

"Who was firing at you?" Ben asked.

Mariah swallowed thickly. Cat could see the woman hadn't quite gotten her bearings yet. The dark-haired man was feeding her what looked and smelled like mint. "Men hired by some jerk named Farrow Pryce."

"Pryce is dead," Ben retorted, exchanging meaningful glances with Cat. Neither one of them had been one-hundred-percent sure that Pryce had died when he took a nosedive off a California cliff, but they'd hoped. The fact that he'd had a magical sword in his hand at the time had possibly delayed his demise.

"Someone forgot to tell him," Mariah shot back.

Cat smiled. It was hard to remember whenever she was around Mariah why she was so jealous of her. She might be a thorn in Ben's side, not to mention his heart, but she was interesting, at the very least. They might have been friends if they hadn't slept with the same man.

"Why's he after you?" Ben asked.

"Same reason you are."

Ben smirked. "I doubt it. I came here to save your life."

Mariah undid her restraints, then gave Cat a look that asked if she could switch places with her. Cat's stare communicated that Mariah and her brass balls had gone a bit too far this time, but Ben's ex responded with an eye roll that made it perfectly clear that her need to talk to Ben alone had absolutely nothing to do with any renewed romantic interest.

Cat shrugged. Only women could communicate so much in so few words. She undid her seat belt and they exchanged seats.

She couldn't hear the argument that immediately ensued between Ben and Mariah, and frankly, she didn't want to. They had their own drama to get through, and her intervention wasn't needed. Besides, she had a more interesting seatmate at the moment.

"She hates him, you know," she told him.

He spared her a dubious glance. "There's often an unclear distinction between love and hate."

Smart man. "True. Your sister, for instance. Did she hate Rogan that last night, or did she still love him?"

His eyes widened, and finally his attention was drawn away from the argument up front. "You know my sister? You know me?"

"No," she said, laying her hand softly on his. "I know your nephew. And it's about time you got to know him as well."

19

"So," Ben said, the word clipped in a way that let Mariah know he was about to ask a question she wasn't going to like. "Who is that guy?"

That was his first question?

"No one you know," she replied.

"Maybe I've heard of him," he countered.

"Actually, I'm one-hundred-percent sure you haven't. But he's not the issue, mate. He saved my life twice tonight. And once a few days ago. He's handy to have around."

"You do generally need lifesaving a little more often than the average woman."

She suppressed an incredible urge to stick her tongue out at him. Instead, she asked, "How did you know where to find me?"

"My father."

"Paschal?" She hadn't seen Ben's father in years. In fact, they'd met only once or twice more than a decade ago, when she and Ben were partners and had sought out the older man's expertise on the value of certain items. Then, suddenly, she made a connection that hadn't occurred to her before.

Rafe was a Gypsy. He'd lived in a Gypsy enclave—a colony created specifically to keep the Romani out of London. Paschal Rousseau's primary area of study was Romani culture, which she'd always thought unusual. Valoren's significance to Gypsy history, however, explained how Ben might have discovered the site.

"So, your father told you about Valoren?"

"Yes," he verified. "He's sort of an expert on it. But the question remains: How did you find out about it?"

Mariah gritted her teeth, not exactly anxious to admit that she'd been keeping tabs on Ben since their breakup. At first, she'd just found it impossible to believe that he was really retiring. His claim to want to pursue his Ph.D. and look after his father seemed like a complicated brush-off at the time. After a while, she realized he'd truly left the biz. But they shared enough friends, colleagues and contacts that when he finally made a move for the Valoren marker, she'd be one of the first to know.

"I heard through the grapevine about your plan to plunder the place," she said, attempting to keep her voice steady and nonchalant. "And since I was on the lookout for a quick take, some unknown site called Valoren seemed as good a spot as any."

"And you found more than you bargained for," Ben said. "Like I warned you."

"If your bottomless ego needs to say, 'I told you so,' just say it already."

He grinned. "I told you so."

"Feel better?"

"Infinitely."

She wanted to tell him to go fuck himself, but Ben had just ridden to her and Rafe's rescue, and she wasn't ungrateful. If he expected a thank-you, however, he'd just have to wait. She was too shaken and too annoyed to be forthcoming with gratitude.

As she and Rafe had expected, Farrow Pryce had left two men behind at the airstrip to watch her plane. She and Rafe had nearly overpowered the goons when the aircraft blew. She supposed she should consider herself lucky that she and Rafe weren't aboard when the jerks detonated the planted explosives, but damn, she loved that plane. And in one night, she'd had to rely on not one, but two men to get her out of a jam.

"How did your father know how to find me?" she asked. "Or that I was in trouble?"

"I'm not sure you'd believe me if I told you."

She snickered and rubbed her eyes, which were starting to ache from the strain. From the moment she'd woken this morning in that clearing by the waterfall, she'd traveled at least fifteen miles through inhospitable terrain, been shot at, beaten up, strip-searched, rescued in a billow of magical smoke and then had her body magically transported back to the beginning. Twice. The sensation had not been unlike having undercooked chicken livers shoved down her throat before riding inside a spinning top for an hour. Upside down.

Admittedly, the second time Rafe had used that mode of transportation to get them to the plane, it hadn't been quite so bad. She'd managed to keep from vomiting up the lining of her stomach. But she still never wanted to do it again.

Ever.

"You'd be surprised at what I'd believe nowadays, Ben. Remember when I used to think I'd seen everything and nothing shocked me? Well, if today proved

anything, it proved how very wrong I was. Trust me
when I say that nothing you tell me about your father
will catch me off guard."

"He's psychic."

She waved her hands dismissively. Why not? She had a
lover who could flit them from place to place in the blink
of an eye. Why couldn't Ben's father be clairvoyant?

"He saw me in a vision?" she asked.

"Something like that. He was actually looking for . . ."

His voice drifted off, and he nearly gave her a crick
in her neck following the quick whip of his head. Without explanation, he unbuckled his restraints, flipped on
the autopilot, then motioned for her to take over. She
wasn't exactly feeling up to it, but he left her no choice
when he abandoned the cockpit.

"Ben, where are you . . ."

Cat, who'd relinquished her seat beside Rafe to Ben,
shook her head warningly. Whatever. Mariah was too
tired to argue. She slipped into the pilot's seat, buckled
in and acclimated herself to the instruments, checking
their heading. Back to Texas. She wasn't sure that was
the best idea. If Farrow Pryce's men had spotted any
identifying numbers on this plane, they could possibly
be waiting for them wherever they landed. Unless Ben
hadn't filed a flight plan, which she figured he hadn't.

Maybe they were safe. For the moment.

She turned to ask Ben about a possible course adjust-
ment when Cat moved into the cockpit.

Ben and Rafe were shaking hands, tentatively, but
with smiles of recognition.

Mariah almost expected them to hug.

Her hand slipped off the wheel just as Cat reclaimed

the copilot's chair. "The family resemblance is amazing, isn't it?"

Suddenly, Mariah couldn't breathe. She might have hyperventilated or asphyxiated if Cat hadn't patted her roughly on the back.

"He's . . ." Mariah started, but the connections eluded her, even though the sudden familiarity around Rafe's eyes caught her entirely off guard. How could she have never noticed? His eyes, except for a subtle difference in the color, were just like Ben's.

Luckily, Cat chatted nonchalantly, as if everyone in the world just found out that their current lover was somehow related to their ex. "Ben's uncle. Looks like you were even a few more beats behind Ben. What's with you people?"

"I don't understand," Mariah admitted.

"Rafe was in the stone you took from Valoren. He was put there by a curse made by a sorcerer named—"

"—Rogan," Mariah supplied. "I know all about the curse and Rafe and who he was, er, is. What I don't understand is, how do you know?"

Cat sat back in the seat and connected her seat belt, but slowly, as if she expected another game of musical chairs any moment. "Do you know about his brothers?"

"And his sister."

"Well, Ben and I don't really know too much about her," Cat said.

"We know she started this whole mess by falling in love and then running away from Rogan," Mariah supplied. "Counting Rafe, at least four of the Forsyth brothers who went after her were trapped by the same kind of magic that holds him now," Cat added. "Three have been freed so far, including Paschal. He was freed over fifty years ago."

Mariah turned to tell Rafe this amazing news, but she could tell by the gloss in his eyes that Ben was filling him in on the same information.

"Where are the others?" she asked, genuinely happy that Rafe would soon reconnect with his siblings.

"The eldest, Damon, is with my friend Alexa Chandler. They're in Poland, but we'll contact them after we retrieve Ben's father in Texas. Damon and Paschal have been tireless in their search for items that might contain their brothers' spirits. So have we, honestly."

"And that's how you found us?"

"Ben's father has a talent called psychometry," Cat explained.

"The ability to read information about a person from holding an object that means something to them."

"Yeah," Cat said, removing a watch from her wrist and handing it to Mariah.

She took it, surprised. She hadn't even realized it was gone.

"You can do it, too?"

Cat wavered. "Sort of. Paschal has actual visions. He saw you in a jungle. Because of your problems with Velez, Ben was able to track down your general location. I'm more like a psychic GPS system. I was able to get a bead on you, so to speak, from holding your watch."

Mariah sighed and relaxed into the rather comfy pilot's chair. "Am I the only one around here who's just normal?"

Cat laughed. "Depends on your definition of 'normal,' doesn't it? A year ago, I was a sought-after debunker of psychic phenomena. It really destroys your whole outlook on life when the one thing you're trying to disprove turns out to be very, very real."

Mariah had no trouble imagining Cat's conflict. She'd spent more than half her life stealing antiquities in defiance of curses, legends and other spooky promises of untold misery. She couldn't help but feel a little humbled when real magic was now turning her life upside down.

"A week ago, I would have thought I was entirely insane for believing any of this," Mariah admitted. "Now, I guess I'm just as crazy as you are."

Cat spared a quick but telling glance over her shoulder. "Looks like we have quite a lot in common, then."

Mariah groaned. "Oh, we're not going to have this conversation tonight, are we?"

Cat patted her reassuringly on the arm. "That conversation is for you and Ben to have. But I am glad you're alive and that you found Rafe. For brothers who spent the majority of their lives in the eighteenth century apart, they certainly are willing to move heaven and earth to reunite. I guess I don't blame them. I'm an only child, so it's hard for me to relate."

"Well, I have brothers, and seeing them once every five or six years is just fine with me."

"All families are different. Still, I'd like to see the Forsyths reunited soon," Cat confessed, with a weariness in her voice that Mariah couldn't help but wonder about. "Four down. Two to go."

"Four down? I thought you said only Rafe and Damon were free."

"Rafe's not really free, is he? We still have to work on that. But Aiden, the second-oldest, was released six months ago. He was in a sword."

"The Dresden Sword?" Mariah asked.

"How do you know that name?"

"Pryce called it that. He had it with him in the jungle. He used it, or attempted to. Tried to make a pyramid come down on top of me in his attempt to get the stone where I found Rafe."

Cat nodded as if she suddenly understood. "That's what Paschal was talking about. We weren't sure what he was saying. The connection was bad, and he was more concerned with us getting to Mexico than he was with filling in all the details. So Pryce is attempting to use the magic. That's not good. That's so not good."

Cat's naturally dark skin paled, and Mariah took that as a very bad sign. Catalina Reyes didn't seem like the type to worry over nothing. Now, not only did Mariah have a ruthless collector after her in Hector Velez, but she had some psycho with paranormal powers at his disposal gunning for her, as well.

She busied herself with checking the instruments on the plane simply for something to do. She'd left the aircraft on autopilot, but again, the closer they got to Texas, the more she thought they might be going in the wrong direction.

Cat, however, was sitting still in her seat, her teeth clenched and her jaw tight.

"If it makes you feel better," Mariah offered, "I don't think Pryce knows exactly how the magic works. If he did, chances are Rafe and I never would have gotten out of there."

"He'll find out sooner or later," Cat surmised, frowning deeply.

"Not if we stop him," she replied. "You said Damon was in Poland, but what about Aiden?"

The tension in Cat's shoulders eased. "You know Lauren Cole, the actress?"

"The Athena chick? Not personally."

"Looks like you'll get a chance to meet her. She originally found the Dresden Sword. She freed Aiden and now he's in Bolivia, working with her on her next flick."

Mariah raised her eyebrows. "He's an actor?"

"He says he's eye candy," Cat said with a laugh. "The Forsyth men certainly don't come standard-issue. Anyway, once he knows about Rafe, he'll head back as soon as he can."

Mariah tried to imagine an eighteenth-century man thrust into the Hollywood world, but the image had her shaking her head. She was having trouble picturing Rafe at ease in the modern world. Or maybe it was just *her* modern world she struggled to see him in. What would he do with himself? She supposed he could continue studying to be a shaman, but why, if he had no clan to guide anymore?

"So that's three—Rafe, Damon and Aiden," Mariah recapped. "You said four."

"Paschal," Cat reminded her.

"Wow . . . when you said 'uncle,' I thought you meant 'great-great uncle' or something. How can Paschal be brothers with Rafe? His name is Rousseau."

"Paschal was born Paxton Forsyth. He was released sixty-plus years ago, near the end of World War II. He took his wife's surname and changed his first name to fit in with the French Resistance, which they were both a part of."

"But I met him in the daylight," Mariah reasoned. "And if he's aged—"

"He's human now," Cat clarified. "Rafe isn't. He's in the phantom state. We don't know how long they can survive that way. Paschal attained human form really quickly. Damon and Aiden each existed as phantoms for less than two weeks."

Mariah's chest clenched. "There's an expiration date?"

Cat shrugged. "We don't know. No one's ever had to find out."

Shivering, Mariah checked the environmental controls, but found the temperature inside the cockpit had little to do with her shakes. She thought she'd understood everything about the curse, but she was wrong. Rafe had asked her to help him break free of the stone, but while she'd agreed, she hadn't had the time to figure out how to do it.

She was starting to realize how incredibly selfish she'd been. She wasn't surprised. She never failed to disappoint. Even herself.

"How does Rafe become human again?"

"Well, he can't do it without you. You're the woman who awakened him to the phantom state. You're the one who can free him."

"How?"

"Oh, that's easy," Cat said nonchalantly. "You just have to fall in love."

20

Ben returned to the cockpit a few minutes later, but Mariah seemed utterly disinterested in any more talking. She relinquished the pilot seat to him, ran her hand along Cat's arm in what seemed like a gesture of thanks, and then drifted back to Rafe. Though his uncle sat forward as if eager to share all he'd learned with Mariah, she touched his lips softly, snuggled beside him, closed her eyes and dropped off to sleep. Or at least, she pretended.

Rafe didn't seem to mind. He ran his hand lovingly across her cheek, then turned to the window and stared out into the purple sky.

Ben readjusted the pilot's seat, put on his headphones and speaker and motioned for Cat to do the same. He wanted a more private conversation this time.

"So, did you tell her?" he asked.

"As you predicted, she totally clammed up. I've never seen a woman get so freaked out about something that's so obviously already happened," Cat said, glancing over her shoulder at the cuddled pair. "You sure you've told me everything about your breakup with her?"

Ben groaned. "While I'd love to take the credit for being so important that I changed the way she's viewed relationships for the past ten years, even I'm not that arrogant. She's always been commitment-phobic. It's the way she's wired."

Cat shook her head. "Avoidance like hers comes from hurt, Ben. Maybe not hurt you caused, but someone did. Probably her parents, from what you've told me. Daddy who didn't know what to do with her. Mommy who abandoned her. It's classic."

Ben wondered if Cat was thinking as much about Mariah as she was about herself. Shortly after her birth, Cat's parents had turned her over to her maternal grandparents. Like Mariah, Cat had turned the lack of parental attention into fierce independence, but unlike Mariah, Cat never lost the capacity to love.

Not so with Mariah. As much as he'd hurt her all those years ago by ending their affair, Ben knew that it wasn't a broken heart that had soured Mariah on him—it was the lost partnership. His disloyalty and abandonment had burned her much more than the fact that he hadn't had deep enough feelings for her to ignore his mother's deathbed request that he give up treasure hunting to take care of his father. Mariah had never understood his choice. Love over money? Obligation over adventure? Totally beyond her comprehension.

His uncle was in a lot of trouble.

"Think maybe we've been watching too much *Dr. Phil*?" he asked Cat, not wanting to consider the consequences for Rafe if Mariah couldn't free him from the stone. Would he have a second chance at life? Could he find someone else to love him? Or was the woman who triggered the initial awakening the only one who could finish the job?

Cat slid her hand over his. "Isn't it funny how pop psychology gives us all the tools to deal with everyone's problems except our own?"

"We don't have any issues we can't deal with," he said.

"But we don't deal with them," she replied.

She was right. After what amounted to a chance meeting fueled by an instantaneous and combustible attraction, Cat had given up her entire life to help him reunite his family. She'd shared his fears, his triumphs and his bed for more than a year. When she'd exhibited misgivings about chasing after Mariah, had he reassured her? Told her how deeply he cared about her? Promised that his past relationship with the Aussie treasure hunter was just that—the past?

No, he'd made jokes.

"Thank you for doing this," he whispered into the speaker.

"Doing what?"

"Everything," he replied. "Flying into the line of fire with me, more than once. Helping find Rafe. He's a little shell-shocked, but excited to know that three of his brothers are alive. But mostly for putting up with Mariah. I know she dredges up a lot of unresolved shit from my past."

"It's your past, Ben, not mine. The only person who can put it to rest is you."

"Mariah and I never had what you and I have. Or what we could have, if my crazy family would stop getting in our way."

"We wouldn't have met without your crazy family," she reminded him, her gaze drifting out into the darkness of the night sky. Her luscious lips turned downward at the corners, and when she turned back to him, her eyes were sad in a way that made his chest hurt. Her inky irises possessed a heart-wrenching melancholy, but her voice, when she spoke, was as strong and forthright as ever. "If you had to put a label on us, what would it be?"

He took her hand in his and kissed her knuckles, then pressed her flesh to his cheek. "We have what we've had from the start—a whole lot of trouble."

She pulled her hand away with a snap. "You're going to avoid this conversation, aren't you?"

Again with the jokes. After a deep breath, he checked the instruments for any sign of upcoming turbulence and, when he saw none, he twisted around to close the small door between the cockpit and the cabin, taking the extra second to engage the lock. Then he removed his headphones, undid his seat belt, did the same to Cat and pulled her onto his lap.

"No," he said, burying his nose against her neck and inhaling the very essence of her. "Up until tonight, I admit, I've been avoiding the conversation, trying to get around telling you how much I care about you in words and relying on only actions. But that's not enough, is it?"

Cat licked her lips, and Ben suddenly wondered why, with all the cross-country flying they'd done in their time together, they'd never made love in the sky.

"Your actions have been very nice," she admitted huskily. "And I haven't exactly been shouting endearments from the rooftops, either. We've both been living in the moment, but with one foot firmly planted in the past. Your relationships with your father and Mariah. Mine with—" Her voice drifted off. Cat's previous boyfriend had died because of the quest for Rogan's magic. Though there had been no love lost between them at the end, she had not come to this point unscathed. "When this is all over, when your family is all together, we'll concentrate on the future. *Our* future."

"You're willing to wait that long?" he asked, surprised. Possibly more shocked because *he* didn't think he could wait for the completion of a task that might never be finished.

Cat pressed her mouth to his and kissed him until he was certain he'd inadvertently spun the plane into an inverted roll.

"Maybe not for all your family to show themselves," she replied. "But let's get this uncle solid and breathing and then we'll take some time off for ourselves. Agreed?"

He didn't bother answering with words, though for the first time, he honestly wanted to say them. He hesitated, not because of the consequences or the expectations of saying, "I love you," to a woman who mattered, but he wanted to say it right—when they were alone, in the most romantic setting he could imagine. Not on a plane. Not while on the run.

But, while he had her here and the skies were clear, Ben decided that now was as good a time as any to practice a bit more of showing his love through actions and not words.

Rafe's experience with hotel suites had been limited, but when he awoke the next day beside Mariah in a bed big enough for a small family, he realized that wealth had its privileges. He'd always eschewed his father's predilection for luxury, even going as far as building a *vardo* at age fifteen out of an abandoned infantry wagon and several splintered doors and dragging the traditional Gypsy dwelling into the middle of his father's carefully tended English garden, where he announced he would follow the traditions of his mother's ancestors.

One rainstorm in the middle of a frigid German winter had convinced him that a solid roof over his head and a blazing fire in the hearth weren't something to scoff at, but moving back inside the manor estate had done nothing to increase his appreciation for comforts like cool silk sheets, downy pillows and room service.

Until now, with Mariah.

They'd arrived in Texas just before dawn, so Rafe had retreated into the stone after watching Mariah stumble into the hotel owned by Cat's friend. Though he'd lost corporeal form, he had not surrendered to sleep until after she'd picked over a plate of scrambled eggs, showered and slid safely into bed. She'd said very little to him during that time, but he'd sensed, from the moment after she'd returned from talking with Catalina Reyes in the front of the small plane, that she was deeply troubled.

Troubled enough to have slept all day.

A knock sounded from the other room, but Mariah merely turned over and placed a pillow over her head. With a grin, Rafe closed the double doors between the bedroom and the living area, then answered the summons. Ben stood there, not with his father as expected, but with a single sheet of paper clutched in his hands and a concerned expression knitting his brow.

"What is this?" he asked, taking the parchment from

his nephew. *His nephew*. He was having a hard time accepting this, since at nearly forty, Ben was older than he was. In normal years.

"A message," Ben replied.

"From Paxton?"

He pinched the bridge of his nose, suddenly appearing as weary as Mariah. "I spoke to my father this morning. He has strong reasons, let's say, to want to avoid any dealings with Farrow Pryce. He's going to meet us in Florida. After we've taken care of this."

Rafe motioned Ben inside as he scanned the paper. The type was small and seemed to contain only a series of numbers underneath Mariah's name, which was printed in big, bold letters.

"It's called a fax," Ben explained. "The plane was recognized in Mexico as belonging to Chandler Enterprises. The entire chain of hotels received this message."

Rafe focused on the part of the situation he understood. "What are these numbers?"

Ben sighed in exasperation. "A phone number, but when I . . . Do you know what a phone is?"

Rafe nodded.

"When I call, whoever answers doesn't reply. The number is unlisted and untraceable. Could be Hector Velez. Could be Farrow Pryce. Either option isn't good. But whoever it is wants to talk to Mariah, and Mariah only."

"She's—" Rafe started, but stopped when he heard the slide of the doors behind him.

"I'm awake," she said softly, a different kind of exhaustion in her voice. As if she weren't just tired from physical activity, but was utterly spent—body and soul. "What is it?"

Rafe wanted to touch her. He sensed waves of indifference rolling off her skin. He both marveled and mourned her ability to contain her emotions so expertly.

He crossed his arms over his chest while Ben explained. As she listened, Mariah continued to look pale and tired, even after nearly sixteen solid hours of sleep. Rafe was about to interrupt to suggest she order a meal before they dealt with the fax, when Mariah accepted Ben's cell phone and started to dial.

She paced as she waited for someone on the other end to respond. She motioned for the two of them to remain silent and then pressed a button that allowed them to hear both ends of the conversation.

"This is Mariah Hunter," she said once a trilling sound ended with a distinctive click.

"I suppose Dr. Rousseau is with you?"

"No," she answered with a saucy smirk, despite her hooded eyelids. "I swiped his phone. Look, doesn't matter who is here, does it? Just say your piece."

"I have your coins," Farrow Pryce replied.

She swore to herself. Rafe had not thought to recover the coins in the jungle. His only concern had been rescuing Mariah and taking her as far away from Farrow Pryce as possible. Once the smoke had cleared, Pryce had taken the coins to use as leverage.

"Of course you do," Mariah replied coolly.

"I'm willing to arrange a trade."

"How very predictable."

"Sometimes, the old ways are the best ways. It's very simple: You give me the stone; I give you the coins."

"Simple except for the fact that I'm not willing to part with my stone."

"That is a problem," Pryce said, exaggerated concern

in his voice. "But you see, I've already been in touch with Hector Velez. I've let him know that not only do I have his coins, but that, thanks to your incompetence, I'm going to melt them one by one until you give me what I want. He did not react well to the news."

Ben grabbed the phone and slammed it shut. Mariah started to protest, but he stopped her quickly with, "He could trace the call. Until we're ready, we can't verify exactly where we are. Now we know what he wants. Now we plan. We need to attack this from an offensive position. The man has money and power—both magical and otherwise. If we play our cards right, we'll have more."

Rafe felt a surge of familial pride. Ben reminded him much of his brothers on the night they'd ridden against Rogan. Perhaps if they'd strategized longer, they might not have fallen to Rogan's curse.

"What are you talking about?" Mariah asked. "Rogan's magic? Because Rafe doesn't like to use it. It makes him—"

Rafe was about to protest when Ben interrupted. "I know what the magic does to him. Maybe there is another option. To find it, though, we need to make a deal with the devil."

Mariah and Rafe exchanged confused looks.

"What devil are you talking about?" she asked.

"A particularly crafty fiend by the name of Gemma Von Roan."

"He's not bluffing," Gemma said, a humorless chuckle in her voice. Paschal held the phone to his shoulder while Ben waited on the other end of the line. If anyone could accurately predict Farrow Pryce's next move, it was his former partner in crime. "He'll melt those coins with glee if he thinks Mariah's going to die a slow and painful death as a result. She's committed the ultimate sin—she denied him something he wants and humiliated him in the process. I've never met her, but tell her she's my new best friend."

Paschal returned to the line and repeated what Gemma said, then added, "I'd advise you to have Mariah free Rafe from the stone and then just trade the marker for the coins, but freeing the phantom doesn't entirely diminish the magic of the object. If Pryce has both the sword and the stone, there's no telling how much power he'll have at his disposal. He could go after the Source, and I'm sure you'll agree that's not a good idea. The K'vr leadership is small potatoes next to what he could do with such extreme power."

His son agreed, but made him promise (again) to be careful and stay put in Florida until he, Cat, Rafe and Mariah took care of the problem. Paschal nearly asked to speak to Rafe, but then thought better of it. He didn't want technology between him and his youngest brother. They'd never been particularly close, and centuries had only added to their separation. He did not wish to exchange small talk. He wanted to look his brother in the eyes and apologize for taking so long to find him.

Paschal slipped the phone into his pocket and watched Gemma twirl Rafe's flute, which she hadn't relinquished since her vision at the K'vr headquarters.

"Anything new?" he asked.

She looked up at him, just as surprised that he was off the phone as he was by the fact that she was still playing with the flute. Below, waves from the Atlantic Ocean ebbed and flowed across the Florida shore in a steady, hypnotic rhythm. The balcony of their suite at the Crown Chandler St. Augustine was lovely, but Paschal longed to return to Isla de Fantasmas, where this entire matter had begun.

"I was just thinking," she said.

"About?"

She balanced the flute on the tip of her finger, a task made more difficult by the insistent night breeze. "The magic. My newly discovered ability. The combination of the two. I mean, I can copy paranormal powers, right? That's what you believe."

"Yes," he answered cautiously.

"Then if I'm in the presence of someone who is controlling Rogan's magic, then I'll be able to steal that, too, right?"

Paschal's mouth dried. He had no idea whether she could steal the magic, but her ambition was precisely what made her so intriguing. The woman was driven and ruthless in her need to rule the K'vr, but just like Pryce, her ambitions could explode, if given the right opportunity.

But he also knew better than to lie.

"I have no idea what will happen when you are exposed to the magic," he responded.

Despite the progress she'd made in finding her authentic self, her grin was every bit as hungry as the first time he'd met her.

"Then what are we waiting for?" she asked, standing. "Let's go find out."

21

"You should let him in," Ben said the moment the door shut behind Cat, who had offered to take Rafe on a tour of the hotel. Mariah was glad for time to think, though she wished Ben had left, too. Gemma Von Roan hadn't been much help. She'd only verified that they had every reason to fear Farrow Pryce if he had magic at his disposal. Even she was scared. So instead of using the rest of the night to sleep, they'd been plotting until now—only an hour from daybreak.

"Who are you talking about?" she asked, not really wanting to hear his answer.

"The man who needs you to love him."

She attempted to quell his interference with a scowl. "You want to give me advice about my romantic relationships, mate? That's rich."

"At least I've learned from my mistakes," Ben said.

"Oh, so now our previous partnership was nothing more than a mistake?"

She said the words, but they lacked true conviction and she knew it. Her reluctance to open her heart to

Rafe went well beyond anything Ben had done to her. She knew that, even if he didn't.

"We never stood a chance," he continued. "I was too arrogant and self-absorbed. You were too eager to get out of Australia. And we were both too young."

"Well, half of that was true," Mariah quipped. "I was seventeen. You were almost thirty."

"You lied about your age, I was twenty-five and that's not the point."

With her elbows on her knees, Mariah dropped her head between her legs and lost herself in the rush of blood to her brain. Their age difference had never been the problem. She'd simply never excelled at discussing her feelings with anyone. Her father practically forbade it, and her mother . . . well, her mother tended to try to associate even the simplest of emotions with some sociological theory or cultural paradigm. Mariah knew she was shitty at dealing with things like friendship and love, and that she was better off keeping things casual and arranging all her relationships so that they met some basic need. Like with the Barketts. They owned an airstrip and gave her access to planes and contacts. Great friends for a pilot to have.

Even with Rafe, she shared a symbiotic relationship. When he used the magic, he needed sex. When she was anywhere near him, the feeling was mutual. When she needed his powers to help her find the coins, he'd obliged. Now he needed her to free him by loving him, exposing herself to the possibility of untold hurts and disappointments. Where was the quid pro quo in that?

Love meant sacrifice, and not just on the big things. That part was easy. She'd choose life over death for any stranger, as long as they weren't trying to take her out in the process. But Rafe needed a woman to love him who was more like Irika—gentle, kind, wise. Not fucked-up from years of keeping her emotions hidden where even the best treasure hunters could not find them—not even her.

Ben slid onto the couch beside her. His jaw was tense, and his eyes, so much like Rafe's that she couldn't believe she hadn't made the genetic connection between the men immediately, gleamed with seriousness.

"I can't do this, Ben. Not now."

"You can never do this. That's your problem."

"Don't tell me what my problems are unless you're ready to hear a damned long list of your own, okay?"

He leaned back into the cushions. "You think Cat doesn't point out my shortcomings on a regular basis?"

Mariah smirked. "She doesn't seem like the fawning type. She's good for you, I think. Takes your ego down a peg."

"I think Rafe could do the same for you, if you'd let him."

Mariah jabbed her hands into her hair, tugging at the roots, trying to make her brain and her heart communicate with each other in a way that could result in Rafe's freedom. She knew she couldn't attempt to undo the curse now. They needed his magic in order to thwart Pryce. But after it was all over, if they succeeded, he deserved a life like the ones his brothers were enjoying—living with beautiful, successful women who'd somehow bridged a two-hundred-and-sixty-year difference in culture to fall madly in love.

Her stomach turned. She wandered to the table and picked through the remnants of Rafe's room-service lunch, scoring a slightly wilted celery stick and chomping on it simply to avoid having to talk.

"Mariah," Ben pressed.

"You think I don't want to let him in?" Mariah asked, washing down the tasteless root vegetable with a swig of her lukewarm beer.

"Have you ever let anyone into that heart of yours?"

"You didn't want in," she replied.

"Fair enough. But this isn't about us anymore. I chose my family over you. I apologized then, but I'm not sorry anymore. My father and I aren't exactly bosom buddies, but we've made strides. You and me? We could be friends. Hell, we could be relatives."

He muttered the last part, but Mariah heard him loud and clear.

"Don't get ahead of yourself," she warned him. "Don't you think your uncle deserves someone better?"

"What's wrong with you? I mean, you're headstrong and full of yourself and single-minded and untrustworthy and coldhearted, but other than that?"

She reached across the couch and slapped him on the back of his head.

"Ow!" he protested.

"I am not *untrustworthy*," she claimed, then swung around to the other side of the room, away from the alcohol, because it would be all too easy to lose herself in the act of getting truly and honestly dirty, stinking drunk. "But I can't argue the rest. Has he told you about his wife?"

Ben's eyes widened. "I didn't realize he'd been married."

Mariah hummed, then strolled to the seat opposite Ben. "Oh, yeah. She died right in front of him shortly after he was trapped inside the stone. Had her throat slit by the soldiers who'd come to murder the Gypsies."

"No," Ben gasped.

She closed her eyes and described to Ben what Rafe had told her, trying to picture what he'd gone through—what it had felt like to watch the woman he loved slaughtered when he was inches away, but unable to save her. If Irika had just walked a few more steps and brushed her hand over the marker, would she have freed him? Would he then have been butchered alongside her, or would he have been able to use the magic to save them both?

They'd never know.

"No wonder he's so brooding," Ben said when she'd finished.

She sat up, surprised. "Rafe isn't brooding. He's surprisingly well adjusted—I mean, for a phantom."

Ben rubbed the stubble on his jaw. "He's got a definite darkness in his eyes. Who wouldn't, after going through that?"

"He's made up for it," Mariah said. "For not being able to help her, I mean. He may not know it yet, but I think Irika would have been proud of him. From what he's told me, she was sweet and quiet and calm. And likely very forgiving. All the things I'm not."

"You can be calm," Ben said, a hint of a chuckle in his voice.

"I'm also *usually* self-sufficient. He's saved my arse three times already. Pathetic, isn't it?"

Ben attempted a smile, but while his eyes lit up with humor, his mouth managed only to quirk up at one corner. "Pretty much. But in the big picture, it should be a sign. What more do you need, Mariah, to convince you that he's the one?"

"But what if I'm not the one for him?" She cursed, deciding this touchy-feely conversation had gone on long enough. "Look, I know I have to love him to free him. But right now, we need to worry about Pryce. And Velez. Once we're clear of them, I can focus on Rafe. Not until then."

Ben pursed his lips, slapped his hands on his knees and stood. "That buys you a reprieve for at least another day."

"Fuck off, mate. I don't see a ring on Cat's finger. You've been together for more than a year. What the hell is up with that, Mr. Romance?"

He nodded as he shuffled to the door. "You're one-hundred-percent right. And since I don't want to lose the best thing that's ever happened to me, I'm going to rectify the situation very soon. What are you going to do?"

If only she knew.

"There isn't much time," Rafe said, charging back into the hotel room shortly after Ben had left.

Mariah jumped and turned away from the window. "What's wrong?"

"This is wrong," he said, tearing off his shirt, sweeping her into his arms and kissing her as if he'd never kissed her before.

He waited for her to surrender to the sensations, to melt into his arms as she'd done by the waterfall or at the cabin. But her resistance was palpable. If he let her go, she'd try to speak. Ask questions. He did not want to hear her voice unless she was screaming his name in pleasure.

During the hotel tour, Catalina had explained how

his brothers Damon, Aiden and Paxton had been freed from Rogan's curse. She'd been entirely certain that it wasn't mere exclamations of love that broke the spell, but the sentiment—the true and honest surrender of one's soul to another, as he'd once had with Irika.

And only Mariah could help him.

He'd never imagined sharing his soul with another woman. And yet, he knew Mariah did not love easily. In another time and place, he might have coaxed and seduced her emotions to the surface. But did he have that much time left?

After centuries of torturous solitude, he had a rare and precious opportunity to rebuild bonds with his brothers. Paxton, known to the others as Paschal, did not have much time left on this earth. When he met the others again, he wanted to do so as a man. Free of Rogan's infection.

But Mariah had to love him. And he knew she didn't.

Not yet.

"Rafe," she said, pulling away from him.

"The dawn approaches." He held her tighter. "I need you, Mariah."

"Did something happen?"

"Is the magic the only reason you believe I would want you?"

She pushed completely out of his arms and turned back to the window. "If you were smart, you wouldn't want me at all."

He wrapped his arms around her middle, standing snug against her so she could feel the fullness of his desire. "My need for you defies the mind. Let me make love to you, Mariah. Allow me to undress you. The sun is less than an hour away. I cannot rest until I've felt you beneath me."

She dropped her hands to her sides in surrender, and one by one, he undid each of the buttons on her blouse, plying her shoulders, neck and arms with kisses. He peeled the material away, and then removed her pants, leaving her in only her lacy lingerie.

She moved to shut the curtains, but he stopped her, blinked and doused the lights behind them, bathing her in the amber lights shining in from outside the suite. He inhaled the sweet scent of her until surrender rolled off her skin and eased the darkness that had sparked within him. That was the last bit of Rogan's magic he'd use tonight. He wanted her elementally, deeply—and as a human man. Or at the very least, as close to a human man as he could be while still ensnared by magic.

He nibbled at the skin on her neck while he unhooked the contraption that buoyed her breasts.

"You taste so sweet," he murmured, invigorated by the sound of her sigh as he dragged the material away from her body. "And you feel," he whispered, cupping her with both hands, loving the weight of her, "like satin."

He flicked his thumbs over her nipples, which were already erect with wanting. When she cooed, he tweaked her harder and took her earlobe into his mouth, sucking to a rhythm that made her push her backside hard against his engorged cock.

"Yes," he said. "This pleases you?"

"Oh, yeah," she admitted.

He nipped at her pulse point, feeling the jump in her blood. "Your heartbeat is quickening. Where else can you feel it? Show me."

She drew one hand down the other arm, wrapping her fingers around her wrist.

He smoothed his palm down her arm, lifted her wrist to his lips and suckled the succulent inside skin where her veins pulsed.

"Where else? You feel it deeper; I know you do. Show me."

With a whimper of acquiescence, she slipped her finger down her panties.

"Oh, yes," he encouraged. "That's where you beat for me the strongest. Where your body slickens. Test how wet you are, Mariah. Tell me you want me as badly as I need you."

He pinched her nipples hard, then soothed the sensitive nubs with his thumbs. He had no idea where his brazen questions came from, except his need to be whole. Human. Real. Not just in the night, but in the sun. He wanted to exist in the light with equal longing to mate with her. The needs were just as overpowering. And just as intertwined.

She moved her hand, but he snared her wrist and guided her fingers back to her panties.

With a moan, she understood what he wanted to see her do. Gooseflesh blossomed across her skin as she slipped a finger inside. Her body quivered. His cock pulsed and he found himself mimicking her rhythm, wanting desperately to join her pleasured crescendo. But not before he showed her—not before he made promises with his body that he could not make in words, knowing that nothing would send Mariah running faster in the other direction than sentiments she could not return.

"Rafe, please," she begged, tugging her panties off and

attempting to pry his hands from her breasts. "You're driving me crazy."

"That's the idea," he replied, turning her once so he could kiss her long and hard. But when she lifted her leg to his waist, he spun her around again. "No, no. Not yet."

"But the sun . . ." Her words faded when he dropped to his knees and kissed her curvy bum.

"Don't worry about the sun. Don't worry about anything. Just feel me all over your body. Touching you. Wanting you. Imprinting your flavors on my tongue."

He turned her then, pushed her up against the slim windowsill and spread her legs so he could feast. And pleasure. His first curl of a kiss started her climax, but he tormented her for as long as he could, suckling and licking and flicking his tongue across and into the soft folds of her sex until her legs nearly gave way. Then he lifted her and carried her to the bedroom.

Once he had her in the sheets, he finished undressing, then pressed the button that opened all the curtains in the room. The view of the hotel grounds and the city beyond wasn't as intoxicating as the jungle, but the sparkle of lights and the soft sway of the tall palms provided the perfect backdrop for lovemaking in this new world.

She held her arms out to him. He stayed at the edge of the bed, staring at her, drinking in every inch of glistening flesh, encircling his sex with his hand. Contact with his rigid state nearly caused him to jump out of his skin.

She moved toward him. "Let me," she begged.

"No," he replied. "I want you to see how much I need you."

She plumped the pillows behind her, her tongue moistening her lips as she drew her knees apart and matched him touch for touch.

The luscious pink folds of her vulva tempted him, taunted him, the moisture clinging there glimmering in the light. He tightened his grip, imagining the snug fit of his sex within hers, of the friction of him squeezing into her tight, hot channel. Her tawny curls drew his eyes and, with the flavor of her still on his tongue, he wasn't sure how much longer he could resist her. When a drop of his seed met his hand, he knew he'd waited long enough. He crawled over to her, took one last long lick of her sex, then trailed a path to her breasts, suckling hard on one and then the other before joining with her in one deliciously long squeeze of flesh into flesh.

"Rafe," she gasped, wrapping her legs tightly around his waist and clinging to him as if her life depended on it, when, in truth, the reverse was true.

He retreated for a torturous second before pressing harder and deeper inside her. "So beautiful. So perfect."

He took her hands in his and trapped them above her head. She arched her back to meet his thrusts and he lost all control. They crashed together, pumping, crying out, pleasuring and taking pleasure until the room began to spin.

He was hard and thick and hot—she was wet and warm and unbound. When she clenched around him and spasmed with release, he drove harder and deeper until his seed spilled and his body shook with unparalleled satisfaction.

When he finally fell, spent, beside her, he was as drenched in sweat as she.

"Rafe," she said, though the sound this time was more like a question.

He glanced up at her, but his vision blurred. The sun would break through the horizon soon. Streaks of pink already taunted him from the skyline outside.

"I don't want to let you down," she confessed.

He forced a small grin. "You've made a living taking valuable items for other people. Maybe this time, it's time to take something of deeper worth just for yourself."

She opened her mouth to reply, but before she could find the words, Rafe faded away.

22

Farrow Pryce stroked the handle of the sword, his head pounding, before he pressed the spot between his eyebrows with the cool metal hilt. Despite months of his trying to retrieve it, Rogan's magic remained elusive. The power had saved him from death, but not injury. His recovery had been hard and long. Pain still plagued him, forcing him to rely on pharmaceuticals for the first time in his life. Until recently, he'd barely had a clear enough mind to access capital from his offshore accounts and summon his most loyal K'vr followers to his cause without alerting the Council.

Now he was stronger. Sharper. He'd returned to the hill country estate he'd abandoned shortly after Gemma's betrayal with Paschal Rousseau. With the old man's expertise, he might have dominance over the magic by now, but the bitch had beaten him to the punch. He'd been left on his own to figure out exactly what the sword was and how it related to the legends and lore of Lord Rogan. His investigations had led him to Mariah Hunter.

Somehow, she possessed magic. He had no illusions

that the mysterious black fog that had eased her escape had been created by natural phenomena. The moment she'd disappeared, the fog had dispersed. She must have had the stone nearby and somehow used the powers within. Or else she'd tapped into the magic in the sword. He'd managed to call upon it once or twice, but without knowing precisely how.

He'd hoped Mariah Hunter would clue him in, but she'd escaped before he could persuade her to share her knowledge.

It would not happen again.

In his wildest imaginings, he'd never dreamed such power could literally be at his fingertips. Just holding the sword, running his hand down the smooth part of the honed blade, caused a ripple of excitement through his body that wasn't unlike good sex. Not that he'd had much of that, lately. Since Gemma had left, he'd found few women interesting, except for an occasional quick fuck to work off pent-up energy. Tab A into slot B. Nothing inventive. Nothing surprising. Even the kinkiest kink didn't do it for him, not when the part of his brain that controlled his lust was obsessed with possessing a magic darker and more powerful than he'd ever believed.

The door to his room burst open and the young punk, Topher Pyle, rounded on him with a mad gleam in his eyes.

"We found her," he exclaimed.

Farrow stood, instinctively covering the sword with the quilt on the bed.

"Mariah Hunter?"

Pyle shook his head, his sharp teeth gleaming in the sunlight. "Gemma."

Farrow eased back into his favorite chair. "Where is she?"

Pyle's smile faltered. "Gone now, but she broke into the K'vr mansion. She and the old man."

So she was still keeping company with the fossil.

"And you know this how?"

Pyle lifted his chin. "I've still got contacts with the elders."

Farrow sniffed derisively. The elders. Pitiful fools. They'd taken their time in choosing a successor to the grand apprenticeship, he now knew, in an attempt to appropriate the vast K'vr holdings for themselves. Farrow should have seen it sooner, but it wasn't until after his so-called death, when they'd attempted to obtain his personal assets as well, that he'd realized their scheme. They weren't merely a half dozen men trying to make the best decision for an organization that had lasted centuries. With no direct heir for succession, they'd been plotting to usurp every drop of K'vr wealth they could get their hands on—including his. Without a designated leader, they were free to rule as they wished.

"Did she take anything from the manse?" he asked.

Since the death of Gemma's father, the K'vr rarely used the old house. Only a small contingent remained to examine and catalog the archives, and even that exercise had been mostly abandoned without a leader to oversee the work.

Pyle's oily grin returned. "Took paperwork. Mostly on the items the K'vr had been looking for under Grand Apprentice David and Grand Apprentice Stuart."

"Her grandfather and a great-great-uncle, if I remember my Von Roan family tree correctly," Farrow surmised. "She took nothing from the archives itself?"

Pyle shrugged. "There's so much junk, no one is sure. She left footprints, and some china shit got smashed, but otherwise, it didn't look like anything was missing."

"Any idea where she went next?"

"Someone saw her driving out of the neighborhood with the old man, but the house had been abandoned. Something to do with radon gas. It was probably a trick, don't you think?"

Farrow arched a brow and remained silent. The answer was obvious, though he had to wonder about the intelligence of the guard left behind if he was so easily fooled. Of course, his cohorts were not much better. He waved Pyle out of the room.

Once alone, he glared at the sword, thinking of how Gemma had betrayed him, how he'd been so blinded, at first, by her blood connection to Lord Rogan and by the inventive sex she gave so willingly. He had not anticipated how she'd turn on him in the end. He'd believed that she wanted the leadership of the K'vr badly enough to help him to it and be satisfied to serve by his side.

Disgusted and infuriated, he imagined ways in which he could get rid of the elders and Gemma when the blade of the sword began to glow cobalt blue. Excited, he reached for the handle, but the light instantly faded.

Fury pulsed through him—how dared this tangle of gold and steel taunt him with promises of power it would not fulfill? He slashed the sword across the neck of a bust situated beside the window and, as the head of the former grand apprentice smashed to the ground, the magical light brightened. The blade shone as if it were forged from sapphire instead of steel.

Power surged up his arm. Images assailed him— striking visions of destruction and violence. Farrow leveled his free hand at the window, and with an ear-splitting crash, shards of glass exploded outward. Fragments of the metal frame spiked like knives into the building across the courtyard, impaling the ancient brick. The blue metallic gleam started to fuse with his arm, imbuing him with what he'd been seeking for so long.

Rogan's magic.

Exhilarated, he whooped in triumph. The glow extinguished. His arm dropped, too heavy for him to lift. The magic was gone, and if not for his leaning on the sword now piercing the carpet, he might have fallen over.

The door behind him burst open.

"What happened?" Pyle asked.

Despite the overwhelming need to collapse, Farrow forced himself to smile. He'd waited so long for this. So very long. To revel in his discovery was a luxury he would not deny himself.

Anger. Anger was the key. And he had plenty of that emotion stored up—particularly for Mariah Hunter, who'd thwarted him one too many times, and whose life he no longer had to spare.

When faced with insurmountable odds against success, Mariah always found it best to keep her plan simple. After arranging for hotel security to stay out of Mariah's way, Ben and Cat had left. They would act as backup if called, but otherwise would remain out of sight. Mariah refused to put them in danger again because she'd left the damned coins behind in Mexico. Just before midnight, she and Rafe rode the elevator to the roof of the hotel alone.

After initially laughing at the selection of time and

place, Pryce had agreed to her terms. She sensed he knew something that she didn't—or at least, he believed he did. Neither Ben nor Cat knew what it could be—not even after checking, yet again, with the woman who reportedly had once been his coconspirator in some scheme to take over a cult Mariah had never heard of. In addition to consulting with Gemma Von Roan, Ben and Cat had tangled with Pryce six months previously, on the very night he'd taken a plunge off a California cliff. Since he was still alive, and after the mini-earthquake in Chiapas, she knew he had a rudimentary knowledge of how the sword worked. But what, if anything, did he know about the stone?

Paschal and Gemma had pored over the documents they'd taken from the archives and had found nothing about the marker. According to them, Mariah's discovery of the youngest Forsyth brother had been pure dumb luck.

Or, as Paschal insisted, fate.

She'd never believed in fate before, but if it helped her get out of this mess, she was certainly willing to start.

Under other circumstances, Mariah might have suggested that Rafe use Rogan's magic to retrieve the coins and finish Farrow Pryce off for good. Damon and Aiden Forsyth, from what she'd been told, would not have hesitated to act against such a dangerous enemy. But Rafe was different. He eschewed the power and the shadowy evil that invaded him whenever he used it. She could not ask a man who'd aspired to be his clan's shaman to use Rogan's magic to commit murder.

Velez had made her a marked woman. When he'd called her shortly after she'd finished setting up the meeting with Pryce, he'd explained in excruciating detail exactly how he would kill her if she didn't cooperate and get his coins back.

If his Mayan treasure were melted to nothing, she would be, too. Images of the Nazis at the end of *Raiders of the Lost Ark* had haunted her all day.

"Are you frightened?" Rafe asked, bursting the images of liquefying skin and bulging eyeballs out of her brain.

"You tell me."

"I'm trying not to intrude."

She wasn't sure she'd exhibit such control if she had the ability to read people's emotions, but then, she wouldn't know what to do with such a talent anyway. Since dawn, when Rafe had faded from her bed, she'd wondered if maybe her heart was made of ice, like in the fairy tales. Or maybe she had no emotions at all. Because, care about Rafe as she did, she couldn't see herself committed to him for years to come. Or more accurately, she couldn't see a man like him staying with a woman like her.

"I'm a little nervous," she admitted. "I don't want anyone to get hurt, least of all you. You may be a phantom, but Ben said you can feel pain."

"But I cannot die," he reminded her. "I am not yet truly alive, so for the moment, I am safe."

"You don't know that for certain," she insisted.

"Don't I?"

He patted the pocket of the dark jeans, which bulged from the stone. Even in modern clothes—jeans, black button-down shirt and slick boots—Rafe still managed to look like he came from another century. Maybe it was the way his long hair was tousled rakishly across his face, or the stoic set of his shadowed jaw, but Mariah could easily imagine him charging across the rocky Valoren terrain atop a powerful black stallion, wet from the rain, desperate to do whatever it took to find his wife and his sister. The tragic ending of that midnight ride could not be reversed, but she had to hold on to the belief that tonight, the conflict with Farrow Pryce at least would go in their favor.

"Pryce thinks he knows something we don't," she replied.

Rafe's brow furrowed for a moment, but when the elevator dinged, he forced a smile. "We know everything he knows, and probably more. He may have the ability to use Rogan's magic, but so do I. Rest assured, Mariah. We will prevail."

She nodded, but the knot of apprehension in the pit of her stomach gave her pause. She took a deep breath and attempted to blow out her misgivings. This had to work. In the last two weeks, nothing had gone her way. She was overdue.

The lift doors parted one level down from the roof. She checked her watch and noted that she and Rafe had barely a minute to arrive at the predetermined location. She wasted no time in using the key Cat had obtained for roof access. Rafe released her hand and, as they discussed, they walked outside together, but without touching. The less Farrow Pryce knew about her relationship with Rafe, the better.

They were met by a rush of wind and the deafening sound of chopper blades. They waited for Farrow Pryce's transportation to set down. Two armed men in sleek black suits exited first, then held the door open for Pryce, who was dressed impeccably in navy blue.

Only in her line of work would a guy treat a blackmail exchange like a cocktail party.

Mariah shoved her hands into the pockets of her khakis and tried to look relaxed.

Pryce greeted them both with a stiff bow.

"Lost your sword?" Mariah asked, raising her voice to be heard over the helicopter, which remained ready to take off at a second's notice.

"Rest assured, it is nearby, should I require it," he replied. "I may not know you well, Ms. Hunter, but you don't strike me as a stupid woman. I'm quite certain you will not attempt to double-cross me."

He gave one of his bodyguards a quick glance. The bulky man produced a heavy velvet bag, which Farrow opened. When he poured the contents into his palm, Mariah's chest clenched. The Mayan coins.

"May I?" she asked.

"Of course," Pryce replied, holding his hand closer.

Mariah flipped the coins over, examining them, though she knew instantly that they were the real deal. The weight of them, the shape and color, had been imprinted in her brain.

She drew her hand back. "Don't you want to keep a few of these until you're sure the stone is authentic?"

His smile broadcast complete confidence. "You've hardly had time to create a copy. And even if you did, I've never laid eyes on the stone. How would I know a copy if you gave me one?"

Mariah narrowed her eyes, reading Pryce as best she could. The sharpness of his gaze, the twitch in his jaw despite his relaxed demeanor—all pointed to his knowing something she didn't. That made her nervous. This whole situation made her nervous.

Farrow eyed Rafe dismissively. "Bodyguard?"

She smiled. "Something like that. Okay, I'm satisfied these are my coins."

With a nod, Farrow's companion shook the coins back into the velvet bag, and then held it possessively, his arms crossed over a massive chest.

"Good. Now let me see the stone," Pryce requested, with entirely more politeness than Mariah trusted. He was too calm. Too confident. She was dealing with someone she was certain aimed to double-cross her. Her heart beat like an aboriginal skin drum.

Rafe produced the stone with a bit of a flourish that made it seem as though he'd made it appear out of nowhere.

Pryce wanted magic? They'd give him magic.

"Bullet catcher or illusionist?" Farrow asked, eyebrow arched.

"Man's got to have quick hands in this line of work," Rafe replied.

Pryce's grin oiled. "And here I thought most ladies liked it better slow."

Mariah kept her expression neutral. "Sometimes we just want to get things over with."

He chuckled and held out his hand. "May I?"

She shrugged. "Go ahead. It's just a rock."

Rafe rolled the stone into Pryce's palm.

He examined it thoroughly. The stone was identical to the one she'd found in Valoren, right down to the hawk etching and the fire opal center. But it had no magic—or at least, no magic that Rafe didn't control.

"Now, Ms. Hunter," Pryce said with a patronizing lilt, "you and I both know that this is not just a rock. It's a piece of history. Magical history. And if I do this . . ."

His words faded away as he grasped the stone tightly and concentrated, staring at the fake fire opal Rafe had magically conjured as if willing something to happen.

Mariah glanced at Rafe.

"What are you doing?" she asked Pryce.

He looked up at her, sneering. "Testing it. It's the only way to know if this is the genuine article."

"The genuine article of what? It's just a rock. It doesn't do anything," she insisted.

His scowl did not lessen. "We shall see, won't we?"

"Return it," Rafe said, clutching Pryce's shoulder.

Pryce's bodyguard pulled Rafe off his boss. They tussled, and the coins fell to the ground with a clank. Pryce continued to clutch the stone, staring so intently, Mariah suspected his eyes might pop out of his head. Just when she saw Rafe go entirely white, an unseen force grabbed her from behind and knocked her clear across the rooftop.

23

As if the sun had suddenly risen, all energy drained from Rafe's body. Mariah skidded across the roof's stony surface, her arms and legs flailing until she slammed against the short wall and fell, unconscious, to the gravel. He glared at Farrow Pryce, not because the monster had used the stone's magic to hurt Mariah, but because Pryce had forced Rafe to do it for him.

The minute Rafe's hand had made contact with Pryce's shoulder, Rafe had felt what the blackguard wanted. The fury and hatred focused at Mariah had been so strong, Rafe had instantly keyed into his intentions. To make the fake marker appear genuine, Rafe had had to turn Pryce's vile desire into reality.

"What have you done?" Rafe shouted, pretending surprise.

Pryce nodded to his bodyguards to return to the helicopter, the coins abandoned.

"I've mastered the magic," Pryce claimed. "I've found what every grand apprentice before me has sought. I control Rogan's magic now. I know the secret. If she ever awakes, do thank her for me."

"You bastard!" Rafe cursed, fully intending to wrap his hands around Pryce's throat, but he brandished the stone, his eyes flashing. Despite Rafe's instinct to tear Pryce limb from limb, he forced himself to stick to the plan.

Rafe made a show of trying to reach Mariah, staggered, then focused the magic on himself. An instant later, he was arching over the edge of the rooftop. He cushioned his landing on the concrete below, but created a scene of blood and gore all around him.

The darkness welling within him was nearly unbearable, but he concentrated on the memories of his last night with Mariah—of loving her, tasting her, moving within her in a rhythm that was as natural as the dance between the sun and the moon in the sky. His palms warmed, recalling the feel of her hands in his as they soared to sexual climax. He clutched that memory like a lifeline until he heard Pryce's helicopter lift off from the roof and soar away.

He returned to the roof beside Mariah. She was just coming to.

"Oh," she groaned, grasping at him uncertainly in her attempt to pull herself up. "What happened?"

"Pryce tried to kill you. Mariah, I am so—"

Though weak and pained, Mariah grabbed his face and kissed him soundly. His attempts to be gentle were met with her bold tongue and a desperate squeeze of his cheeks.

"Don't say it," she ordered, breathless. "You did what you had to do. We're both okay. Is he gone?"

Rafe caught sight of red taillights in the sky. Despite Mariah's kiss, he concentrated a blast of wind at the flying machine, which tottered uncertainly in the air.

"Leave it," she said, tugging at his shoulders. "You don't want him coming back, do you?"

"He won't return if he is dead."

"You're not a murderer. Pryce thinks he has the real stone. He thinks he knows how to use it. And he believes I'm dead, or at least seriously injured. He's wrong. You put a lot of power in that punch of yours, but you cushioned me, too. Just like you did in Chiapas."

"I could not bear to hurt you. Not when I—" He cut himself off, knowing that despite all they'd shared, admitting the strength of his emotions for her was not yet prudent. "Not when I care deeply for you."

She smiled, then kissed him again, slowly and languorously. She broke away, he noticed, when the helicopter could no longer be heard.

"He will determine that the stone is fake," Rafe reminded her as he stood, then helped her up beside him.

"Yes, but by the time he does, we'll have reunited with your brothers, who understand this magic better than we do. Now, where are my coins?"

They found them scattered on the ground near the door, abandoned, as Mariah suspected they would be, likely left for Hector Velez to retrieve, along with Mariah's bruised and battered body. Well, Velez would at least get half of what he expected. She returned the coins to the velvet bag and hid with Rafe behind an air-conditioning unit until, an hour later, two men arrived on the roof. Quickly, they retrieved the coins and then looked for Mariah. Rafe's magic ensured that she was not found, and, after making a quick phone call to their boss, Velez's men left.

"Do you think they'll keep after you?" Rafe asked.

"They have what they want. Getting me as a punching bag would only have been icing on the cake. Let's bail out. My name is bog water in the treasure-hunting game now anyway."

Rafe arched a brow. He was becoming quite accustomed to the vernacular of the twenty-first century, but some expressions still eluded him.

"In other words," she said, grabbing his hand, "let's get out of here."

With that, he could not agree more.

They rendezvoused with Ben and Cat at an airstrip not far from the hotel. Ben had had a helicopter ready to go, prepared to follow if Farrow Pryce had decided to take Mariah with him as some form of collateral or as an extra prize. Luckily, the wannabe magician had decided she was totally expendable. While Mariah ached from her flight across the roof, her primary pain came from Rafe's expression whenever she grunted or hissed from residual soreness.

She'd reassured him that he'd had no choice but make Pryce's magic look real, but his frown remained. She strongly suspected his feelings for her ran deeper than mere caring, and for that, she felt exponentially worse.

Ben flew them to Dallas, where they traded up to a private jet that delivered them to Florida. They arrived at the Chandler property in St. Augustine sometime after sunrise, so Mariah carried Rogan's marker inside a courier bag Cat had given her, wholly aware that while Rafe had disappeared from sight, his self-recriminations and regrets had not.

From the expressions of the people in the lobby, she guessed she looked scary, with her bloodshot eyes and dirty clothes. She longed for a bath and a couple of hours' sleep before she had to confront her inability to make the man who'd saved her yet again solid and whole.

"He's not here," Cat said shortly after talking to the front desk, and just as Mariah's foot was about to cross the threshold into the elevator.

Ben grabbed Mariah's elbow and pulled her out before the sliding doors shut.

"Who's not here?" she asked, annoyed.

"Paschal. We'd asked the hotel staff to keep an eye on him and Gemma after they arrived," Cat admitted, then exchanged a worried look with Ben. "They left before dawn."

"They'd only just arrived," Ben said. "Where did they go?"

Cat's mouth thinned. "They wanted a ride down to the pier."

"The island? Damn."

"Why damn?" Mariah asked, completely confused. She couldn't imagine why Paschal Rousseau or Paxton Forsyth or whatever his name was would leave this luxurious, completed hotel for a reportedly sparse, unfinished one on an island off the coast, especially when he knew that his long-lost youngest brother was on his way. Rafe had risked life and limb, both his and hers, to attend this reunion, unhampered by her drama with the coins or Farrow Pryce. The least his brother could have done after searching for sixty years was to exercise some patience.

"There are things on that island that Gemma Von Roan doesn't need to be near," Ben said, tugging Mariah toward the exit.

She pulled out of his grasp. "Hang on," she insisted. "I'm dead on my feet, Ben. Swear to God, I don't want to do anything to mess up this Forsyth family blowout, but I've got to get some sleep."

The closer Rafe got to reuniting with his family without her being able to free him entirely, the closer she got to throwing up. She needed a soak. She owed Rafe some serious soul searching, at the very least. And for that, she needed to be alone.

"I have to make sure he's okay," Ben insisted.

She placed a hand on his shoulder and then did the same to Cat. "You guys go on. I swear, I'll join you as soon as Rafe is, you know, solid."

Ben looked at Cat with reluctance, but Cat nodded and took him by the hand. "We'll call you if anything isn't right. Stay safe."

Mariah patted the bag and pressed the elevator button. "I can't seem to do anything but, since Rafe came into my life."

After a moment's hesitation, Ben and Cat left, and a minute later the elevator dinged and Mariah practically threw herself inside. Though Rafe could usually speak to her even while in the phantom state, he'd remained quiet since sunrise. He'd gone through as much as she had in the past twenty-four hours. He deserved a good nap before meeting his brothers, too.

She noticed the opulence of the suite long enough to decide that Alexa Chandler had exquisite taste. She could only imagine what the woman was going to do with a castle. For Mariah's part, though, all she required of a room right now was an unlimited supply of hot water.

She headed straight into the bathroom, turned on the faucets, then stripped out of her clothes, brushed out her hair and used the complimentary toothbrush to scrub away the last of the gritty taste in her mouth before she eased her aching muscles into the steaming water and turned on the jets.

So much had happened since she'd succumbed to her whim to fly to Germany and try to beat Ben out of some unknown treasure. For the first time in ten years, that particular chip had completely dissolved off her shoulder. Ben wasn't such a bad guy. He just wasn't for her. He had a family he cared about—a father he was willing to sacrifice everything for, including a chance for a real relationship with a great woman.

Catalina Reyes struck Mariah as patient, but Mariah couldn't see her waiting forever for Ben to make a permanent commitment. Funny how she could sympathize when she'd never in her life made as much as a pinkie promise to anyone except herself.

She squeezed two travel-size bottles of lavender-scented bath gel into the water, which was now level with her stomach. The hot water and the soothing perfume of the liquid soap helped her ease back into the curved porcelain. Her mind drifted to Australia, where this whole mess had started.

If there was ever one thing her mother and father had both given her in spades, it was distance. Even when she'd lived with one or the other, she'd never quite fit in. But she'd always been connected to them, even after she ran away. Suddenly inspired, she leaned across the bubbles floating atop the scalding water and reached for the phone.

Once the hotel operator answered, she asked, "Can you put a call through to Sydney, Australia, please? The Jasper Museum. Thank you."

Mariah's chest tightened with every ring. She had to steady her hands just to push the buttons for her mother's extension. It was after seven o'clock at night down under, but as she guessed, her mum was still in her office and answered the call absently.

"Hey, Mum."

"Mariah? Is that you? Darling, what's wrong?"

A thick lump formed in her esophagus. "Do I only call you when something's wrong?"

"What do you think?" Dinah asked. "Last time you called was to wish me a happy birthday six months ago."

"Actually, it was my birthday," Mariah countered with a nervous laugh. "But since you did all the work, I figured you deserved a bit of credit."

The cadence of Mariah's speech instantly changed, picking up the inflections and rhythms of her homeland.

"When are you coming home? It's been too long since we've had a proper visit."

Mariah nodded, her throat constricting. Had her mother ever said anything so motherly, and yet so unexpected? Did she ask this question as a matter of course, or because she truly wanted to see her only daughter?

"That's not a bad idea," Mariah answered. "Maybe a trip home is just what I need."

Her mother hesitated. Mariah's eyes suddenly stung with humiliation.

"Are you in trouble again?" Dinah asked. "With the law, I mean?"

Mariah laughed, though somehow the sound nearly

came out like a sob. "Nah," she replied. "I can't say I wasn't in some trouble recently, but I got it all worked out. Well, the law part anyway. Mum, what do you know about Gypsies?"

It was almost automatic, engaging Dinah on a professional level, where it was safer than digging into the emotions they both protected so fiercely.

"What Gypsies, sweetheart?"

"Eighteenth-century. London or thereabouts. Germany, maybe. I heard tell recently of a colony of sorts called Valoren. I was wondering what you knew."

She should have made this phone call weeks ago. On the other hand, she might not have stumbled onto Rafe if she had. Angst aside, she did not regret knowing him or making love to him or even battling Farrow Pryce with him. She regretted only being unable to break his Gypsy curse.

"Hold on," her mother said, and even though they were half a world away, she could hear her mother's fingers flying over the keyboard of her computer. She had access to databases that ordinary people simply didn't have—scholarly collections that the general public wouldn't much care about. If not for her mother's work at the museum, Mariah would never have met Ben. Seventeen and angry and anxious to not only spread her wings, but to do so in a way that would scandalize her mother, she'd left without so much as a note.

And yet, a decade later, the woman still took her calls.

"I see only one reference here," Dinah announced. "A scholarly article written by a Paschal Rousseau. Valoren was a secret enclave of banished Gypsies. Pervasive magical mythology. Why? Planning to steal something from there?"

"Already did," she answered.

"You don't sound happy about it," her mother observed wryly.

Mariah allowed a tiny smile. She could have done without falling off a cliff, but otherwise, things hadn't worked out so badly, had they? Except for Rafe needing what she wasn't sure she was capable of providing.

"It's been a load of trouble, as usual, but it could work out."

"It will," her mother said with a lighthearted laugh. "With you, Mariah, it always does."

"How can you say that? I'm a thief, Mum. I don't even make my living stealing for myself. I do it for other people. I don't give a damn about what I take or whom it hurts. I just—"

"*Survive*, darling. That's what you do. I'm not going to condone your lifestyle. You and your like are the bane of the existence of curators like me. But I've been telling myself all these years that at least you were happy. Living an exciting life, not trapped on some dusty desert ranch in the middle of the Northern Territory, pregnant and penned in . . ."

"Like you were," Mariah filled in.

Mariah's mother cleared her throat. "Yeah, like I was. I know you and your brothers paid a hefty price for my leaving, but I had to go. I thought marrying your father would be one great adventure. I'd have access to digs in parts of Australia that few have been able to explore at their leisure. And for a while, I was the happiest woman north of Alice Springs. But, honey, it wasn't enough, and I—"

"You don't have to explain, Mum."

"Maybe I do," she contradicted. "Maybe if I explained, you would stop running and would find what will really make you happy. Before you make the mistakes I did. Trying to be someone you're not."

Mariah's eyes stung. She must have splashed herself with a soap bubble. Or else she was breaking through barriers in her heart that she'd erected so long ago. She'd never thought about being a mother herself, but she supposed her childhood was a prime example of how not to parent. Maybe she could pull off the whole nurturing thing someday if she had the right man to balance out her imperfections.

Someone patient. Kind. Honorable. Someone who would encourage their children to explore the world and be honest and authentic about who they really were.

Someone like Rafe.

A sob broke through from her chest, unwelcome and unbidden.

"Mariah, sweetheart, you tell me what's wrong right now."

She couldn't do this, could she? Open up to a woman she'd distrusted for so long? Was this what Ben meant about letting people in? About putting family ties above all others, even when her mother had not?

"I'm messing it all up, Mum," she confessed, deciding she no longer had the strength to hold on to her resentments from the past. "He respects me for exactly who I am. He doesn't compare me to his wife or want me to be like her. I'm the only one who does that, and I'm not sure why. He wants me for me."

"His *wife*?"

Mariah swiped away the tears she now acknowledged

were streaming down her face. "She's dead. It was a long time ago. But I'm pushing him away. I may have already lost him."

Her mother's laugh was something between a bark and a cry of relief. "Sweetheart, you're the expert at finding things that other people have hidden and protected. Use your own talents on yourself. Whomever you've lost, you'll find—if you want to badly enough."

24

Rafe emerged from the stone to find Mariah asleep in a chair near the window, dressed in a fluffy white robe, a telephone cradled in her lap. A tray of food sat beside her, heartily picked over, though Rafe did manage to snag what he now knew to be called a french fry. Even cold, the delicacy pleased his palate. After draining the last of Mariah's beer—now warm and more familiar than the questionable American preference for serving the beverage cold—he grazed his fingers over her cheek until she woke.

"Hi," she said, struggling to sit when she must still be sore from their encounter the night before. "When did you, um, wake up?"

"Just a moment ago," he said. "I might have suspected I'd finally died, I slept so soundly. I dreamed of you."

She snatched a half-filled glass of water and drained it in one long gulp. "I hope I was doing something fun."

"You were weeping."

And from the condition of the skin beneath and around her eyes, he realized that he might not have been dreaming at all. She blinked and he noticed thick, red veins streaking toward her amber irises.

"Was I?" she asked.

Her nonchalance betrayed her.

"What happened while I slumbered?" he asked.

She poured herself more water from a sweating silver pitcher. "Just had a long talk with my mother. I learned a lot."

"About?"

"About me. About her. I think, when all this is over, I want to go home to Australia for a while. It's been too long."

He heard a change in the melody of her voice, as if wanting to return to her homeland had struck a chord deep inside her—a tune of measured optimism. He forced a smile. He could not imagine going anywhere so far away when he was about to reunite with his brothers—and yet, he hated the idea of Mariah traveling continents away without him.

But he had no right to indulge in melancholy. Night had fallen. It was time for him to meet his brothers.

"Where is Paxton?"

"Who? Oh, Paschal. I don't know," she replied. "He was supposed to be waiting for us here when we arrived this morning, but he and that Gemma woman must have gone to the island."

Rafe's chest tightened. "The island with Rogan's castle?"

She nodded and yawned, then stood and stretched her limbs. "Yeah. Ben and Cat went after them. Ben said he'd call if anything was wrong, though I suppose he might not have been able to get through. I was on the phone for a while. I'll call the front desk and see if we have any messages."

"No," he said, pointing her toward the bedroom. "Dress. I will call."

Mariah's eyes widened, but she obeyed nonetheless. When she'd closed the door behind her, he stared at the phone, wondering precisely how to make a call, when the device rang.

He picked up the receiver and held it to his ear as he'd watched Mariah do so many times. "Yes?"

"Rafe? Rafe Forsyth. Is that you?"

The voice was female, husky, deep and wholly unfamiliar.

"Who is this?"

"Your destiny, lover. I'm the woman who can set you free."

Paschal snatched the phone from Gemma. "Who are you calling?"

The old man could be damned stealthy for someone who should be walking with a shuffle. Or a cane. She supposed she should be happy he didn't have the latter or he might have thwacked her over the head with it.

"None of your business," she snapped.

He grabbed her roughly by the arm, and though she tried to tug away, his grip remained steady. She was starting to think it was a major mistake to come to this island. Ever since they'd arrived, Paschal had become stronger and incredibly more stubborn. Though he'd given her free rein to explore the island, which was really nothing more than sea grass, palmetto bushes, palm trees, sand, rocks, birds and crabs, he'd hardly let her look around the castle at all. When he'd finally allowed her enter, he'd kept her corralled in the downstairs rooms—a grand dining hall, new modern kitchens, several studies and a lounge. All had been scrubbed and renovated to far above current architectural standards—meaning, they'd lost some of their authenticity. Besides examining some beautiful mosaics and stained glass reportedly original to the structure, she'd been bored out of her mind.

The furnishings were mostly antique, but Rogan hadn't sat on a single chair or touched any of the various vases, candelabra or portraits. She'd skimmed a few books on Romani culture from the library, which had kept her entertained while the construction work continued on the upper floors, but she longed to explore the towers and turrets and secret hiding spaces. Now that Ben Rousseau and Catalina Reyes had arrived, Paschal had reinforcements to keep her in check. What she needed was a distraction. What she needed was his brother.

"Tell me whom you called," he insisted.

She handed him the damned phone so he could check the caller ID. "I called Rafe at the hotel. He and Mariah should have been here by now."

Paschal's silver eyes narrowed suspiciously. "Why do you care if he's late?"

"You want to meet him, don't you?"

"I've waited sixty-five years. I can wait another half hour."

"I'm bored," she admitted. And antsy. Before calling the hotel, she'd experienced an ominous sensation that had descended with the darkness. She'd attributed the phenomenon to frustration, but maybe it was something more.

"You're the one who wanted to come here," he reminded her.

"To look around," she argued. "Explore my forbear's legacy."

His clever smile sliced away any chance she might have thought she had of rooting around with no supervision. "Construction workers have been swarming this site for over a year. Do you think we'd leave anything of value just lying around? Like, perhaps, the legendary Source of Rogan's magical power?"

Frowning, she grabbed her phone back and trudged up the beach toward the path to the castle. He wasn't lying—but he wasn't really answering her question, either.

"Maybe it's the walls," she supposed. "Those are original, aren't they?"

"The walls, the windows and the mosaics. Not much else."

"Then why won't you let me go upstairs?"

"You don't have a hard hat," he replied.

The wind had kicked up around them. Though the small strip of land several miles east of St. Augustine in the Atlantic was called Isla de Fantasmas by the locals, Gemma had yet to meet a single ghost. Or phantom. She was anxious to see for herself if the stories Paschal had told her were really true. A curse that could trap a man's soul and the essence of his body inside an object for over two centuries would require substantial magic. And she wanted it. It was, after all, her birthright.

That much hadn't changed. And Paschal knew it. Ever since she'd learned about her psychic gift, he'd taken to keeping his own counsel. Even when reviewing the documents from her former family home, he'd remained close-lipped about any information he'd discovered. He did not trust her, and while logically she couldn't blame him, she had to admit that the sudden distance stung.

So instead of focusing on that angst, she'd imagined the grand possibilities of meeting his youngest brother, who, still trapped by the curse set by her ancestor, possessed what could be a great and terrible magic. If she got him alone . . . if she spent time with him . . . could she absorb his magic as she did other paranormal gifts?

She glanced over her shoulder. The water rippled over the shoreline, spewing white foam that glistened in the moonlight. Clouds scuttled above them, but she could see quite a distance. Not a single boat approached. And yet, why did she feel as if someone were about to pop up behind her and say, "Boo!"

"Did he answer?" Paschal asked.

"What?" she said, startled.

"Rafe? Did he answer your call?"

"Oh," she said, inhaling a calming breath. "Yeah, they'll be here shortly. What about Damon and Alexa? I thought you expected them hours ago."

Paschal frowned. "Bad weather delayed their flight. They won't arrive until tomorrow."

He turned, his gaze suddenly lost across the inky dark water. The sound of the waves lashing at the rocky shore did not quell what she suspected was his great anxiety. It certainly hadn't done much for hers.

"I'm sure they won't take off in dangerous weather," she assured him.

"That's not what I'm worried about."

Almost instinctively, she touched his arm. With a moment's concentration, she caught an image of boys playing in a garden. Twins with golden streaks in their hair and a third boy with a black ponytail standing on the perimeter—watching, but not running with the others.

An outsider.

"Is that why you're so nervous? Meeting a brother who . . ." She concentrated harder. Images she could see. Emotions were harder to pinpoint, since the faces of the people in the visions were often blurred and the sound muffled. "I know now. Didn't quite fit in? You know what they say about time and wounds. Besides, he's your brother."

Paschal took a great inhalation of ocean-scented air. "When's the last time you visited your brother in jail?"

She snorted. "Keith and I were never close. We were pitted against each other from childhood."

"In many ways, so were we."

He spoke without an ounce of malice, but a boatload of regret. A thrill of a secret scurried through her. "Really? Why? Was it because he's only your half brother? Or was it something better? Like an old rivalry? Perhaps over a woman?"

Paschal's frown deepened. "You assign your gender too much credit for the discord between men."

"Ha! Women have been starting wars since Helen of Troy. Is that it? Was it a woman?"

He started walking toward the castle. "Some wars rage much deeper."

"This sounds interesting," she said, purring her words as she sidled up to Paschal in the sexy way that had once been such second nature to her. Now, she wasn't flirting as much as she was trying to get under his skin.

Paschal ignored her.

Once inside, the soaring ceilings, carved buttresses and sparkling stained-glass windows, illuminated by exquisitely crafted gas torches, stole her breath. Nightfall had definitely added to the beauty of the place. She had no trouble imagining herself the queen of this castle, though she continued to struggle with the sense of entitlement that had haunted her since her arrival. This would get her nowhere. Rogan had existed a very long time ago. She was only the great-times-twenty-granddaughter of Rogan's grabby younger brother. No one was going to hand her the keys to this place anytime soon.

But under the circumstances, she couldn't resist posing the one unasked question that had hung in the air like an unpleasant smell since they'd arrived.

"Do you think Rogan is still alive?"

Paschal gave no hint of surprise. He merely gestured her into a lavish library to the right, directly away from the dining hall where Catalina and Ben had spent the day poring over the documents Paschal had brought from the archives, looking for something the old man might have missed. "I'd rather talk about Rafe."

"I want to know about both," she said. "You've regaled me with tales of this castle and of your childhood in England and Valoren, but you somehow managed to neglect to tell me anything interesting about either your brother or my ancestor. Your brother, who is still alive after two hundred and sixty-odd years. Like you. And Damon. And Aiden. There has to be a chance, at least, that Rogan's alive somewhere, too."

"We've no indication of that," Paschal said, a bit of a snap in his voice.

"Actually, the indication is talking to me. You lived. Why not him?"

"It was his magic that trapped us."

"I believe that," she assured him. "He was powerful.

That much we've all figured out. But why would he save you and not save himself?"

"Save?" His volume rose. "Is that what you think he did to us? *Save* us?"

"You didn't die that night," she insisted. "Or the next morning when that army descended on the village. No one died. No one was there to die."

"You're wrong." A voice from the doorway sliced into the echoing quiet all around them. Ben and Cat came into the library behind the man who had to be Rafe Forsyth.

Gemma's heart skipped a beat and she gulped painfully. She'd thought Ben was on the hot side, and the natural attraction she'd felt toward Paschal in spite of their age difference had been undeniable, but Rafe's dark skin, penetrating eyes and proud mien captured her fantasies in an elemental way. Unfortunately, he had a woman attached to his arm whose eyes, the moment they clashed with Gemma's, warned her to stay away.

Gemma forced herself to stand up taller. "I'm sorry?"

"You said no one died in the village, and that is a lie. My wife was murdered hours after I was captured by Rogan's curse. Her throat was slit and her blood soaked into the ground not three paces from where I was trapped, unable to save her. Unable to avenge her. Thanks to your ancestor's black magic."

His eyes flashed with something inherently more frightening than anger. For an instant, Gemma thought she felt the floor beneath her feet shake, but the woman beside him, Mariah Hunter, she assumed, tightened her grip on his arm, and the unsteadiness stopped.

"Rafe?" Paschal said, his voice tremulous.

Gemma bit back the myriad questions that tumbled in her brain and instead allowed the brothers to greet each other. They clasped hands at first, and then embraced, and the fire she'd seen flash in the Gypsy's eyes melted away with warmth for his long-lost sibling. Mariah watched, her eyes glossy, until the two men sat to talk. She then turned and left, a little unsteady on her feet and suddenly looking a little green. She disappeared with Ben and Cat into the dining hall. Gemma considered hanging around the library and seeing what she could pick up from the brothers' conversation, but she couldn't resist an opportunity to explore the castle without an escort.

She headed toward the main hall, but found her way blocked by an invisible barrier just beyond the threshold.

When she spun around to complain, Rafe was directly in front of her. She jumped back. Taller, broader and twice as intimidating as he was from a distance, he would have made her stumble if he hadn't caught her by the wrist.

"Don't," Paschal warned. "Don't touch her."

"What?" she asked, insulted. She might have the ability to soak up his magic, but she didn't have damned cooties. "I'm not going to hurt him."

"Explain," Rafe demanded, turning on his brother after breaking eye contact.

Paschal traded the fearful look on his face for a mask of indifference. "Let her go. She can do no damage up there."

Rafe stared at her long and hard, as if searching for signs of Rogan's face in hers. Cold tendrils of apprehension ran sprints up and down her spine. She had the strong suspicion that if she shared so much as the same nose, Rafe might tear her in half where she stood.

Then the atmosphere shifted. He turned away, and she guessed she was free to go.

She headed straight for the stairs, leaping around crates and heavy machinery, getting away faster than her cool demeanor normally allowed. In a collection of tools on the landing, she found a flashlight. She shone the beam up the grand staircase, which turned sharply to the left and into total darkness. The ominous feeling she'd experienced near the beach returned full force. No matter what Paschal said, she knew there was something in this castle that belonged to Rogan. Something that belonged to her.

"Well," she said, "I wonder what I'll discover."

A familiar male whisper curled around her ear.

Come and find out.

25

"Someone's here," Cat said, glancing up at the high ceiling, half expecting something unwelcome to float down from above. She'd heard a voice. A disembodied voice. And her insides had immediately chilled.

Ben looked up from the architectural plans he'd been studying, and Mariah, who'd been examining the mosaic that spanned the entire opposite wall, whirled around.

"Who? Where?" Mariah asked.

Cat held up a hand, concentrating. For a split second, while staring at a kaleidoscope of color on the stained glass, Cat had experienced a strong sensation of foreboding. And then something like an echo of a voice had teased the outer edges of her consciousness. Her arms had erupted in gooseflesh. But now she felt and heard nothing. Had it been her imagination? The offshoot of being inside a place that had possessed dark magic for centuries? Where, not long ago, she'd been shot in the arm?

Cat cursed. "I'm not sure. But something's not right."

Ben came up beside her and wrapped his arm around

her shoulder, saying nothing while she closed her eyes tighter and attempted to key back in to whatever had invaded her consciousness.

The three of them had been alone in the great hall for only ten to fifteen minutes. Rafe and Paschal had remained in the library. The sounds of their discussion, peppered with bursts of laughter, broke the castle's unnatural quiet. The renovation workers had cleared out early on Alexa's orders, but both Ben and Cat had explored the building and the island shortly afterward to make sure no one had been left behind. And yet, Cat sensed a presence that had slipped under her skin, turned her bones to ice, then slithered out again, leaving her shivering from head to toe.

"We need to check on Rafe."

They sprinted into the library, with Mariah following. Paschal and his phantom brother remained where they'd left them, hunched together on a tarp-covered couch. Their talk ceased the minute the trio had entered the room.

"Where's Gemma?" Mariah asked, immediately noticing the absence of Paschal's unlikely sidekick.

Gemma Von Roan had been avoiding Cat, which she couldn't help but find suspicious. Everything about the woman screamed *turncoat*. Up until six months ago, she'd been Farrow Pryce's right-hand woman. Now she'd taken up with Paschal. Yet Rogan's long-lost relative had sworn no allegiance, and Cat doubted she knew how.

Rafe blinked at them, as if he had to register who Gemma was. "She went upstairs."

Paschal's stare met Cat's. He'd already told her, albeit in rushed tones on the phone prior to their arrival, that Gemma should be kept away from Rafe. She had some sort of ability to gradually assimilate paranormal powers—an ability they could not risk her using while Rafe was still in the phantom state and had so much magic at his disposal.

"I'll find her," Cat volunteered.

"No, I'll go," Ben said. "You said someone was here."

Cat quelled him with her best, oh-no-you-won't glare. "I don't think whoever I felt is in the castle. Rafe?"

Rafe's eyed widened. Poor guy didn't realize that Cat had dealt with three of the Forsyth brothers while they were still tied to the magic. She knew their powers just as well as she knew her own.

He closed his eyes and concentrated. "There is no one upstairs but the Von Roan woman."

"A disaster waiting to happen, if you ask me," Cat concluded. "I'll find our runaway traitor. Every time she sees me, she rubs her jaw. She must remember my roundhouse kick."

She exited the room, but Ben caught up with her before she'd taken a half dozen steps toward the grand staircase.

"What?" she asked. The K'vr bitch was probably digging into stuff, hunting for the immense fire opal that was the source of Rogan's magic. As if they'd just leave it lying around.

"Be careful," Ben said.

"You're telling *me*?" she asked, with exaggerated shock. "I'm so not the daredevil in our little twosome."

He wrapped his arms possessively around her waist. "I like that we're a twosome."

An increasing hardness in his groin area made her regret that there was a threesome in the adjacent room and a wandering onesome somewhere upstairs. When the renovation was complete, this castle was going to end up one of the most romantic getaways owned by Crown Chandler hotels. She'd have to work it so Alexa gave her and Ben a night alone here before it opened. As a wedding gift, perhaps.

"Me, too," she replied, keeping her marital musings to herself. "Think Rafe and Mariah are ready for that next step?"

He frowned. Yeah, that was what Cat had been thinking, too.

While Mariah wasn't quite as prickly as usual, she was quiet and contemplative, and from all she knew about the woman, she wasn't the quiet and contemplative type. Rafe had been focused on reuniting with his brother. Understandable, but troubling. They'd arranged to come to the island because Rogan's magic was strongest here—and could, hopefully, be used to help break the curse.

"Maybe we should lock them in one of the finished bedrooms upstairs and let them work out whatever is holding them back," Cat suggested.

"I don't think sex is the problem."

"Might be the solution," she encouraged.

Ben grinned in that lopsided way that made her heart melt into a puddle at her feet. "I find it cures all my ills. Only with you, of course."

"Of course," she said with a laugh. "I'll be back. Now that Rafe and Paschal have had time to reconnect, I think we should get the ball rolling." She leaned in closer and whispered in Ben's ear. Not only did it give her a chance to take a heady whiff of his intoxicating cologne, it ensured that they weren't overheard. "Once Rafe is free, we can seal the marker in the same hidey-hole as the Source. That will keep them both safe."

"You really think it's a good idea to store them to-gether? We've been trying to avoid allowing both the sword and the stone to fall into Pryce's hands. If he gets the stone and the Source, too—"

"Then we're royally screwed," Cat finished.

"Who are you?" Gemma asked.

Don't you recognize me, or have we been apart so long?

Farrow.

She turned off the flashlight and threw herself flat against the nearest wall. She trained her ears to register any sound of his approach. Her throat constricted and her heart slammed double-time against her chest. After a full minute, she sensed no one. And yet, she'd heard what she'd heard—and she knew Farrow's voice. Ten-tatively, she continued down the hall. Her shoes scuffed over the dusty marble beneath her feet.

"Where are you?"

Find a window that faces the ocean.

She stopped. Wasn't he here? In the castle? How was he talking to her? Acid churned in her stomach and shot up her esophagus, nearly choking her.

The magic.

Farrow had caught up with them. He was contacting her. Rafe and Mariah had warned that he was gaining knowledge of the magic, but how had he known she was here?

"I don't trust you," she said, trying to keep her voice quiet even though she wanted to scream at the top of her lungs.

Of course you don't. But you can come to me of your own free will, or I can make you. Which do you prefer?

She stopped. If he had defied death despite throwing himself off a steep California cliff and now could speak into her mind, maybe revealing her exact location by going to a window wasn't the best idea.

I don't want to hurt you, Gemma. I need your help. And as you can see, I have quite a bit to offer you, as well.

She swallowed deeply. He was telling the truth. Still, her instinct to turn and run was strong—stronger than she'd ever want to admit.

Of course, he didn't know about the power she'd inherited from dear old Dad. He would expect mistrust.

"Why should I believe you?"

He did not answer. She walked farther down the dark corridor, turning two corners and flashing the light into rooms with open doors to guest suites in the midst of renovation. One or two were nearly finished, with plush beds and paintings on the walls, glittering glass cases filled with bric-a-brac that matched the eighteenth-century time period of the decor. The room at the end of the hall had a large, ocean-facing window. She paused at the threshold. Farrow could hear her, but did he also know what she was thinking?

Because if he did, she was in serious trouble.

Mariah jumped when Ben stepped back into the library and gained their attention with a clap of his hands. "Okay, people. I think it's time for us to get this show on the road."

"What show?" she asked.

Ben exchanged a nervous glance with Rafe. He and

Paschal stood, and Mariah felt her heart drop to her toes. The time had come.

Surprisingly, her heart seemed to bounce back into her chest just as quickly as it had dropped, lighter than it had felt in a very long time.

"Oh," she said with a smile. "Think we could be alone for a few minutes?"

She held out her hand to Rafe. Despite the personal inroads she'd made in the last twenty-four hours, she had a few private confessions to make before she outwitted a curse that had held him for nearly three centuries.

With a grin that made her insides liquefy, he took her hand in his and marched them into the dining hall.

Then he jerked to a stop.

"What's wrong?" she asked.

"This room. It is exactly as I remember it."

He led her deeper inside. Incredibly impressive, the space was dominated by a long, carved table that could easily sit fifty people. The walls to their immediate left sparkled with clouded stained glass. In front of them, a fireplace large enough to fit a small car (or roast a whole cow) sat amid one of the most glorious mosaics Mariah had ever seen. Made up of tiny tiles in various sizes and colors, the scene depicted featured a small Gypsy camp with multihued houses and even more vibrant villagers.

Something about the artistry was so alive, so compelling. Mariah had seen a lot of native art in her life, but nothing had compared to this.

"Is this Umgeben?" she asked.

He managed a nod and tugged her along when he crossed the room. The mosaic started just above the fireplace, so they had to stand back to take in the full picture.

"This is my village. This is my home."

The surprise and wonder in his voice caught her off guard. "I thought you'd been in Rogan's castle before. Wasn't this mosaic always here?"

"Yes, I believe so."

He shook his head, as if breaking the hypnotic draw of the artistry in order to speak with her. "The mosaic did not have such detail. Not that I remember. However, Rogan was still having work done on it the last time I visited him. I refused to enter his house long before it was completed."

"Why? Because of Sarina?"

Rafe turned away from the wall and flexed his fingers open and closed. He noticed the nervous gesture immediately and shoved his hands into his pockets. "I knew about Sarina's infatuation long before my brothers, but no, that was not the reason."

"You and Sarina were close," she provided.

He nodded. "We shared our Gypsy heritage. Our playground was the forest and caves of Valoren, not prim English gardens. We had a mother to raise us, not nurses. We loved our brothers, but we were often separated from them. They spent months at a time in England. Damon studied abroad and tended to our father's holdings. Aiden, Colin, Paxton and Logan each went to school away from Valoren, leaving Sarina and me to play with the other Gypsy children."

"The Gypsies were your family, too."

His gaze drifted back to the mosaic. "Not all of them."

"I thought Rogan was a nobleman of some sort."

Rafe lifted an eyebrow. "Are the two mutually exclusive?"

"In most countries, yeah."

"Rogan kept his roots hidden well. He preferred that men of power and influence, such as my brother Damon, or my father, consider him royalty of some small Slavic country. But he was Romani. I saw it in his eyes the first time we met."

"Why would he hide his bloodlines from your father? I thought the earl loved the Gypsies. Your mother was Romani. And wasn't your father the one who came up with the idea to colonize your people rather than imprison them in London? Or worse?"

Rafe frowned. They'd discussed all this before, but she knew he struggled with his feelings about his father just as she had fought her emotions for hers. And her mother. And her brothers. And Ben. She'd pretty much had issues with everyone she'd spent prolonged periods of time with.

Watching Rafe tussle with his own emotional demons made her anxious to say the words she'd never imagined she'd speak. But she hesitated. Rafe's eyes glazed as he stared at the mosaic—as he stared at his past.

"My father cared for the Gypsies, yes. But he mistrusted Rogan from the moment they met. I doubt his revealing the carefully guarded secret of his lineage would have engendered faith or confidence. Rogan needed my father so he could have access to the Gypsies, so he could build this massive castle on promises of bringing wealth and security to the colony. Before we had a single hint of his magical abilities, he had enthralled the entire encampment with his charisma. He was a nobleman who paid homage to our *Chovihano* upon his arrival and who brought flowers daily to my grandmother—buds that did not grow in the valley and yet stayed fresh for days on end. He charmed us all."

"Including Sarina?"

"Worse," Rafe said. "He completely enraptured my Irika. If I had not married her, I might have lost her to him forever."

26

Emotions Rafe had thought he'd cleansed from his soul long ago came raging back. Jealousy and guilt battled for dominance. Rafe had loved his wife. He'd loved his sister. But in the end, he'd lost them both.

Mariah ran her hand along his shoulders. Her sympathy caressed him, and he needed the sensation too desperately to shut her out. He'd already told her about his inability to save Irika, and he'd confessed how he'd failed to discourage his sister's affection for the sorcerer whose magic had led him here. But he had not shared how his own actions had helped create both tragedies.

But he could no longer deny his past. Not if he wanted to live again.

"Irika was very beautiful," he said.

"To have the handsomest man in the village—that would be you—and a powerful nobleman both desire her for their own," Mariah said, her voice soothing, "she must have been stunning."

His gaze swept the mosaic for any sign of Irika's long, dark hair and penetrating eyes. Instead, he spotted the old woman who painted intricate landscapes on thimbles. Cinka. Cinka Dobravich. Nearly blind, she could not see to greet a visitor from across a yard, but her talent in miniature had been striking. And near the center of the display, he caught sight of the strapping young lad, one of four sons of Ivo and Esme, who'd so often disrupt Stefan's naps by drumming on the fence outside their cottage. In an upper corner, nearly out of his line of sight, he saw a gray-haired man in a bright red shirt who wore the thoughtful, determined expression of the *Chovihano*, right down to the mole on his left cheek and the downward curve of his lips. Belthezor wore a bundle on his back, which was odd, but otherwise, he could practically feel the man's gentle gaze as if he stood right beside him.

"I don't see her," he said.

"These are actual people?"

"Yes," he said, equally amazed. Why would a man as self-indulgent as Rogan have this intimate masterpiece in the most public space in his castle?

"What did she look like?"

Mariah stepped back, her stare lost in the collage of faces. The scene was the village viewed from atop one of the mountain cliffs. Colorful *vardos* and festooned, ramshackle homes anchored a portrait brimming with action. The tiles on the communal fire at the center of the mosaic glittered, picking up the light from the chandeliers in the dining hall. Pieced together with expert care, the representations of children and animals evoked movement, even when they were entirely still. The artists had captured the weary, hunched shoulders of the butcher and the sprightly step of his much younger wife. But no sign of Irika. And no man at all who looked like him.

"Dark skin and hair," he explained, hoping to find her—to know that something, however small, was left of the woman he'd loved. "Slim and almost fragile. She was a storm cloud hovering above, but never producing a single drop of rain."

"Whereas I'm thundering all the time," Mariah cracked.

He laughed, but for only an instant. Irika and Mariah existed on opposite ends of the world of women, but he suspected that if they'd met, they would have liked each other. Even Mariah's rough edges would not have frightened Irika, who had been born with an angel's soul.

"And you never saw this mosaic before tonight?" she asked.

He shook his head. "After Irika and I were married, we avoided invitations into Rogan's inner sanctum. I did not flaunt temptation in front of a man such as him."

"Didn't you trust her?"

"Irika? Implicitly," he said, surprised by her question. "But Rogan? No. When he heard of our marriage, he presented us with a generous gift—a house, solidly built up against the mountainside." He scanned the mosaic and found his home, surprised to see the windows dark and the yard where he'd once raised goats entirely empty—dead, whereas the rest of the mosaic overflowed with life. He pointed at the structure for Mariah's sake. "There."

Mariah levered up on her tiptoes. "And you took it?"

"Irika's father insisted," he complained. "He thought it unwise to insult Rogan. But we stayed away from any gathering that forced us inside his domain. I remember talk of the great mosaic, but I do not recall knowing that the villagers would be represented."

Thinking back so far was a futile exercise. It was hard enough to remember all the major events, much less the minutiae, after two hundred and sixty years.

Mariah's hand slipped down his arm, her fingers tangling with his. He could not miss the shiver of uncertainty that preceded her question. "Were you already promised to Irika when Rogan came to town, or did she pick you over him?"

Rafe slipped his hand free of Mariah's and continued searching the mosaic, recognizing the woodworker, Lazar, and his wife, Natasha, surrounded by their trio of daughters. He did not want to feel Mariah's insecurity when asking about his past. He had enough doubt of his own in providing the answers.

"Irika and I were promised to each other at birth. A marriage between the son of the governor and the daughter of the *Chovihano* ensured good relations among the Gypsies and their jailer."

He expected her to contradict his classification of his own father, but she did not. He gained some measure of comfort by unburdening his conscience while in such close proximity to the mosaic, which seemed to emanate the same emotional warmth the village had provided when it was thriving and alive.

"Irika and I played together as children, knowing that someday we'd wed. We loved each other long before we exchanged promises with the blessings of our families."

"You say that as if you're sorry," Mariah observed, her head tilted quizzically.

Rafe closed his eyes, remembering the day he'd stood beneath a canopy of colorful scarves, exchanged bites of bread doused in salt and vowed to remain faithful to Irika until death.

"I am not sorry I loved Irika, but I will never forgive myself for rushing our marriage. Once Irika was my bride, Rogan turned his charms on my sister. She was so young. He was a man of the world. And I was not there to protect her."

Mariah stepped away, her arms hooked behind her back. He knew instantly that she was about to say something he would not want to hear.

"Sarina might have been young, but I've never heard you say she was foolish."

"She was not," he replied. "Just . . . innocent."

Mariah's eyebrows lifted, as if she doubted any woman, young or old, could be quite as guileless as he professed. He supposed that in this century, the notion would be difficult to accept. But he knew his sister. He knew Irika. Neither could have fought off Rogan's charms for long.

"Women of my day were not like you or Catalina," he explained. "Even the *puri* grandmothers who possessed the sight did not see Rogan for what he was. Not, at least, until it was too late."

"I'm not denying that he was a scary guy," she said. "Anyone who could devise the magic he did that trapped you for all this time had a seriously warped outlook on the world. But I don't think you're giving your sister much credit, and you're taking too much blame for yourself. Maybe Rogan truly cared for her. Maybe he was trying to make a good marriage, too. Sarina was the daughter of the governor, and you said he wanted a position of power in the village—"

"Yes, but ask yourself," Rafe interrupted, "why did he care about Valoren? Why settle in the village of Umgeben when he could have resumed his travels to the far corners of the world? Our village was small and remote. What had we to offer him to make him want so desperately to stay that he'd erect this monstrosity?"

He gestured at the castle, but Mariah did not follow his hands. Her eyes bored straight into his and held him captive.

"Love," she answered simply.

"He knew not how to love," Rafe snapped.

At this, she glanced aside. "Okay, then. Maybe just the company of people who shared his blood?"

He shook his head wildly. "My people had been in Valoren for over two decades when Rogan arrived. For all those years, we survived, but we chafed under the laws that kept us from wandering the land, making our lives wherever we saw fit. He changed all that. He took away the Gypsies' desire to explore and travel and control their own destinies. Everyone ... changed."

"Everyone?"

"Nearly everyone," he clarified. "But even Irika no longer spoke of leaving the valley. She wanted his house. His roots."

"Maybe it was *your* roots she wanted," Mariah offered. "Something steady and predictable and safe. I'm no expert, but I hear that a lot of women find that very attractive."

She smiled, but Rafe could not see the humor.

"You don't understand. Rogan possessed magic unlike any ever conceived of by the Romani. He influenced them all. Changed them all. You saw what Farrow Pryce could do with just the sword and a half-wit's knowledge of how to use it. With the skills he possessed, Rogan could have taken over the world. But he didn't. Why?"

"His motives don't matter anymore," Mariah reminded him. "You have to let go of the past. If there's one lesson I've learned recently, that's the one."

Painfully, Rafe tore his eyes away from the mosaic and the loss it represented. Hatred and fury surged inside him, as if he'd just conjured something massive with Rogan's tainted power.

"How can it not matter?" he asked. "He set my fate in motion. He insulted the king, who sent the army, who killed my wife. His magic ensnared me, prevented me from helping her. He forced me to watch blood stream from her neck and . . ."

Before Rafe knew it, his vision blurred and his face was wet. He slashed at his tears, tempted to gouge out his eyes if he thought the act would erase the torturous images from his brain. But he knew it would not. Nothing would assuage this agony. Not as long as he remained here, in Rogan's lair. Not as long as he was tied to Rogan's cursed marker.

Mariah slipped her arms around his waist and pressed her cheek to his chest. "What happened doesn't make sense. Murder never does. But Irika's death was not your fault."

"What of Sarina?"

"You don't even know that she died. She could have become trapped, like you and your brothers. But you need to accept that she had a mind of her own."

"She was running from him, Mariah. She was terrified."

"I know," she said softly, but then spoke no more. What more could she say? They might never know what happened to Sarina. But Irika's fate was indisputable. Rafe had not realized until now that time had not erased even the tiniest detail of that tragedy from his heart.

"Perhaps I did not trust Irika's love. If I had, we might have taken our time with our marriage. She might not have become pregnant so young and remained weak for so long afterward that she couldn't—"

"Fight the soldiers?" Mariah supplied, staring into his eyes incredulously. "Rafe, she wouldn't have lived even if she'd been armed to the teeth and trained to fight. She was outnumbered. And even if you had been able to escape the stone, you would have died, too."

He jammed his hands into his hair, pulling the strands from the queue he'd tied at the back of his neck. He had no answers, only questions. Fortunately, Paxton came in behind them and cleared his throat.

"What's wrong?" Mariah asked.

Paxton glanced behind him. "Ben went to go find Cat, but they've both been gone quite a while."

Mariah turned to Rafe. "Can you feel them? Are they here? Are they in danger?"

He did not want to call upon Rogan's magic, but the tug of the darkness was too powerful here for him to resist. He reached out as if with a thousand hands and felt the emotions surging through the atmosphere. Ben's concern. Cat's annoyance. Gemma's confusion.

"They are here and they are safe, but this place reeks with Rogan's evil." He opened his eyes. His brother now stood beside Mariah. "Paxton, you above all the others understand. You know what exists here. The vibrations darken me."

So unchanged from the unflappable older brother with whom he shared special abilities, Paxton patted him on the shoulder. "This old place can be a little creepy in the dark. But like it or not, it's Rogan's magic that flows through this place and through the stone that keeps you tethered. It can also set you free. If Ben and the girls are all right, then we need to get on with things." He turned to Mariah, who stepped back at the fierce look in his brother's stare. "The time is now."

Rafe saw the undulation of Mariah's throat as she swallowed, but he saw not a flicker of hesitation in her amber eyes. In fact, they softened, almost glossed as she took his hands in hers. The emotions flowing from her skin instantly battled with the icy cold remnants of Rogan's power.

"I love you, Rafe Forsyth. I want you to be free."

She didn't give him time to bend his head to kiss her. Instead, she stood on tiptoe and crashed her lips to his. Love flowed like water, dousing him with a thousand soothing sensations.

And yet, when he broke the kiss, he felt dry and parched, and the silken threads of her love snapped and fell aside.

27

Mariah waited, her breath tight in her chest, desperate for any sign that the curse had been broken. When Rafe stumbled back, she expected ... what? Fireworks? Explosions? Beams of light dousing him from above? She didn't know what she'd thought would happen, but she certainly expected something.

"Rafe?"

He gazed at her, his silver eyes so cold, they might have been forged from steel.

She turned to Paschal, but the older man simply shook his head.

"What's wrong? I said the words," she insisted, reaching for Rafe. "And I meant them. I love you. We've known each other for only a short time, but look at what we've accomplished together. I've let you into places in my heart I never knew existed. You've saved my life and I've saved yours. The thought of being without you for the rest of my life hurts more than being flung across a hotel roof or falling off a cliff. My fear kept me from seeing how much I care for you, how much I want to be with you. We're connected. We have been since the day

I touched the stone. Maybe it was fate. Maybe I finally earned some good luck. I can deny a lot of things, but I can't deny that I love you with all my heart and soul."

No matter what she said, his expression did not change. Finally, he broke away from her and stalked to the fireplace. He gripped the mantel so hard, his knuckles turned white.

"Leave me," he ordered.

"Excuse me?" She'd just opened a door more heavily guarded than any tomb in the Valley of the Kings and he was pushing her away without even looking her in the eye?

"Fate has made fools of both of us," he replied, his back still turned. "Leave now, while you still can."

Part of her bristled at his dismissive tone, but the whole of her wanted to collapse. Or perhaps throw herself into his arms? Had he been infected by Rogan's magic again? But how? He hadn't made anything appear or disappear.

Except, perhaps, her trust.

She grabbed for the one emotion that never let her down, and used her fury to stretch to her full height and tilt her chin up.

"I just did something pretty damned selfless, you arrogant son of a bitch. The least you can do is look me in the eye when you tell me to get lost."

Paschal clutched her shoulders and gave her a little shake that might have earned him a black eye and a busted groin if he weren't Ben's father and just a few centuries shy of matching ages with Methuselah.

"Mariah, please," Paschal begged. "Give him a moment."

"I'll give him a moment, all right," she said, tearing

off the bag she wore over her shoulder. "I'll give him a bunch of moments. As many as he needs. My part in this drama is over. Have a nice life—or whatever."

She dug into the bag, retrieved Rogan's marker and thrust it into Paschal's hands, hardly registering how hot the stone was in her palms. She expected that anything she touched right now might burn to cinders from the magnitude of her anger. She'd just offered Rafe her greatest and most elusive treasure—her heart—on a bloody gilded platter. Her confession hadn't made any difference to the curse, but it could have at least made a difference to him.

"Mariah, wait," Paschal called as she stalked out, but she waved him off. She was finished. Truly and utterly finished with this whole freaking family. She should have known. She should have realized that having anything to do with this bunch wasn't going to turn out in her favor. Not much had lately. Why should this be any different?

Except for the groundbreaking conversation with her mother and a few nights of incredibly mind-blowing sex, Mariah had been on a downward spiral since she'd lost those coins in Mexico. Maybe the curse had been on them and not on the Valoren stone. Maybe she just wasn't destined to be lucky in love. Ever.

The humid sea air slapped her in the face the moment she stepped outside, instantly chilling the streaks of moisture she hadn't realized were streaming down her face. Then the wind kicked sand directly into her raw eyes. She cursed, but as she raised her hands, someone grabbed her by the wrists. She kicked out, but her legs were immediately bound by several beefy hands, and no matter how she tried, she could not scream.

"Take her. Quietly."

She barely registered Farrow Pryce's soulless laugh before her eyes rolled up into her head and the world went dark.

Cat plunged her hand into Gemma's spiky hair and snatched her away from the window. The short strands slipped from her grip, but not before she'd grabbed the woman's undivided attention.

"What the hell are you doing?"

Gemma pivoted, her arms flailing, but Cat sidestepped her pathetic attempts at punches, snagged the woman's wrist and twisted it behind her back. Gemma Von Roan might be related to a major-league, eighteenth-century badass, but she fought like a girl.

"Let me go," she said, her voice surprisingly soft and fearful.

The emotion caught Cat off guard, giving Gemma the split second she needed to break free of her grip. A heartbeat later, the air was jammed out of her midsection by Gemma's shoulder, and both of them tumbled to the dusty, gritty floor.

Cat moved to get her feet under her, but Gemma shoved her flat. "Stay down!"

"Wha—"

"Shh!"

With a shake, Cat tried to make sense of the situation. The moment she'd spotted Gemma at the window of the finished suite, she'd been overwhelmed by the impression that Gemma was signaling someone outside. Well-deserved mistrust spurred her to act. She'd expected Gemma to put up a fight, but she hadn't counted on her genuine fear.

Gemma crawled back to the window, slid her hands up to the sill and then slowly stood, but only halfway. Had there been light, only the tips of her hair would have been visible on the other side on the glass. But it was darker inside than it was outside. No one would be able to see her. And who the heck would be looking up to an ocean-view window from several stories down anyway?

Intrigued, and not at all thrilled to have been tackled to the ground by a woman whose allegiances were entirely foggy, Cat joined her, but kept her back pressed against the wall. If she was going to figure out what Gemma Von Roan was up to, she had to play along.

"What are you looking for?"

"I'm not sure," Gemma replied.

"Care to hazard a guess?"

"Farrow was in my head."

Cat's eyes widened. Paschal hadn't mentioned that Gemma Von Roan was crazy before now, but she was a descendent of a known megalomaniac and the former lover of a certified freak—one who had apparently taken up residence in her brain.

"Does he hang out there often?" she asked.

Gemma shot her a quelling look.

"Sorry," Cat replied, rubbing her tailbone, which had taken the weight of her fall after Gemma's tackle. "Sarcasm is my natural mode of communication when I'm in pain."

"Better a sore ass than dead," Gemma snapped.

"I can't disagree. Paschal said you had some sort of psychic mimicking power. Is that why you're suddenly hearing voices?"

Gemma shook her head. "I've never heard voices before, so if I'm mimicking someone, it's a new development."

"From Rafe?" Cat asked, suspecting that while still tethered to the stone, Rafe Forsyth possessed a wide range of magical abilities. Damon and Aiden had both had a relatively unlimited capacity to draw on Rogan's magic and make all sorts of nifty things happen. But Paschal had been very careful to keep Gemma away from Rafe, just in case her power to absorb the paranormal abilities extended to a full-fledged magical phantom.

Gemma stood up a little straighter. "Maybe it's not me. Maybe it's him. He's here. On the island." She visibly shivered. "Maybe he finally figured out how to use that damned sword."

Cat allowed herself one brief moment to cradle her head in her hands. Hadn't she been here before? On the brink of a showdown with some big bad while holed up in Rogan's castle on this remote island in the middle of the night? Pain buzzed below the scar on her arm. Yup, the last time she'd been shot, and the Von Roan involved—Gemma's brother—had been the advancing enemy. What would they face if Pryce had magic on his side?

"What did he say while floating around in your skull?" she asked.

Gemma frowned. "He just wanted me to look out the window. I was about to do that when you snatched my hair. And that hurt, by the way."

"Wish I could say that wasn't my intention," Cat answered. "So, you're taking orders from him again?"

Gemma glared at her, but Cat forced her expression to remain stoic. If they were on the brink of another war, she needed to know whose side Gemma was on. And even if she claimed allegiance to Paschal, Cat was certain they couldn't trust her.

"I'm not going back to Farrow, if that's what you think," she snapped. "He'll use me and then he'll kill me. If not tonight, then soon."

"You're sure?"

"I'm positive." The decisiveness in her voice was unmistakable, and so was the fear. "I'm a threat to him—to everything he's ever wanted. And I betrayed him, so I'm also a reminder to his followers that not everyone does what he says. My only option, if I want to stay alive, is to continue my alliance with you."

"You don't sound happy about it," Cat pointed out.

"Are you?"

"Point taken. Okay, let him into your head again. Pretend you're his new best friend if you have to, but keep him busy. I'll get Ben."

Cat turned to leave, but Gemma grabbed her by the wrist. "No!"

"What?"

With moonlight streaming in from the window, Gemma's face was pale.

"Stay. If he gets into my head . . ."

Cat blew out an uneasy breath. Cat had heard voices in her head before, and the experience wasn't exactly warm and fuzzy. Apparently, Gemma found it just as invasive.

"Don't want to do anything you'd regret later?" she asked.

Gemma squeezed her eyelids shut. "I've never regretted a damned thing, and the hell if I'm going to start now because he got hold of Rogan's magic before I did."

"At least we know where you stand," Cat quipped.

"Haven't you always?"

She still couldn't trust Gemma, but she could buy that the woman didn't want to act on Pryce's influence. If she was going to betray them, Cat guessed she'd do it on her own terms.

Gemma took a deep breath, stood, then turned to the window. She peered into the darkness, leaning until her nose pressed against the glass.

"I don't see him," she said after a long minute. "I don't see anything out there but waves. Why would he call me and then not show himself?"

Cat looked for herself. On a whim, she put her hand on Gemma's shoulder and focused on the silence.

"What are you doing?" Gemma asked, nonplussed.

"Shh," Cat admonished. "I'm doing my psychic thing."

"And that is . . . ?"

Cat quieted Gemma with a glare.

"Geez," Gemma mumbled. "Are you naturally this cranky or is it just with me?"

"Bit of both," Cat replied through clenched teeth. "Now, reach out to him."

"Why?"

"Because, just maybe, I can figure out precisely where he went."

"How?"

"Watch and learn," Cat replied.

"You know I'll do more than just learn, right?" Gemma asked.

Yes, Cat knew. She was taking a big risk using her locating ability with Gemma, but she didn't have much of a choice. Gemma's stealing Cat's power was worth the risk if it kept Farrow Pryce from yet another attempt at taking Rogan's magic and killing them all.

Because this time, he might just succeed.

"Go after her," Paxton insisted.

Rafe took in great gulps of air, each inhalation calming him, each exhalation bringing him closer to understanding what had just happened. Had Mariah lied? Had she said the words simply to free him and not because they came from her heart?

He did not believe so. He heard the honesty in her tone, felt the love shimmering off her body like light from the sun after a torrential rainfall. And yet, his own body had acted like a shield, blocking the warmth from penetrating his defenses.

From behind him, he heard his brother shout for Ben. Paxton's voice echoed through the main hall and up the grand staircase. Rafe managed to pull his head up and look at the familiar faces of the Gypsy villagers in the mosaic. How could he have been so blind and unaware?

Mariah did love him.

He simply did not love her in return. How could he when he still mourned his wife? His child? His people?

The sound of someone running toward them made his stomach ache. How could he have hurt Mariah so willfully? She'd done nothing to deserve his rejection except open her heart.

"What happened?" Ben asked, breathless.

Rafe turned to see Paxton gesturing his son into the library.

"I failed," Rafe announced, stopping them from leaving.

"What?" Ben asked, his confused stare alternating between his father and Rafe. "What are you talking about? Where's Mariah? What happened?"

"Gemma and Cat shouldn't be left alone together," Paxton said almost at the same time. He started toward the stairs, but Ben grabbed his arm and held him in place.

"Mariah has left," Rafe announced. "She did as you instructed. She confessed her love to me, and she meant it. Yet I am still bound by Rogan's curse."

Ben frowned. "Maybe she just couldn't—"

"No," Rafe interrupted. "She loves me. Or loved me, up until a moment ago, when I could not return the sentiment. I do not deserve liberation. I do not deserve her."

A female voice from the top of the stairs drew them into the entranceway. Gemma was dragging Cat across the landing, then stumbled and fell hard to her knees.

Ben took the stairs three or four at a time, but Rafe beat him to the top by using Rogan's magic. Why shouldn't he? Denying the power would not free him. The anger that the sorcery spawned hungered to be fed. He lifted Gemma by the arms.

Ben slid Cat onto his lap. "What did you do to her?"

"I didn't," Gemma said, her body folding down on itself, despite Rafe's attempt to hold her up. "I didn't ... do anything. Farrow. On the island. Waiting. For you. He has Mariah."

As if a block of stone had just formed in the pit of his stomach, Rafe lowered Gemma gently to the floor.

"Where?" Rafe asked.

Gemma pushed herself to a sitting position. "Not

sure. He's using Rogan's magic. He's good at it now. He will destroy you and take the stone."

Caring not about Gemma's warning, Rafe started down the stairs. Paxton met him at the bottom and stayed him with a hand to his chest.

"I didn't go to all the damned trouble to find you to lose you to some power-hungry idiot," Paxton said.

"I am not unarmed," he reminded his brother. "I still have Rogan's powers at my disposal. If he has hurt Mariah, I will kill him."

"Sounds to me like you love her," Paxton said, his voice a whisper.

If only his brother's assumption were true, he'd be free.

"I am responsible for her."

Paxton pursed his lips. "You're more than that. If he took Mariah as leverage to get you and the stone, he won't harm her while he waits. That gives us time to plan."

One-half of the most cunning pair of twins Rafe had ever encountered, Paxton had once possessed the mind of a master strategist. Mariah was the same way. Always a scheme up her sleeve. Always working out ways to come out on top.

And yet Pryce had her. He'd allowed his men to molest her in the jungle. Beat her. How could Rafe wait and give the bastard time to abuse her again?

Cat stirred, her eyes blinking until she was able to hold them open. "He's here somewhere. And he knows I felt his presence. Then he did something. Like a psychic backdraft. I think I might have two heads now, because they're both hurting like hell."

Her gaze locked with Gemma's; then they both turned to stare at Rafe with utter terror in their eyes.

"He wants you," Cat said. "And the stone."

Gemma finished: "And he's willing to kill Mariah to get both."

28

What do you want with me?

She could only wonder, and not out loud. Since Pryce's men had dragged her down to a lush lagoon where they'd grounded their boat, she had remained unable to speak. Even after they'd removed the gag from her mouth, her vocal cords would not work. They hadn't even bothered to bind her with rope, and yet, somehow, she could not move. Pryce stood five feet away from her, the sword at his side.

He had not broken eye contact with her once since his men had tossed her on the sandy shore. Tears streamed down her face, but only to dislodge the sand kicked up at her. Rafe's betrayal jettisoned her well beyond weeping. And yet, if Pryce interpreted her crying as weakness, then he was in for a big surprise.

Not that she was any less shocked by the turn of events—all of them, from Rafe's inability to return her love to Pryce's sudden appearance less than twenty-four hours after they'd escaped him on the hotel rooftop. Pryce had seemed formidable when he'd attacked her in the jungle, but now he was downright scary. He gripped the sword he'd stolen from Rafe's brother as if the handle were an extension of his arm. The weapon glowed bright purple as the fire of the opal in the handle met the cool cobalt of the blade.

"You are bait, Ms. Hunter," he told her. "Your ruse last night was clever, but you forgot that I'd dealt with a guardian of Rogan's magic before. I knew you would ultimately end up here, where the magic began."

She still could not speak, but her eyes must have betrayed her confusion.

He smiled at her indulgently. "Your companion last night was no mere bodyguard. Shame on me for not recognizing him sooner for what he was. The guardian of the stone cushioned your landing on the rooftop and then faked his own death. He was quite convincing. I bought his theatrical demise—until I attempted to use the stone. Then, when Hector Velez called to complain that you'd disappeared before his men could collect you, I realized I'd been tricked. You must care for him deeply to risk your life on his account."

Mariah kept her eyes focused, her heart stoic. Up until a short time ago, she had cared for Rafe more than she had for any other person in her life. But not anymore—and never again.

"When I acquired this," he continued, lifting the sword, "I was confronted by a man who looked not unlike your companion. Dark and forbidding, violent and sharp. He bested me. But now I realize he was not human. He possessed magic unlike any I'd ever seen. Lord Rogan must have imbued his objects with a manifestation of the magic itself, to protect them. Guardians, so to speak."

Mariah looked down at her lap. This asshole couldn't

be more wrong about the men who were cursed by Rogan's sorcery, but she certainly wasn't going to correct him. What would be the point? She just wanted out—out of this situation and off this island and, if there were any justice left in the world, out of the States and on the first plane to Sydney.

"I might have pursued him, but I found it prudent to allow certain people to believe I died falling off that cliff. But I still had contacts. I had you followed in Germany and learned from the locals that you'd left in a hurry. You'd found something significant, hadn't you? And if one item associated with Lord Rogan could keep me from dying after plunging into the icy Pacific from ten stories up, then imagine what I could do with two."

She glared at him defiantly, as if the thought of his having more magic at his disposal didn't terrify her to her core.

"But you have thwarted me. Twice. However, since Rogan's guardian went to such trouble to protect you last night, I will simply wait for him to rescue you now. He knows I am here. When he arrives, I will destroy him and take the stone."

Had she been capable of making a sound, she would have snorted.

The grin faded from his face.

"What do you know?"

That she was a whacker for falling in a love with a man who didn't give a shit about her feelings. That she'd put her life on the line for a phantom whose ability to appreciate her sacrifice was equal to the amount of drinkable water in the waves lapping a few inches from her feet. That Farrow Pryce was going to have a hell of a long wait if he expected Rafe Forsyth to ride to her rescue.

He wouldn't come. And she didn't want him to. She'd get herself out of this on her own, damn it. And if she didn't, she deserved whatever she got.

Pryce lowered the sword. The glow emanating from it dulled, and the tightness that had kept her from speaking loosened.

She cleared her throat. "He won't come for me," she said, her voice hoarse.

"Why not?"

"Why should he? If you didn't notice, I was leaving the castle when you snatched me. Our deal was that he would use the magic to help me find my coins, and then I would return him to Rogan's castle. Our transaction was complete."

Farrow's eyes narrowed. "He cared about you on that hotel roof. He was devastated that you were hurt."

"But I wasn't hurt," she reminded him. "We were acting, mate. These guardians have a talent for putting on a show. It was a trick. If you want him, you're going to have to go after him."

She didn't know why she was lying for Rafe, except that telling mistruths was second nature to her. And while she was pissed off at Rafe until she was seeing redder than the stone embedded in the sword's handle, she didn't wish harm on Ben, Cat, Paschal or even Gemma. The poor woman had a past with Pryce. If the bastard acted like every other man Mariah had known, his ex would be his very first victim, simply out of spite over his wounded pride.

She also knew that Pryce must have had a very good reason for not infiltrating the castle in the first place. He had what looked like three thuggish men on his side. And he had the sword, which he seemed to be getting pretty good at using, magically speaking. Still, he wanted to flush Rafe out into the open. Why?

He stretched the blade forward. She scrambled out of his way, but a second later, she was again bound by the magic. With a malevolent grin, he touched the tip of the blade to the top of her hand, piercing her skin.

"What the hell are you . . ."

But her question died in her throat as the blue light shot into her body. She gasped. Her lungs seized, and a split second later, she could no longer see.

"Tell me the truth, Ms. Hunter, or quite soon, you'll be dead."

"Bet I can do it."

Rafe glanced down at the woman, Gemma Von Roan, the descendent of his blood enemy. After recovering from her episode, she had joined him in the great hall. She reached out to touch him, but he jerked away.

"You can save Mariah?"

Gemma lifted one shoulder indifferently, but humiliation cascaded from her like an unpleasant smell.

"What advantage would that be for me?" she asked.

"No, I can free you from Rogan's curse."

"How?"

She sidled closer. "You made her fall in love with you, didn't you? And I don't think she's the type to just give that away for free. Trouble is, she didn't spend any time trying to get you to love her back. Seems to me that if you were raised Romani, you need someone a little more . . . compliant. Old-world. I can be whatever you want me to be. All you have to do is ask."

Her hand was sliding up his chest now. Her right hand. Her left had curved around to the small of his back and was drifting lower until her fingers spanned over his buttocks and then squeezed.

Disgusted, Rafe pushed her away—not with his hands, but with the magic. She stumbled back several steps, then smiled so that her eyes lit like stars.

"Rafe, don't!" Paschal warned, jogging away from where he, Ben and Cat had been plotting Mariah's rescue.

Gemma clutched her chest lovingly, as if he'd just given her his heart rather than repelled her with evil magic.

"It's remarkable! So strong. Do it again," she ordered.

Paschal planted himself in front of her. "Don't! If you use the magic on her, she'll steal it."

"I can only steal psychic powers," she countered.

Paschal whirled on her. "You don't know what you can do. Stay away from my brother. You can't free him. Only Mariah can."

Gemma yanked herself out of Paschal's hold. "Well, at least we know why Farrow isn't just attacking. If that push was any indication, he knows Rafe's magic is stronger, especially here in the castle. He wants a more balanced battlefield."

"But he hasn't taken Mariah off the island," Cat argued. "I know she's still here."

Cat guided Rafe to the dining table, where she and Ben had been poring over a map of the island. When Rafe attempted to disengage himself from her grip, she stopped him with a quelling glare.

"Concentrate," she ordered. "Just think about Mariah. I can find people. It's what I do. But I need to connect through an object that is close to the person who is missing. I can use you to pinpoint precisely where Mariah is."

Despite the cool blackness of the magic tearing through him, Rafe pictured Mariah in his mind, trying to remember her face in the jungle lagoon or in the cabin during the rainstorm. But no matter how much he tried, only the blush of expectation that had colored her face just after her confession of love came to his mind. She loved him. Why, then, could he not love her in return?

"I have her," Cat said, her free hand floating toward the map. "They are at the lagoon."

"We can use some of the renovation tools as weapons," Ben said. "It's the best we can do."

"Farrow can use the magic!" Gemma insisted.

Paschal pointed his finger at her. "You! Stay out of this. Your loyalties are suspect at best."

"I told you Farrow was here," Gemma insisted, fury in her eyes. "I could have sneaked out and joined him if that was what I wanted to do."

"You only want Rafe to use the magic so you can mimic it," Ben replied.

"So what if I do? It's Rogan's magic, isn't it? I'm his heir. I'm the one who deserves to have it. My whole life has been about the pursuit for that power. Why would I stop now?"

"Because you've grown a conscience?" Paschal said hopefully.

Gemma crossed her arms tightly over her chest and laughed. "Whatever made you think I'd done that?"

"Wishful thinking?" Cat replied.

Rafe pulled away from the argument. None of it mattered. If Gemma Von Roan wanted the magic, she was welcome to it. He simply wanted it out of him. He glanced up at the mosaic and wished he had been there that night—that he had died at the hands of the soldiers. Death would be a release, at the very least. Returned to the earth, he would not suffer knowing that, yet again, he could not save a woman he loved.

And then, suddenly, he could not breathe.

29

"Like ... hell ... I ... will," Mariah said, shoving each word out of her mouth. Each syllable tasted of burned cotton and mercury, but when she strung them together, she regained her defiance.

She was not going to die like this. Not that succumbing to a power-hungry madman wouldn't be the perfect capper to the worst couple of weeks of her life. First, she'd had to kowtow to Hector Velez, who'd wrecked her reputation and threatened to burn her alive. Then she'd had to run away from a former lover who'd lured her into this mess from the beginning. And after she'd stolen a rare Gypsy artifact that should have bought her out of all her troubles, she'd ended up with an arrogant, cold-as-ice opportunist who had taken the detritus of her emotions and compacted it into a tiny, insignificant square of scrap.

Blood from her wound leaked down her arm as she thought about Rafe. Rafe, who'd seduced her. Who'd wanted her so desperately when he'd been infected by this dark and evil magic but, in the end, couldn't love her. How dared he treat her no better than he might a common whore? Who the hell did he think he was?

Suddenly, the blue light that had held her as if encased in ice began to melt—not to the consistency of water, but to the viscous texture of hot wax. It clung to her insides, solidifying and edifying her until she could stand against Pryce's attack. She grabbed the blade and, though her hand was sliced open, she felt no pain. Instead, she imagined Farrow dropping to his knees in subservience, and seconds later he complied.

Her eyes seared with heat. She gulped in great breaths and pushed the air past her thickened trachea and into her heaving lungs. The more she inhaled, the more aware she was of the rush of blood pumping through her veins—the more she remembered how Rafe had spurned her. He hadn't even faced her after he'd sent her away. He had not deigned to acknowledge how she'd plumbed the depths of her psyche in order to find the slit in the armor she'd erected around her heart. She'd broken down her barriers, opened herself up to ultimate rejection—which was precisely what she'd gotten.

"You will not hurt me," she said to Farrow, her voice echoing as if nothing existed inside her skull except pure, white heat. He released the sword and dropped to the ground, his hands digging into the sand, sweat pouring from his face and soaking his back. Her gaze darted to the men he'd brought with him—the ones who had dared to grab her, paw her, manhandle her. Suddenly they were on their knees, too, and their eyes bulged and their faces turned bloodred.

Mariah was in control of the magic—and she would finally have her revenge.

On Pryce.

On Ben.

On Rafe.

*   *   *

Rafe crumpled to the ground. Pain scorched through him as his insides attempted to burn their way out of his body. He howled, barely aware of the others standing around him—Ben holding Cat back, Paxton frozen in place and Gemma inching her way closer. He attempted to push her away, but he no longer had the power. After a flash of blinding light, total darkness engulfed him.

Light taps on his face brought him back to consciousness. He blinked to find Cat standing over him, smiling broadly.

"Welcome to the land of the living," she said.

His neck ached, but he managed to turn and see his brother and his nephew standing over him, their expressions of happiness just as bright as Cat's. He relaxed, and his head hit the ground with a thump. A painful thump.

"Ow," he said.

"Yeah," Cat said wryly. "You're going to have to be a little more careful about things like pain now. You're no longer invulnerable to little things like, you know, dying. You're just human like the rest of us."

"But I can't . . ."

Ben reached down, offering his hand, which Rafe took. His nephew pulled him up, though Rafe wavered in a flux of dizziness until Paxton braced him on the shoulders and his equilibrium returned.

"You are alive again," Paxton assured him. "Mariah's confession must have had a delayed reaction."

"I don't think it was Mariah's fault," Cat snapped.

Ben turned to argue, but Rafe stopped him with an unsteady hand on his shoulder. "Catalina is right. I was so engulfed by my guilt and grief over the fate of my wife and the Gypsy villagers"—he gestured to the mosaic—"I could not open my heart and accept Mariah's love any more than I could return it. But I do love her—desperately. I cannot allow another woman I worship to die because of me. If Farrow wants the stone, I shall bring it to him. We'll have to find another way to stop his quest for power—one that won't cost Mariah her life."

They turned to the table where Paxton had left the stone after Mariah had left, but it was gone.

And so was Gemma Von Roan.

"You want the stone?" Mariah shouted at Pryce, who was now prone on the ground, his legs soaked by the waves in the lagoon, which had swelled in her fury. He'd crawled on his elbows to her feet, attempting to snatch at her with feeble hands, but she kicked sand in his face, laughed and backed away.

She now held the sword by its handle. The gold fused around her hand. The metal was red-hot, but the burn invigorated her and sealed her wounds. She possessed the magic now. Her insides writhed with the dark power of pure anger and rage. Rafe had despised the sensation, but Mariah had never felt so strong and invulnerable.

And she wanted more.

"I call to the stone," she shouted.

In the distance, she heard a feminine scream and a thrashing in the palmettos. She expected someone to spill onto the beach with the Valoren marker, but no one came.

How dared the magic defy her?

"I call Rafe Forsyth!"

And suddenly he was there.

The violet light burning on the blade and hilt of the sword flickered.

"Mariah," he said, clutching his stomach and doubling over.

She buoyed the sword with both hands and remembered precisely how she'd felt when he'd turned his back on her. Betrayed. Enraged.

"Where's the stone?" she asked, her voice shrill to her own ears.

"Gone," Rafe replied, attempting to look up at her even as he fought against dry heaves. "I apologize ... for using the magic ... to transport you. The aftermath is sickening."

Again, the sword light dimmed, and Mariah battled against the darkness inside her to hurry to Rafe's side. Then Farrow clutched her ankle, and the three men who had taken her hostage climbed to their knees.

"No!" she shouted, and the four of them were blasted back into the water and disappeared beneath the surface.

"Mariah, stop," Rafe begged her, taking in a great gulp of air.

"Don't tell me what to do," she said with a hiss. The glow on the sword brightened, and the blackness inside her thickened again. "You had your chance to be a part of my life. To *be* my life. And you threw it away."

"No," he said sternly, forcing himself to stand. "I was just, as I have been since you rescued me, behind the times. I love you, Mariah. And because of that love, I'm human." He reached out for her, but she blocked him with the sword, swiping the blade so that it slashed across his hand. He winced, and blood spurted from the wound. "I'm alive, Mariah. I'm flesh and blood. I am no longer trapped in that cursed stone."

Her throat constricted, and the sword suddenly grew heavy in her hand. Even in the moonlight, she watched red streaks slither down his arm. She looked down at her own hand, where blood had caked and dried from the wound Farrow had given her, only he'd jabbed her with the sword, injecting her with magic that had instantly invaded her soul and had given her the power to protect herself. Protect her heart.

"That's impossible," she said. "I bared my soul to you. Nothing happened."

Rafe took a step forward, but Mariah raised the sword higher to keep him at bay. The thought of his touch repulsed her, and yet made her ache for him at the same time. She'd given him everything she had—heart, soul and body—and he'd spurned her. She could never allow a man to harm her again.

Especially not Rafe.

Never Rafe.

She'd loved him.

So deeply.

Deeper than any cut.

More destructively than any wound.

She could no longer keep the sword raised. The blade thudded to the sand as her brain swam with dizzying images of light and dark. A split second later, she felt strong hands on her arms and, in a haze, watched mesmerizing silver eyes come closer and closer until lips crashed onto hers in a kiss that sapped the last of her resistance.

His love injected into her like pure adrenaline. Whatever evil sludge had occupied her body was zapped away by the electric need now stirring in her veins, making her sizzle from the inside out. She speared her hands into Rafe's hair. Her tongue and his battled and mated and pleasured until she felt certain she would combust if he did not strip her down and make love to her right then and there.

Splashing noises interrupted them. They flew apart to see Farrow Pryce and his men coughing and flailing, then dropping down beneath the surface of the shallow lagoon as if a creature had snagged them by the ankles and pulled them down.

"What's happening?" Mariah's vision wavered as her mind and body throbbed with an undeniable need to be with Rafe, now and forever.

"I don't know."

Rafe grabbed the sword, but the color had drained from the metal. It was nothing but sparkling gold and steel. Even the fire opal in the center of the handle had dulled to darkest red. And yet the lagoon seemed to have solidified. The waves stopped midroll, and when Rafe tried to enter the water to rescue the men, his foot became encased as if in ice.

Mariah grabbed his arm and attempted to pull him free.

Muffled screams and pounding were barely audible over the sudden swirl of the trees and bushes around them. A chill dusted over the icy surface, making her teeth chatter.

"They're drowning," she said, surprised that she cared. Farrow had tried to kill her. Twice. The men who obeyed him had treated her like a punching bag. Had Rafe not appeared when she called him, she might have murdered the men herself. But she wasn't doing this.

Rogan's magic was responsible, but she had no idea where it was coming from.

She continued to pull on Rafe's arm, trying to free him, but not daring to enter the water herself. The seconds ticked by in slow motion, and only after she realized that the men below the surface had stopped struggling did she notice someone standing on the other side of the lagoon, her hands gripping Rogan's marker until her fingers bled.

The fire opal within the center of the stone blazed and her eyes—Gemma's eyes—matched the stone in fiery glow.

"Gemma!" Mariah shouted. "You're killing them!"

Suddenly the water unfroze. Rafe nearly tumbled into the lagoon, but Mariah tugged him free. They stumbled onto the beach, but by the time they stood, Gemma was gone.

Four bodies floated to the surface of the lagoon. One of them was Farrow Pryce's.

30

"We have to stop her," Rafe said, but Mariah hung on tighter, refusing to let him leave just yet. The shock of realizing that four men had fought for their lives only yards from where she stood quelled the lust that had spiked through her, but she still could not bear to let him go.

"We can't," Mariah said, her voice husky, as if she'd been screaming for hours. Her temples pounded and her stomach roiled as if she'd just magically been transported here from Valoren itself, yet she summoned the strength to hold him in place. "It's too late."

She didn't have to turn around to know that Pryce and his men were dead. Gemma had held them beneath the surface until they'd stopped moving. Still, when Rafe insisted on dragging them to the shore, she did not stop him. She even assessed whether any of them would have benefited from CPR.

None would have—which worked out for the best. The thought of pressing her lips to Farrow Pryce's mouth to breathe life into him made her drop to the sand and will the contents of her stomach to remain in place.

She should have mourned the dead men, no matter what they'd done. But she saved her grief for Gemma. She'd have to live with her actions—with what Mariah had helped her do. Infected by the magic, she'd thrown Pryce and his men into the lagoon, giving Gemma the perfect means to commit cold-blooded murder.

Rafe, soaking wet, dropped onto the beach beside her. Her gaze instantly went to the streaks of red on his hand.

"I'm sorry," she said, her fingers grazing over where she'd cut him.

"I'll live," he replied, his smile so gentle and brimming with love, she finally released the emotions she was trying so hard to keep inside.

More powerful than any curse, Rafe opened his arms, and she immediately fell into him. They'd deal with the death and destruction later. Right now, she had to concentrate on life.

Her life, reclaimed. Rafe's life, renewed. Her love had freed him. And his love had saved her. Now they just had to figure out how to build a life together—or, possibly, how to survive a lifetime apart.

"Now I know what you felt when the magic invaded you," she admitted. "It was impossible to fight. Not that I tried very hard. I was so angry."

"Angrier than Pryce," he said, sparing the man's corpse a rueful glance over her shoulder. "The rage allowed you to take the sword and its magic from him. Had he known what you'd just been through, he might not have attempted to hurt you."

"I'd never felt so . . ."

She grimaced, but Rafe took her chin and forced her to look at him, then brushed away the residual effects of the magic with a kiss so real, so invigorating, she thought she might lose herself in him for eternity. Not that this would be a bad thing. In fact, blending her soul with Rafe's until the end of time suddenly seemed like a perfect plan.

Shouts and the crashing of bodies through the underbrush tore them away from each other in time to see Ben and Cat spill out onto the crescent-shaped shore of the lagoon. Soon after, Paschal appeared. They smiled when they saw Rafe and Mariah alive and entwined on the sand, but all three stopped short at the bodies a few yards away.

"What happened?" Cat asked.

Mariah leaned into Rafe, closed her eyes and concentrated on the sound of his heart beating in her ear while he recounted how Pryce had cut her with the sword while it was gleaming with magic, and how her anger, more powerful than his, had allowed her to usurp the weapon and hold him at bay. Rafe told them about how Mariah had summoned him, how he'd professed his love and broken the curse—for both of them.

"Gemma stole the stone," Cat told them.

"We know. I tried to call it here," Mariah explained. "But she must have already had some control, because she fought me. The magic is like venom. She must have been furious, and her anger fed the magic. I'd tossed Pryce and his men into the lagoon when they attacked, and Gemma froze the surface until they drowned. There wasn't anything we could do."

Paschal dropped to his knees. Mariah knew Ben's father had counted Gemma as an ally, if not a friend. But she'd killed in cold blood. Magic or not, the act reinforced what they'd all wanted to deny: She was Rogan's blood heir—in every way.

Mariah did not argue when Ben suggested that Cat and Mariah return with Paschal to the castle. Only after she had the older man ensconced in the library with a glass of brandy and Cat at his side did Mariah wander into the great hall to wait for Rafe's return.

At first, she tried to ignore the space around the fireplace, but the mosaic glittered under the lights, making it impossible to look away. Before she'd poured her heart out to him—standing right in front of those tiled images—he'd shared jagged pieces of his past with her, slivers of his daily life. She spotted the small, dark house near the mountains, where he'd lived with Irika and his son. Had Rogan never interfered in Valoren, Rafe might have grown old and gray there, never knowing that a woman existed in his future who would love him desperately, despite her heavy emotional baggage.

She shivered and suddenly craved a shower—if someone had invented one that worked from the inside out. Yet she knew that when Rafe returned and wrapped her in his arms again, the effect would be just as cleansing. She took her time, studying the faces of the people in the mosaic, trying to imagine what Rafe's life had been like centuries ago, when he finally slipped his hands around her waist and pulled her close.

He smelled of sweat and seawater, a combination she suddenly found very mortal, very human and very alluring.

"Ben has alerted an organization called the coast guard," he explained. "He reported a boat in trouble and men in the water. He says when they arrive, he'll claim we tried to rescue them, but they'd drowned."

Mariah sighed. "It's a more believable story than trying to convince them that a woman with a magic rock froze the surface of the lagoon in eighty-degree Florida weather. Did you check on Paschal?"

His voice dipped with sadness. "He's deeply disturbed about Gemma's actions."

She tilted her head to the side and reveled in the way he nuzzled her neck. "As much as he didn't trust her, I don't think he ever expected she'd kill. Those men were no threat to us."

"You don't know that," Rafe said. "I was mortal, and you were no longer infected by the magic. For all we know, she saved our lives."

"That's an interesting spin," she said, exhausted.

"She was Rogan's heir. Her bloodlines led her to a darkness she could not resist. I do not wish to give her credit for what she did. She'll have much to account for at some point. But it is her cross to bear, not yours."

Mariah hooked her hands behind Rafe's back, just in case he got any big ideas about trying to let her go. "She was infected by the magic. Just like I was. Just like Farrow was."

"Farrow chose to use the magic. He sought its secrets and paid the price. You defeated him, and the sword is now back in our possession."

"Yeah, well, hell hath no fury like a woman scorned," she said wryly. "The poor whacker didn't know that you'd just broken my heart or he never would have messed with me."

Her weak attempt at humor, not surprisingly, didn't work. His scowl might have frightened her if she didn't know the gentleness of his soul. "I concentrated so hard on trying to make you love me that I had not allowed myself to love you. I didn't realize how deeply I was still entrenched in my past."

"Meaning?" she asked, suddenly shaking inside.

Rafe kissed her forehead, then held her closer. "I still mourn Irika, but until tonight, I never truly let her go. I had not opened my heart to you, and I nearly cost you your life."

She snuggled against his chest, once again hypnotized by the amazing sound of his heart, which seemed to beat a bit faster than it had on the beach. He slid his hands up her back and into her hair, tilting her head.

Unlike any other kiss they'd shared, this one was filled with promise. His lips were soft, but his tongue was not. He made love to her mouth so thoroughly, she experienced a weakness in her limbs that might have pulled her to the floor if he hadn't held her steady.

And for the first time in her life, she didn't mind leaning on a man for support. Rafe offered his strength with no strings, no expectations. He wanted nothing from her but her love.

He had that in abundance from now until eternity.

She whimpered when he broke the kiss.

"We should check on Paschal. If he's strong enough, Ben advises that you and I retreat upstairs with him before the authorities arrive. He said something about my not having 'proper identification.' "

Mariah grimaced. "Yeah, that can be a problem with law enforcement types. I'd bundle up the sword, too. Wouldn't be good for anyone if that baby is taken as evidence."

She moved away, her hand still hooked with his, until she realized he hadn't moved. When she turned, she found him gazing up at the mosaic again, not with longing in his eyes, but with curiosity.

"What?" she asked.

"This mosaic is not right," he replied. "It has struck me as odd since we first entered this room."

"It's beautiful," she said, surprised.

"Yes, of course, but I feel . . ." He took a step back. "Emotions. Many more than I can take in, but mostly . . . hope. My friends. My family. It's as if . . ."

He retrieved a chair from the dining table and dragged it to the fireplace so he could reach up to the community fire that sparkled in the center of the tiled village. The moment his fingers brushed over the tiny red slivers, Mariah felt his body seize up. Though she'd braced her hand against his back as he'd climbed up, a bright blast of power sent him flying to the floor, unconscious.

"Rafe. Rafe, please. I didn't go through all this to lose you now. Besides, you sort of have a lot of people waiting for you. Rafe, please wake up."

Mariah's voice drifted into his consciousness, and it took him a long moment to figure out what she'd said. He could feel her hair brushing against his face, and when he forced his eyes open, he saw that she was cradling his head on her lap.

"What happened?" he asked.

"Since you passed out? Quite a bit," she said with a smile.

He had the sense of being surrounded by many people. The jingle of jewelry and the crackle of boots against the stone floor echoed all around. Voices suddenly broke into his consciousness, many of them talking in the Romani dialect he had not heard for centuries.

Pushing up to a sitting position, he saw dozens of Gypsies roaming about the great hall. Most were hugging one another in celebration, swinging children in their arms, attempting to venture into the rest of the castle, though they were blocked in the room by Ben, Cat and Paxton, who looked utterly and entirely shocked.

He opened his mouth to ask who all these people were, but suddenly he knew.

They were the Gypsies of Valoren.

He moved to stand, and Mariah helped.

"Looks like you and your brothers weren't the only ones caught in Rogan's curse," she said.

"Curse?" repeated a deep, wizened voice from behind him.

Rafe turned and saw a man shuffling toward him, his gray hair and quick brown eyes instantly recognizable. Rafe gave a little bow in deference to the *Chovihano*. Irika's father. His mentor in the shaman arts of the Romani.

His people were alive.

"Belthezor," he said in greeting.

The *Chovihano* reached out both hands, took Rafe's and gave Mariah what amounted to a disapproving glare. Rafe wasn't surprised that Mariah did not quail, but hooked her hands possessively around Rafe's arm.

"Who is this woman? Where is Irika?"

"Where did you come from?" Rafe asked, not anxious to break the news of Irika's death to her father so soon after his reappearance.

"Rogan saved us," the older man insisted.

"Saved?" Mariah and Rafe asked in unison.

He cast Mariah another spiteful glare. "Yes, *saved*. We received word from the governor's messenger that an army was advancing to the village to reclaim the king's land. I was moving the villagers to the caves when Rogan and Sarina begged us to come to the castle. Rogan spoke an ancient spell, and suddenly we were trapped within the tiles. That's the last I remember, until you touched the center fire tonight with so much love in your heart for us." The old man's face brightened in a gentle smile. "You freed us, Rafe. You freed your people. You freed your son."

Rafe staggered as the *Chovihano* reached behind him and unbuckled the bundle he was wearing on his back. Inside, Stefan dozed, unaware of and unconcerned with the celebration of freedom kicking up around him.

Mariah gasped. Rafe's knees nearly buckled as he looked on the slumbering face of his infant son. He took the child and pushed away the swaddling, freeing his tiny limbs. The baby whined in protest, but did not wake. Rafe cradled him against his chest, fighting the instinct to squeeze him too hard.

Through clouded eyes, he watched Mariah take Belthezor to a quiet corner away from the crowd. The *Chovihano* frowned, but followed. Rafe found the chair he'd dragged from the table and sat in front of the empty fireplace, relearning his son's face. His ink-dark hair. His round cheeks. His thick fingers, which curled under his dimpled chin as he slept.

Only the sound of Belthezor's grief ripped his gaze away from his son. He was immediately surrounded by family and friends, and Mariah soon slipped away and returned to Rafe. She knelt at his side. His love for her grew exponentially as he realized she'd taken on the difficult task of telling Belthezor about his daughter's death.

"He needs to mourn her," Mariah said. "But he'll be okay. He has his grandson, right? A piece of her."

She gazed at the baby with an expression that was

halfway between fear and wonderment—the same exact expression he'd seen on Irika's face when she had looked on Stefan for the first time.

"Wow," she said.

"I could never have imagined," he said, brushing his hand over his son's warm cheek. "I thought I had won the greatest gift of good fortune when I reunited with my brother and fell in love with you. I never thought I could have my son back."

"We're going to have a heck of a time explaining all this to the authorities," Mariah said, but the sardonic tone of her voice was softened when she reached out and swept a lock of Stefan's hair off his forehead. "But we'll figure something out. He's beautiful, Rafe. I guess we both got more than we bargained for tonight."

Rafe's heart clenched in his chest. He loved Mariah with all his soul and knew she felt the same for him, but they'd never discussed the future.

"Does this change how you feel?" he asked.

"What?" She looked up, her eyes wide, but glossy. "The instant family? Automatic motherhood? I'm probably going to screw him up terribly. It's not like I had much of a role model. But luckily," she said, her voice rising an octave and taking on a singsong tone, "we have something in this century called *psy-cho-anal-y-sis*."

The baby squirmed in Rafe's arms. Rafe had no idea what Mariah was talking about, yet again, but he knew his son would be in good hands with her. She was, if nothing else, incredibly resourceful.

Suddenly she laughed. "Isn't my mother going to be shocked when I go home to Australia with not only a husband, but a child? That's what she gets for making nice with me. Instant grandmotherhood."

Rafe's heart soared at the thought that Mariah wanted to marry him, and though he suspected she did not require a traditional proposal, he would make one just the same. Soon. There was so much to consider. So much to comprehend. That fact that she loved him and adored his son made all the rest insignificant.

Mariah slid one hand onto his shoulder and, with the other, caressed Stefan's pudgy arm. When the baby curled his fingers around hers, she gasped, then cooed. He could feel her apprehension, but her love was more powerful. Now that she'd opened the doors to the emotion, he suspected her capacity for it would build to an immeasurable store. For both of them.

In the next half hour, Belthezor returned and, still mourning the loss of his daughter, took Stefan and guided the villagers upstairs while the authorities investigated the deaths of the men on the beach.

But as the sun rose, Rafe could not resist venturing outdoors. Basking in the sunlight from a balcony overlooking the sea, he allowed the sunlight to warm his face for the first time in two hundred and sixty years.

"The coast guard is at the lagoon," Mariah warned, though she joined him outside and tilted her beautiful face toward the bright morning sky. "We should stay inside until they're gone. I promise you'll have a thousand more mornings of sunshine to enjoy once we put all this behind us."

Rafe was almost afraid to believe that circumstances had turned out as they had. In the rush of rounding up the Gypsies, mourning with his family for Irika and cuddling with his son, he'd been unable to fully understand something the *Chovihano* had said. He had not had a chance to discuss it with Mariah until now.

"He said Rogan saved them," he said.

She bit her lip. "Maybe Rogan wasn't as evil as you thought. Because of him, the Gypsies are alive—and so are you. And your son. All ready to start new lives."

"I have absolutely no idea what to do with this new life," he admitted.

Mariah slid her arms around his neck and kissed him long and leisurely, making sure she touched every single part of his mouth with her tongue and every part of his soul with her love. "We'll figure it out. We always do."

He held her tightly, lifting her in the jubilation of all he'd gained on account of Rogan's curse. He now had a woman to love again, his child returned and his Gypsy family restored, as well as part of his *gadje* one. What more could a man want? What more did a man deserve?

"This could not have been the future you foresaw for yourself when you stole that stone from Valoren," he said as Mariah led him to the grand staircase, a twinkle of desire lighting her amber eyes.

"It's exactly what I foresaw," she insisted. "I am a treasure hunter. And you, sir, are the greatest treasure a woman could ever find."